ANGEL PARK

Also by C.J. Booth

OLIVE PARK
CRIMSON PARK

ANGEL PARK

The Park Trilogy – Book 3

By C.J. Booth

This is a work of fiction. Names, characters, places, and incidents are either the product of the author's imagination or are used in a fictitious manner. Any resemblance to actual persons, living or dead, events or locations, is entirely coincidental.

This one is for Dad

It is no worse, because I write of it. It would be no better, if I stopped my most unwilling hand. Nothing can undo it; nothing can make it otherwise than as it was."
— **Charles Dickens, <u>David Copperfield</u>**

PROLOGUE

Plainfield, New Jersey

Three months before the Marston murders.

"More goddamn shoes?! You're killin' me here, Katherine. Why the hell does she need another pair of shoes for chrissakes? I've told you we cannot afford this shit-"

On the concrete front stoop of her parents' row house, Anna Chase, eleven years old, waited for her mother who had promised she'd be right out. Anna leaned down and admired her reflection in her new shoes. Idly, she fingered the hem of her dress, a hand me down from Bella, her sister three years older. She pulled at it, fluffed it out. Off-white with a little blue bow, it set off her fine blond hair. Her parents' friends were always telling her she resembled a young Britney Spears.

Anna sniffed.

Spears. Like. So yesterday.

Today is Anna's day.

Her mother came blasting out the front door, trailed by Anna's father's expletive-filled reaction to the latest Visa bill.

"Did you hear me Katherine!"

Anna's mother slammed the front door.

"Let's go, Anna. Now!"

"I'm ready. I've been ready."

"You didn't get that dress dirty, did you?"

"You didn't forget all the papers the lady said to bring, did you?" Anna answered with attitude.

Her mother put the two bags she was carrying in the back seat and stopped to think what she might be missing.

"Papers mother?"

Her mother dismissed her, concentrating on what she might have forgotten. Finally, she slipped behind the steering wheel and slammed the door.

"We're good. Let's go."

"And you have everything?" Anna was suddenly nervous. She didn't know whether it was her anxiousness about her first video shoot or whether it was her dependence on her forgetful mother.

Anna closed her eyes and mouthed something she knew her favorite singer, Elaa, would say. It was a mantra the young singer used when she was about to go on stage. She'd read about it on Elaa's website.

'Where there is talent, there is no fear.'

Elaa always said it every time she went on stage, according to the website. Anna whispered it three times and felt her uneasiness slip away.

Her mother pulled out onto Bergen Avenue and sighed.

"Whew! Yes, I have everything. All the stuff whatshername said to bring; then I brought two extra outfits, just in case. Your make-up case and another pair of shoes."

"I don't have a make-up case."

"Well, I put one together for you." Anna's mother looked over and gave her a quick smile.

Anna pulled out the dog-eared page of the TV commercial that she had spent all last night studying. She had rehearsed and rehearsed, trying the lines every way she could think that they could ask her to do them. They were now memorized so well, she knew that even when she was like forty years old, she'd remember them.

Anna rolled and unrolled the script. She tried not to imagine how good this would be and what it would mean for her.

She had never heard of a TV commercial being shot in Plainfield. The Chases had no extra money to fly to L.A. to let her audition for anything, even if Anna's father believed in her. Which he did not. She and her mother were never even allowed train fare to get to New York to show up at the incessant cattle calls for everything from Broadway stuff to films to TV.

This time, though, Hollywood had come to her. The thought made her hitch up a breath.

She mouthed her mantra a few more times.

"I wonder what the other kids are going to be like," Anna said.

Anna's mother turned onto Oak Tree Avenue headed toward South Plainfield.

"There won't be any other kids there when you are, probably. Remember, they're shooting each one of you by yourselves."

"I know, I know. I hope I look okay, you know, next to 'em."

"You'll be the prettiest, I'm sure. Besides, she said they're just shooting you from the shoulders up"

Satisfied, Anna was quiet the rest of the way to the warehouse, nervously flipping between the pages of her script and the photo of the "drink" they were supposed to "enjoy". The commercial was for some perfectly horrid looking stuff, OrangeSquish.

Anna had seen the picture of the juice concoction yesterday when Cassie, the producer, had met with them and told them Anna had been chosen for one of the kid's roles. It looked pretty yucky, not really orange, more brownish. It reminded Anna of what would happen if she mixed an orange soda with mud.

Oh well, she didn't have to drink it, one of the other kids was going to have to do that, she heard. She just had to hold the glass.

"We're here," announced her mother. "All set?"

"'Course."

Mantra.

Anna waited a moment for her mother to come around and open the door for her like a star and when she realized that wasn't going to happen, opened it herself and stood in the parking lot waiting for her mother to gather up her things.

At that moment, Cassie, pulled in next to them. She got out, gathered up a briefcase and waved to them.

"There you are! Let's go. We have four kids to shoot today. You're first."

The commercial shoot didn't make her much money, just $50, not like a real star. Before, the most she's ever been able to collect from doing anything resembling acting was $48.22. It was for a childcare center brochure and she had been one of the three kids featured on the cover of the brochure. Whoop-de-doo.

Still, it was something. A start maybe.

She'd hoarded the money for a week, but then she spied a few things she absolutely had to have – a carrying case for her iPod and a pair of shoes, of course. That shot it all. She had to borrow from Bella the extra few dollars for the sales tax.

But money aside, as Cassie explained, it was a fantastic opportunity.

'Outside of Hollywood, girls your age almost never get a chance like this. You're very lucky.' Cassie had said.

The 'studio' was nothing more than the corner of one of the offices in the empty building. The 'set' was a kitchen table with the lower edge of a window frame in the background.

The camera was as small as a laptop. In fact, it was connected to a laptop. Behind the camera were a few canvas chairs and an old table. The only other people there were two men who were standing around sipping water from plastic bottles. There was no other water for Anna.

Anna had looked at her mother. It was their first video shoot, and this did not look like any Hollywood video set-up Anna had ever seen in the magazines.

Cassie noticed the look.

"Doesn't look like much, does it? You were probably expecting," she waved her hands and head in exaggeration, "Lights, Camera, Action stuff, huh?"

"Well…" Anna's mother drawled.

Cassie pulled files and papers from her briefcase. "Things have changed. Everything's smaller. Miniaturized. Sensitive. Hardly need any lights. We shoot in high def with that little beauty," she raised her chin, indicating the camera.

"The signal goes to some kind of card in the camera and also to the computer, so we can edit immediately."

"I see," said Anna's mother, but she didn't really.

Anna watched the two men fiddle with the camera. They kept exchanging glances, quickly flicking their eyes up at each other when they thought no one was watching.

"I brought other outfits," said Anna's mother without conviction.

Cassie dismissed her. "We're good."

Anna was placed behind the table on a rough stool and given an empty glass to hold. There was one light and one of the men tilted it upwards and it bounced it off a white card. It gave her face a stark, uneven slash. A small microphone was clipped to Anna's dress just out of camera range.

The man behind the camera, as if repeating a prewritten script, quietly encouraged Anna to repeat her lines just three times, then turn and repeat them as if she was talking to another child off-camera.

Cassie moved to Anna's mother's side and whispered, "We can cut you a check now or have it mailed. Which?"

Anna's mother hesitated, but only for a second. "Today would be great. So why is the glass empty?" She pointed at Anna on the stool, smiling and holding the glass.

"It's called CGI. Computer stuff. Later, when they edit, they'll fill the glass electronically with whatever the marketing schlubs decide the final drink color will be. Anyway, no concern of ours. Fill these out, model release and everything else and I'll have it ready in a sec."

Anna's mother pulled out several documents. "All done. You gave us the forms yesterday."

"Oh. Right," said Cassie dismissively, taking the papers. She looked up and whispered. "She's doing great. Almost done."

"Already?"

A minute later, Anna slid off the stool and joined her mother. The two crew men stood next to the camera and the laptop, watching Cassie. Neither did anything with the playback on the camera or the computer.

"Here you go." Cassie ripped the check out of her book. "$50. The first of many checks I'm sure for you, little girl."

Cassie stood back and looked at her watch.

"You're done. And just in time. One of the other little girls will be here any minute. We're on a bit of tight schedule."

When Anna hesitated, Cassie began walking them to the door. Anna's mother went out first. Anna started to follow when Cassie took hold of her arm and turned her around.

She knelt down to Anna's level, touched her gently on her nose and said, "You're going to be a star young lady. You just watch. People will be speaking your name. I just know it."

Anna and her mother had been quiet on the way home. The shoot was not what either expected and Anna felt a little disappointed at the lack of fanfare. It wasn't like their experiences with the tiara pageants a few years ago or the few Optimist talent shows, or the school plays she'd participated in. Today, there were no busy assistants scurrying around. No one to help her get made up, though she'd been all ready. No one to ask her if she needed anything, just as she imagined assistants were doing for kids on her favorite shows. Still, it was okay, she reasoned. She was paid $50 and as her mother reminded her twice, she was just doing a TV commercial. Maybe next time.

Had either Anna or her mother lingered at the warehouse they would've known there were no other kids coming to the video shoot. That there was no such thing as OrangeSquish juice, the camera and microphone were props and the 'crew' were two, relatively clean, unemployeds selected from the group at the entrance to the nearest Home Depot.

When Cassie was sure Anna and her mother had left, she took Anna's model release and the rest of the paperwork and slid it into a silver Haliburton case. The case now held complete names, addresses and social security numbers of the hundreds of other star-struck New Jersey kids who had responded to the enticing ad from the 'Hollywood' production company and who had already paraded through the warehouse with various parents or guardians in tow. All excited, assured that this was the first step to stardom.

Cassie loaded the cases into the back of her rental car. She peeled off $50 for each of the 'crew'. Her clothes were already packed into the backseat and now she threw her jean jacket on top and slipped into the driver seat.

She made it to I-78 in ten minutes and pushed her rental hard. Her flight out of Newark was leaving in a few hours and she wanted time to have a nice glass of champagne in the airport lounge before the flight. It had been a good East Coast swing.

The last thing 'Cassie' did was strip off her brunette wig and toss it out the window. It landed squarely on the windshield of a yellow cab.

As if wigs resembling a bag of dead squirrels were a common sight on his windshield, the Jersey cabbie turned on his wipers and the wig slipped off past the driver's side and fell to its death in the center lane of I-78 under the wheels of a semi.

CHAPTER ONE

"Stan!"

Mallory Dimante sat bolt upright, her heart pounding. She desperately searched her dark room, terrified that someone had shouted at her.

She pulled the blanket close.

Her bed shook with her hard breathing.

Then she understood she had been the one yelling.

"Get a righteous grip, will you."

She closed her eyes to stop the world from rotating and, like a train roaring through the station, she let the whoosh of the memory of the nightmare play out.

She remembered why she yelled. Why she had to yell. Why she had to get Detective Stan Wyld's attention or anyone's in Sacramento's cold-case division.

"Aahhh, Ohhhh God."

Mallory threw herself sideways, flopping over the edge of the bed trying to secure her stomach from erupting because the remembrance of the bottle of Tanqueray she'd tried to conquer last night was front and center and she really, really didn't wish to have to clean that up.

She braced herself with her hands against the floor and let the cold sweat drip off while she talked herself into not throwing up. Last night, nursing her gin, she'd plowed back into Peter Berlin's notes, which were also now scattered all around her bedroom.

Possibly it had been the other way around; nursing Berlin's notes and plowing into the gin.

Her position on the bed was, if not a favorable one, it at least afforded her the ability to identify, through tearing eyes, the notes she'd taken last night, that were now distributed haphazardly before her. Notes that made sense of the curious scribblings of the deceased private detective Peter Berlin. Of course, only an immediate field trip would tell her for sure. And while she was anxious to get up and go, her body voted no.

After ten minutes, assured she was safe to be mobile, she slithered off the bed and went to the bathroom and ran the shower.

She stood inhaling the steam long enough to clear her lungs before she got in, then let the spray buffet her head, hoping it would drive out the memory of seeing herself on the surveillance tape shooting Ilsa Pokovich.

She straightened up abruptly.

"Shit!"

Berlin's notes. Those locations. They had always sounded familiar.

And she was sure she was the only one that knew this because neither of her two partners, the two detectives in On-going Investigation Division, Stan Wyld nor Jake Steiner, had put it together.

Of course, neither had she, until now.

She rubbed her nose, stopped the shower and cleared her eyes. In the bedroom, she found her cell.

She couldn't call Stan. He was out of commission, concussion protocol. Besides, she'd have to explain to Stan's wife, Bea, why she wanted to drag him out on a wild hunch.

She dialed Jake's number.

It rang and rang.

Mallory stabbed her phone to end the call. "What do I need him for? Really." Her voice sounded way more confident than she felt.

She sat on the bed hoping now he wouldn't notice it was her who had called and call back.

Stan's out. Most certainly Jake is out. She thought about the phone ringing and ringing. A detective gets a call in the middle of the night, he doesn't ignore it.

"Unless he's otherwise occupied." She stopped herself. "Cut that shit out. He's just... really, really, really asleep." It was a statement borne of 72% self-assurance, 15% uncertainty and 3% abject, soul-crushing fear.

"Yeah. Jake's out."

She couldn't call Rodriguez or any of the Robbery-Homicide crew because there was the small matter of her being officer-involved-shooting material, sort of, and she was not to do anything in an official capacity, departmentally or OID-related until they sorted out what had taken place. Who had shot whom.

Anyway, even with the glowing preliminary report showing otherwise, she knew most of the Robbery-Homicide crew were still certain she had wounded Stan. Shot him, causing him to bounce his head off the desk and end up not remembering what had happened. Tough, let 'em think that.

Wrapping herself in a towel, she dialed the only person left. It was picked up after endless rings. Mallory sensed a muffled response. With that as her invitation, she thrust forward.

"Hey... it's me... yeah, I know what time it is. Listen... just listen, I need you to pick me up... Soon. Now is better... am I drunk? Why do people keep asking me that? No, well, I was, but I'm not, so come get me... it is important... because I want a witness. I'd rather not say... just come... no, it won't be long... do I promise? Yeah, I think so... so when? I'll be out front. Oh, and bring some tools."

Mallory ended the call before she could be interrogated further. She thought about what she said.

"Because I want a witness? Bullshit. Because I'm scared, and I don't want to do this alone."

She ran to the bathroom and finally rid herself of her gin martinis.

"So, how's OID's faithful assistant doing?" asked Susan Spruance when Mallory slid into the Lexus' passenger seat.

"This OID assistant is knocking them dead, thanks."

"Humor at three in the morning."

"And how's my replacement in the IT department doing?" countered Mallory.

"Unlike you, I haven't shot anyone in the last few days, but they haven't fired me, so yeah, I guess they think I still have value. Now wondering why you've dragged me out in the middle of the night."

Mallory regarded her companion. With Susan's hair pulled back into an aggressive ponytail and the signature black turtleneck and black jeans, she looked perfect for the marginally illegal operation Mallory had in mind.

"You'll see," replied Mallory as she rolled down her window.

"You okay?" asked Susan.

"Adrenaline and booze wore off a few hours ago."

"'Bout time."

"What do you mean?"

"You called me last night."

"I did?"

"Four times. Not that I was counting. Seriously, I didn't need to relive seeing that tape again of you shooting that broad and the dog being shot and all that."

"Shit, sorry. Really. Yeah, well, I'm okay. I've stopped shaking and throwing up."

"Speaking of, you do smell a little like the night before."

"I gargled. Twice. Hey, nice car."

"My ex's. Mine's in the shop. He still thinks we're going to have sex. Roll down your window a bit. I'm hypersensitive to smells like that when I first wake up."

Mallory did as she was asked and stuck her head out the window. She let the early morning air whip past her face.

"Hey, so okay I'm just driving here. I have no idea where I'm supposed to be going!" shouted Susan. Mallory brought her head back in.

Susan flicked on her brights. "And why did I have to bring my whole toolbox?"

"Because I don't have any. You bring the gun too?"

Susan looked over with delight. "Always packin'. What's wrong with yours?"

Mallory shrugged. "They pinched mine. Evidence. So, um, head straight. I'll tell you when to turn."

She pulled the wad of paper out from her jeans, located one particular scrap, and found the address on her phone's map.

"Head across the river. West Sacramento."

Susan looked at her sideways. "At this hour?"

"Get off at Jefferson."

Susan shifted her shoulders and bore down on the wheel.

"Now I know why I brought the gun."

"Orleta, just off Jefferson after the canal."

Susan glanced at her.

"Sure about this?"

"Right here. Go right."

Susan turned onto Orleta. The sparkling white Lexus stood out against the abandoned storefronts and rusted sheet metal that secured many of the vacant buildings.

"I can't see any of the addresses," said Mallory, squinting into the darkness.

"That's because they shot out all the streetlights."

Mallory's phone finally came to life.

'In 200 feet, your destination will be on the right.'

"Slow down. I can't see."

"I'm just going to pull over. Lock the doors."

Mallory looked at her. "Lock the doors? There's nobody around."

"They invariably say that just before the zombies smash through the window."

"If they're coming through the window, locking the doors won't help."

"You'll see." Susan guided the quiet car to the curb. Mallory opened the door and got out.

"What are you doing?" hissed Susan. She reached up and turned off the dome light.

Mallory stuck her head back in. "We're here. C'mon. And, where are the tools?"

"Backseat."

"Where's the gun?"

"In my hand. Where else?"

Mallory reached into the back seat, opened the toolbox and rummaged until she found what she was looking for.

Susan's eyes widened. "A crowbar? What are we doing?"

"Putting two pieces of a puzzle together," said Mallory, closing the door and checking the flashlight she'd brought. "Right after breaking and entering. It'll be fun."

"No doubt." Susan slipped out and stood next to the car, guarding it. She checked both ends of the street. "What's wrong with daylight? You allergic to being safe?"

Mallory knelt in front of the weathered, graffitied plywood that sealed the entrance to a storefront office. Nails, long rusted, were pounded deep through the plywood.

"Mallory?"

Mallory paused, scanned the length of the street, both ways, as if seeing it for the first time.

"We're fine. Nobody's around."

Susan sniffed. "You can't see 'em, but they're around."

Mallory found a sliver of space between the plywood and the building structure and shoved in the short end of the crowbar. She put her weight against the other end and worked it back and forth. The ancient nails screamed with every move of the wood.

"Hey Mal, you'll wake everybody."

"Give me a hand then," puffed Mallory. "Grab and pull."

Susan added her hands to the edge of the plywood and together they worked the board back and forth until they could raise their grip along the side of the door's covering, enlarging the gap.

"Brace the crowbar against the doorframe. We can squeeze in."

"Is this a felony or just a gross misdemeanor?" questioned Susan. "I mean, I remember going over this during training, but it's a bit different when you're actually committing the crime."

"Neither. This is investigation." Mallory turned and smiled. "This is field work. C'mon. You can slip under."

"What size do you think I am? Have you even seen my ass?"

Susan checked the car and the street and the dark before she inhaled, turned sideways, worked her butt and followed Mallory into the tenuous opening.

"Don't touch the bar," admonished Mallory. "It slips and the wood springs back into place, and we're stuck."

"I'm not touching anything."

The door glass behind the plywood had long ago been victim to a rock or a heel. They crunched on dusty shards and splinters of wood as they stepped through the door frame. Susan caught a glance of the faded gold lettering atop the door as she followed.

'Acme Distributing'

"You kidding me?" whispered Susan. "Are we in a cartoon? Acme Distributing? Some safe going to come crashing down?"

Mallory was already steps ahead and had switched on her flashlight.

They were in a reception area. That much was evident. Comfy chairs, albeit ripped to shreds, were along one wall. A high desk which someone had graciously put a foot through, stood guarding a dark hallway.

Evidently, whoever had decided to trash the place had decided not to urinate or shit anywhere, which was surprising. But there was a raw mustiness to the place that made her nose twitch.

"What is this place?"

Mallory turned.

"This used to be owned by Marston or one of his companies. Probably a distribution point for many of his old films. Closed it a few years ago."

"How do you know this?"

Mallory sighed and turned. "Because a good friend who I hardly knew gave his life to tell me about this."

Susan did a short take to make sure Mallory was telling it straight. Finally accepting it, she gave the moment the minimal required solemn respect.

"So," ventured Susan, as she kept close to Mallory's back. "I'm afraid to ask, why are we here?"

"A hunch."

"And you called me?"

"Who else?"

"Thanks so much. Look, hasn't this been cleaned out? I mean, if it's closed, didn't they take the films?"

Mallory stopped before a padded double door. She raised her flashlight to the sign.

'Screening Room'

"We're not looking for films."

Mallory was about to open the door when she stopped. She pulled her sleeve up over her hand and with the cloth against the door, pushed it open.

A complete darkness loomed. No light from anywhere except the meager beam from Mallory's light.

They moved forward, and the door swung closed behind them. The room's feel was large and spacious. The raw musty smell was stronger, riper.

"Mal?"

"What?"

"I hear something moving."

Mallory swung the light to her left revealing a door, half sprung from its hinges, beyond which her light revealed a projection room. There was a massive steel base that sat before two angled windows. There was no 35mm film projector anymore, just the base which was anchored to the floor.

"Look. The glass of the windows."

"What about it?"

"Somebody's cleaned the glass."

A rough circle had been wiped clear of dust on one of the projection windows.

Mallory's light swung back to the room. She took a few steps forward and touched the back of an upholstered seat. She played the beam along the row of seats. There were six seats in the back row.

Mallory knelt and inspected the back of the seat on the aisle. A faded stencil, 'MPP', for Molten Pitchers Productions, was there.

She raised her light, letting it reach as far ahead into the gloom as possible.

There were five rows of seats. Each seat had the stencil and each seat had the short, curved headrest, except one.

One seat in from the aisle on the front row, something stuck up above the back of the seat.

Then she knew.

Susan moved closer to Mallory. "What is that?"

"Stay here," said Mallory as she moved forward along the aisle.

"Fuck that." Susan kept glued to Mallory's back.

As they advanced, Mallory kept her light trained on the front row.

It was the legs they saw first as they passed the second row. They were splayed out. Frantic heel marks furrowed the plush carpet.

Mallory raised the narrow beam.

The torso, clothed in a bloody tuxedo, was unnaturally contorted. The arms were bent back and appeared to be broken.

She raised the light higher.

The stump of a spinal column stuck above the seat.

"Holy shit," whispered Susan. She clung to Mallory.

"This is what I thought-"

"Oh my God!" Susan shrieked. "Move! Move back!"

Both women jumped back as the chest heaved in a spastic pumping.

An enormous bewhiskered rat, its maw stained crimson, worked its way out of the ruffled shirt and down one pant leg and sauntered away, but not before looking Mallory straight in the eye.

"Ohhh Shiiit!" Susan turned her face to the wall and stood shivering. "Jesus, that was bad. Is it gone?"

"We scared it away."

"We scared it away? Bullshit. Bullshit, it didn't want to hear me scream. Jesus Mal, I can't believe you brought me here."

"I'm sorry. I needed backup."

"You shoulda told me."

"I wasn't sure."

Mallory held onto Susan and tried to slow her own breathing. She was equally unsuccessful in generating any kind of spit in her mouth.

Susan kept her forehead against the wall. "Listen, I really think I'm going to lose it Mal. We gotta get outta here. Now!"

"You go back to the lobby, okay? I need to check something else."

"You're crazy."

"C'mon."

Mallory guided Susan back to the reception area. She let her slump into one of the torn-up chairs and watched as Susan lowered her head between her knees.

A small sliver of light came in past the plywood. Mallory saw the crowbar was still in place.

"I'll be back in a minute."

Susan didn't look up but waved her away.

Mallory once again pushed through the padded door and started down the aisle of the viewing room. She kept her light trained on the floor. She would be prepared if anything tried to run across her feet.

She wondered if the rat had come back for dessert because she had a strong feeling of being watched. It was so quiet, she could hear her feet on the carpet, could sense her own breathing. It was as if someone was watching, holding their breath and waiting as she approached.

She made it to the front row again and checked to see if the rat had returned.

All quiet. And still.

Mallory tried to lick her lips. There was so much darkness and her light was weakening. She tapped it with her hand and the brightness jumped a notch.

The hairs rose on her neck and she shivered. She was being watched. From deep in the shadows, someone, something was watching her.

Mallory gripped and re-gripped her light in sweaty hands and started a slow scan of the room. She moved the light off the bloody tux and down to the floor. She started the beam toward the screen.

This wasn't right.

She froze when something shiny glinted back at her.

"Shit."

Whatever it was was on the floor. And not moving.

Mallory wiped the back of her hand across her mouth. The light waved wildly, then settled back.

Slowly, she found it.

In the center of the beam, placed prominently and proudly on a large silver tray with scroll handles, was a human head. Staring back at her with gouged-out eyes was a silently imploring Peter Berlin.

Mallory cut the light as a crippling flood of remorse and regret and light-headed nausea rocked her. She lowered the nearest aisle seat and slumped into it.

The only phrase that kept running through her head was, 'a series of unfortunate events'. One bad thing follows another, like lethal dominoes.

She was tempted to turn the flashlight back on but decided she wanted to remember Peter Berlin as she last saw him, at the coffee shop near headquarters, earnestly waxing on about the latest investigation he was plowing through.

She hadn't really been paying attention that day, still, none of what he had mentioned in their last meeting had hinted at being dangerous. It wasn't until Danni had identified his headless torso in Marston's car did they all realize Peter Berlin had been chasing something way out of his league.

And then he'd tried to contact her, but she'd been too busy. Maybe if she'd taken his call to find out what he wanted. Maybe if she'd returned his call.

She rested her head on the back of the seat. Sitting in the dark, she didn't know exactly how but she was certain, in the unfortunate series of events, it was her fault that he was dead. Yes, she'd agreed to let Berlin help her with finding her brother so long ago. Yes, he had persisted on his own, believing, somehow, there was a connection between this location and whoever killed her brother. It had all been in the cryptic notes that Jake had found in Berlin's office.

She kicked the seat in front of her.

"Shit!"

The thought kept returning. She'd dismissed the yearnings of an old man because she shamefully thought him a Quixote-ish character, pursuing insignificant ghosts.

Well, what he'd found and what he'd seen had left him here.

She rose and spoke into the dark. "I'm sorry," she whispered. Her words disappeared in the sound dead room as if they'd never been spoken.

"Mal," came Susan's strained plea from the lobby.

"In a sec," answered Mallory, as she flicked the flashlight back on.

She took a few steps down the aisle into the center of the screening room, keeping the light trained on the head of Peter Berlin.

It was obvious from the crawling flies that covered him that Mallory was not the first to discover it.

The tray looked to be a dulled silver serving tray, the type the maid would carry as she circulated with the hors-d'oeuvres, smoked salmon on one side and the little crackers with small shrimps and melted brie on the other. Only this time, it was two-month-old rotting sweetmeats with a side order of bloated tongue. Assuming the tongue was still there.

Mallory traced the beam around the perimeter of the tray.

"Oh shit."

She rose too quickly. Her head swam, and white streaks shot across her vision for a few seconds. She could see why the tray wasn't shiny. Hundreds of tiny frenzied dried blood rat prints and black rat turds covered the tray with a vigorous colony of maggots, squirming their way around the private detective's identification jammed between his teeth.

Shit. Rats and cockroaches. They were always around, even in the best of places. And they'd be around forever, even when the Apocalypse had been and gone. They'd find some way to survive and even prosper.

Truly, God's chosen ones.

She stood and scanned the rest of the projection room, ending on the large screen.

Someone had taken the time to bring Marston here, dress him in a tux, had to make him watch one of his movies and then had sawn his head off.

The absurdity of it hit Mallory. But, then not.

This is not a dumpster. James Marston and Peter Berlin didn't have two small execution holes in the front or back of their skulls.

You want to eliminate someone, you just do it. You do it and dump them wherever. A trash bin, a ditch, a shallow grave in the desert.

You don't put them on display unless there is a reason. And this is a display. It was meant to be seen by... us.

For a reason.

What are we missing?

"Mal...?" Susan, from the lobby. A weak voice from between two legs, staring at a dirty floor.

"Mal, c'mon. You still alive in there?"

Mallory Dimante flashed her light one last time over the dead inventory in the Acme Distributing projection room.

Head.

Torso.

Not connected yet interconnected.

And still there. Not going anywhere.

She hit Jake's number on her cell.

"Wake up you bastard. I don't care who's there. We've got work to do."

CHAPTER TWO

Mallory and Susan stood guard outside waiting for Jake.

"You hungry?" asked Mallory.

"Don't even," muttered Susan.

"Just thought."

"Just don't."

"You put the gun away?"

"Oh yeah," said Susan, recovering some energy. "Back in the glove box where it belongs."

"That's not very convenient, is it?"

"For what?"

"I mean if you need it quickly."

"What? I should have it sliding around on the floor? Jammed between the seats, ready for that never-in-a-lifetime pursuit where I must drive and shoot at the same time? You mean like that convenient?"

Mallory shrugged. "You need it, you need it."

"I think I'll have enough time when the time comes." Susan glanced over Mallory's shoulder.

"Uh. Company."

Two fully loaded inebriates, rousted by the rising sun, having spied the plywood pried away from the door frame and obviously believing they had reservations at the Acme Distributing hotel, were now making a staggering beeline for the opening.

"Hey! Guys!" shouted Mallory. "You can't go in there."

The shouted warning only made the first one, a mega-sized chunk of flammable lard, attempt to squeeze past the crowbar faster. However, his inability to balance on one foot as he tried to place the other leg inside past the crowbar proved to be his literal stumbling block.

The crowbar, dislodged by his slow-motion teetering, let the wood snap back, capturing his leg, and allowing him, like a California redwood, to fall backward, bouncing then settling neatly in place at Mallory's feet.

The back of his head made contact with the sidewalk rendering him eye-rolling disoriented.

The other one, a smaller version of the first, turned his head to confront Mallory. His eyes, coming from their own time zone, followed.

"The hell you doin'?" he slurred.

"This is police business. Help your buddy up and move along." She tried to sound macho, all the while wondering if she should call an ambulance.

"Police?" He swayed. "Police my ass. You ain't no policeman. Damn man, you're just a woman."

She closed her eyes briefly, afraid his putrid wino breath would cloud her vision.

The little guy began a valiant effort to pull the big guy up off the ground, but only succeeding in getting him to a sitting position.

"I'm gonna sue you, you bitch. You killed my friend. You killed him. Sue you and the whole goddamn police. Nothing but a bunch of Nazi lesbos. Right, Big Wally?"

Big Wally managed to raise an arm to rub the back of his head.

"The... fuck" is all Big Wally could manage.

The little one let go of Wally's arm, dropping his head back to the pavement, and started a swaying advance on Mallory.

"Bitch... I'll kill you."

Mallory stood her ground, except to get out of the way when the little guy tripped on Big Wally's knee and went forward, face first, his nose making that crunching sound when it met concrete.

A moaning cry of pain made it through the clouds of alcohol fog and he rolled onto his side, blood decorating the sidewalk next to his head.

"Here he is," said Susan, as she spied Jake's Corvette turning the corner.

Mallory straightened and moved to the curb to flag him down.

"You don't need to wave," quipped Susan. "He'll see the car. It's the only clean thing on the street."

Jake pulled up, alone.

Mallory half expected a string of SacPD squads behind Jake, but there was no one else.

Jake got out, stood next to his car and surveyed the whole scene. A dirty teal two-story warehouse. Windows broken and boarded with weathered plywood, a graffitied garage door savagely dimpled from repeated attempts to kick it to death, broken light fixtures askew and Mallory and Susan next to a pile of beaten up drunks. He could see both drunks were conscious and didn't appear in need of receiving mouth-to-mouth.

"Good work girls. Looks like I'm a little late. Like you have everything wrapped up."

"Funny guy," said Mallory as she handed him her flashlight.

"All the way back."

Mallory pretended not to notice Jake taking proper crime scene precautions by donning a pair of latex gloves, something that hadn't even crossed her mind.

Both women gripped the side of the plywood and pulled, holding it open long enough for Jake to squirm through. They let the wood snap back into place.

"Steiner."

"What?"

"Knock when you want out."

Jake was gone for ten minutes. Long enough that Mallory considered going in after him.

Then they saw the board move. "Let me out."

With Jake pushing and the women pulling Jake made it back out on the street. The sun was out full now, blasting the front of the building. Jake squinted against the glare as he handed the flashlight back to Mallory. She didn't expect him to say what he did.

"Good find. Good job." He sounded so sincere at first Mallory thought he was being his usual sarcastic self.

"Thanks," she said, her uncertainty obvious.

"I mean it."

She was surprised his praise meant so much. Embarrassed by it. She looked away.

"Maybe we should call it in."

"Did that from inside. Ambulance too." He nodded to Big and Little Wally, both of whom had taken refuge next to a concrete bus bench.

Then he surprised her.

"You want me to take this?"

At first, she didn't understand.

"You mean take credit for what I found?" Her voice rising with growing indignation.

"No, Mallory. Do you want me to take the heat?"

Then she got it. Like an obedient member of SacPD who was involved in an Internal Affairs investigation, she was supposed to be off the street, out of circulation, pending final resolution. Not out busting into places in the dead of night, beating up drunks.

"Oh. No. Thanks Jake. This is mine. All the way. I had a hunch and didn't want to bother anybody with it."

"Yeah? Well, then that wasn't you who called me earlier?"

Mallory smiled. "Might've been. Thought I could use the company."

"Well, I'm here now."

"Yeah. You are."

Approaching sirens usually had a calming effect. Help was on the way. All would be better now.

Except Mallory knew that wasn't going to happen.

CHAPTER THREE

"What the hell was she doing here?" Carruthers was right in Jake's space.

"She came on a hunch," Jake shrugged. "Just a feeling, she said. She wanted to see if the place was still open."

"For chrissakes, she came in the middle of the night and she dragged a completely inexperienced and unprepared staff member along. No backup. No alerting anyone else she was here."

"She called me."

Carruthers ignored Jake. "Like goddamn Nancy Drew. Playing goddamn amateur Hardy Boys."

"Yeah, well, look what she found."

"I still want her out of here, Steiner. Out of OID. She's a loose cannon. Who knows what she'll do next. Who knows who she'll shoot."

Jake started to object. Carruthers stopped him.

"I know, I know, you say she didn't shoot Stan. Maybe, maybe not. Maybe she got lucky."

"It seemed to be pretty good, smart shooting Captain."

"Still, let's look, see if we can find someplace more... appropriate for her."

"Not now. I need her."

Jake leveled his gaze at Carruthers.

"I need her. Stan's out for a while, we still are functioning as OID. We have open cases we've started and can't stop."

"I need her," Jake repeated.

"Steiner, we've hardly started the officer-involved investigation and now this," stated Carruthers, beating the same theme he couldn't relinquish. He looked at Mallory, slumped on one of the brown, ripped chairs in the reception area next to Susan Spruance.

"And I'm not sure we can trust her."

Mallory kept her eyes closed and rested her head back on the torn velour reception room chair, too tired to care how many drunks and heroin-fueled drug heads had vacationed in Acme Distributing over the last few years and used this very chair as their personal bedstead. She also didn't need to see Carruthers continually glancing her way as he grilled Jake. So, she was surprised when she opened her eyes and saw Jake kneeling before her.

"Hey," he said as he touched her hand. "You okay?"

Mallory sat up. "Yeah. Sure. Why wouldn't I be?" It came out harsher than intended. She tried again. "Yeah. Thanks, I'm fine." This time she smiled.

Susan nudged Mallory.

"We're both fine," Mallory added.

"Good. Listen-"

Before Jake could continue Mallory interrupted.

"Jake, where are the Cooper kids? You must know where they are."

Jake started at the abrupt change of subject.

"No," he said as he checked his phone. "No idea. Told you. CPS felt we were putting the kids in mortal danger and they pulled all the rank they could and swooped in took 'em from my place. What's going on?"

Mallory rushed on. "Yesterday, I spent hours cajoling, threatening, nearly bribing any and all I could find in the CPS fortress to relent and give me the location of those two kids, but no dice. You must know someone who knows. You're connected."

"Not connected enough," replied Jake. "Listen, CPS is an inept organization mostly, until they decided to take their job seriously. In this case, they must've banded together. Look, those kids'll be okay."

"No! That's not it. We have to get them back here."

"Whoa, what's the rush?"

"Jake! It was on the security footage. The cameras saw it all. Except for the one you covered up."

"I didn't cover-"

"The camera you covered because it was aimed right at your desk, remember? So, in fact, the security cameras really were connected to downtown. I know you didn't think they were, but they were. And the tape had everything. Stan, Pokovich, me and poor Jake dog too. It was all there. I saw it. Audio too. And I know."

Jake stopped her. "Hey. I saw the tape too."

"And?"

"I'm not getting out of it what you did."

Mallory sat up as if slapped. "Wait! You didn't hear what I..." she turned to Susan. "What we both heard? About the bear? The kids' bear?"

"It wasn't clear to me."

"Jake! That was what this Ilsa Pokovich was there for. To get a goddamn bear which we don't have but she thought we did and is probably with those two Cooper kids."

"Maybe. Maybe you're right."

"I am," answered Mallory defiantly.

"We'll figure it out tomorrow. The three of us."

"Stan too? He's mobile?"

"He thinks so. Listen, tell me. How did you find this place?"

Mallory smiled. "Hell, Jake. You found it."

"Me?"

"Berlin's notes. The ones you found in his office. The ones we couldn't make sense of. It was there. We weren't seeing it. All that looked like gibberish to us. It was the locations. Those were locations on his notes. When I researched Marston and his whole production operation, I remembered he had this place at one time. The location clicked as one on Berlin's notes."

Jake struggled for some parting words and ended up with, "Good work." He was looking straight at Mallory, then included Susan. "Both of you."

He went and rejoined Carruthers. Both women watched him walk away.

"We in trouble you think?" muttered Susan.

Mallory sighed. "No. We're in that special place."

"The unemployment line? That special place?"

"No, it's where we will be professionally, and probably publicly, excoriated, then later, we'll be very quietly and privately forgiven."

Mallory turned her head and regarded Susan. "And because it's all men above us in the SacPD food chain, there will be a steaming pile of female bashing, some to our face, but mostly behind our backs, all because we are strong and threatening women who actually did some solid police work."

"Bastards."

"It's okay. They can't help it."

"Here's to brains and boobs." Susan held up her fist. Mallory bumped with hers.

"You're gonna be a busy girl, you know," continued Susan. Officer-involved shooting investigation, gun questions, now this. They'll smother you in paper and endless rounds of interrogations."

"I'll live. 'Sides a girl's gotta keep busy."

Both women were quiet as the swirl of crime scene investigators came and went.

Eventually, Susan stirred. "Well, this was fun. What do you want to do tomorrow?"

"Find the two Cooper kids who nobody else seems able to find."

CHAPTER FOUR

The farmhouse was white clapboard with a pinewood porch, in the middle of Nowhere, California. That was fourteen-year-old Michael Cooper's impression when he surveyed the land all around the farm. Corn, corn and more corn. It was then he knew they were truly in deep. It would take a Marine platoon to affect a rescue of him and his seven-year-old sister, Jessie. That was if the military could even find the place.

The only thing he knew for sure was they were somewhere west of Sacramento. He knew his geography, at least California's. That put them somewhere near Davis. When the para-military CPS goons had swept into Detective Steiner's place and scooped them up he had put up a fight, but there was no reasoning with determined people who believed they were doing right by the kids they were supposed to protect.

Plus, they were bigger than he was. And they had Jessie by both arms. He didn't want to set a bad example for his sister. On the other hand, he was fucking weary of being pushed and dragged as if his and his sister's life was not their own. So, he had done his best to make his opinion known. The gash on the one guy's arm and the solid connection to the other CPS guy's shin at least gave them something to think about.

Yet, here they were. In the land of cornfield OZ.

At the kitchen table, he regarded his sister who sat slumped in the hard-backed chair. Not crying but probably wanting to.

"Where are we M?" Jessie Cooper prodded her brother Michael on the shoulder and was about to ask again when he answered.

"Where are we? Hah! We're in foster hell, that's where."

"We're not in hell. I know what hell is," whispered Jessie proudly.

Michael looked at his sister. He kept his voice down. "You're just a kid. How can you know what hell is?"

"I just do."

"Okay," smirked Michael, looking around the tiny kitchen they were in. "If this isn't hell, you tell me what it is then."

Interrupting, Rachel McCardle scuttled into the kitchen. Michael loved old movies, and he was certain Rachel McCardle was channeling the veteran actress Marjorie Main, but without the humor. She had unruly hair, a sloppy dress, an unkempt apron, and managed an alarming lack of sparkle in her eyes.

"Eat up, you two." Looking at Jessie's plate, she addressed her. "Little girl, you haven't taken but one little bite now. It's peanut butter and jelly."

Jessie lifted the edge of the top bread and looked at Michael.

Michael took up the slack. "Her name's Jessie. She likes butter with her PB and J. That's all."

"Nothing we can do about that now. Just have to tough it out. We've had plenty a kids through here. You're the first to complain about the food we serve you. Just eat up. 'Bout time for bed."

"I'd like to make a phone call," said Michael.

Rachel looked startled. She brushed some flyaways from her face. "To who?"

"I'd like to call my aunt."

"Whoa. Well… I don't know if I should tell you this… But ya gotta know sometime."

Michael pushed out some good old fake innocence. "What is it?"

"Well, kiddies, sad to say but it seems your aunt has landed herself in the... jail. Not sure what the story is there, but pretty sure she won't be takin' any calls."

Michael pretended to be shocked. Jessie turned to watch another of Michael's performances.

"What's this I hear about makin' a call?" asked Sy McCardle from the kitchen doorway.

This was the first time Michael had gotten a good look at the Mister of their pair of foster care wardens. His shoulders filled the doorway and the grin that slathered his face was a grin Michael knew was the type you not only didn't believe, but you also didn't return. Sy McCardle looked like he wrestled locomotives for a living and usually won.

"Just tellin' em.," explained Rachel. "No call to their aunt 'cause their aunt is indisposed, like."

"Right," agreed Sy. "And it's time you kids were in bed."

Michael glanced at the soiled yellow wall clock. "It's not even eight, yet. We usually stay up-"

"Usually? You're not in 'usually' anymore," interrupted Sy. "Chop, chop."

Jessie looked at Michael. Tears appeared at the corners. "I'm not done," she whispered.

Sy made it to the cupboard in two strides, found the bottle and poured a half tumbler. "Gotta get up and do chores. You two gotta earn your keep."

Michael gathered up the rest of Jessie's sandwich in a napkin. "You get paid for having us here. Foster kids don't have to work. Especially temporary ones like us."

Sy looked at Rachel. "Who says you're temporary? 'Sides, you're here, you'll work. Don't work, don't eat. That's our motto ain't it?"

Rachel nodded. "Always has been."

In bed, Michael remembered Jessie's question. 'Where are we?'

He had a keen sense of direction and he felt good about his Davis, California guess, but they had driven out of Sacramento in the night. Looking out the car window he couldn't really see, but he sensed the vegetation change as they drove. Probably over an hour away from town. He'd have to check a map tomorrow, that is if Mr. and Mrs. Sodom and Gomorrah even had one.

He listened to Jessie's deep, even breathing. Resilient little kid. With almost nothing of her own except the backpack with some hastily packed clothes, the stuffed bear, and her precious hair ties.

Past Jessie, out the window, the moon shone on fields. The distant hills were blue in the moonlight.

The last thing he thought of before he fell asleep was how tired he was trying to escape every place they landed. Like a basketball. Tossed from point guard to center, back and forth, never getting a shot at the rim. Well, this shit would have to change, and soon.

His dream-nightmare saw him delivering a solid kick to the chin of the little brown man at the church.

Over and over. Solid each time. Damn betcha.

CHAPTER FIVE

"We'll start you out easy. You can tend the horses with Jody." Breakfast done, Sy McCardle led Michael and Jessie out the back door across to one of the three barns. They nearly ran to catch up.

Jessie grabbed Michael's arm. "Not horses, okay?" she whispered. "Promise?"

"What do you mean? You always said you were eager to ride a horse when we got to Arizona. You know, riding the range. Roping them doggies. All that fun ranch stuff."

Jessie shook her head. "I didn't know how... big... they are, M."

McCardle must've overheard, Michael thought, because he responded before Michael could convince Jessie that she would be a master horsewoman.

"Not you kid," growled McCardle. "Don't want you trampled by any we got here. You're too little. We'll find something else for you."

"Okay, thank you," said Jessie, in a relieved voice.

Michael swung back toward his sister and gave her a 'thumbs up'. He didn't know why she was being a such a scaredy cat.

"This looks like a farm to me, not a horse ranch," observed Michael as he looked out over fields of knee-high corn.

"Best damn corn and beans in the county. Can't live on beans and what they pay us to feed and house stray kids like you two. We board a horse or two for some city people. Pays better than corn, square foot by square foot."

McCardle slid back the barn door. Michael followed him into the gloom. Jessie held back by the door.

Michael couldn't see, but he could sense the shifting bodies alive in the stalls, and the smell of warm oak, leather, dung and urined straw.

McCardle strode on, pointing to the array of harnesses, saddles and grooming brushes that were haphazardly arranged in a makeshift tack room.

"First, straighten all that shit up," said McCardle. "Then help Jody with the feeding watering and ya gotta groom 'em too, don't forget."

"Who's Jody?" Michael asked. "Another prisoner?"

McCardle spun and confronted Michael. "Do not get smart with me kid. We're pretty forgiving but we give what we're given. You give us shit, you'll get shit. And you," continued McCardle, pointing at Jessie, who was already backing out of the barn, "You stay right here until I figure where I'll put you."

Michael looked past McCardle and saw another boy about his age lumbering in the other end of the barn, weighed down with two water pails.

"Jody'll show you." McCardle tilted his head toward the boy.

"Another prisoner," muttered Michael.

But, McCardle had moved on. "I'll be back in half an hour. You better be done."

"I don't like him," sighed Jessie as she took two hesitant steps into the barn.

"No one does," said Jody as he approached them and dropped the two pails. Half the water sloshed out of each bucket and darkened the barn wood floor. He didn't seem to mind or didn't seem to care.

Michael could see him clearly now. Skinny, black mop of hair, glasses that kept slipping. He had on jeans torn at both knees and a ratty, faded T-shirt that used to sport the logo of some winery.

"Hey."

"Hey."

"I'm Michael. This is Jessie."

"Jody. Jody Foster. Don't even," he sighed. "Better get to it. What'd he tell you to do?"

"Help you." Michael pointed to the tack room. "And I'm supposed to straighten all that crap up in there."

"What about her?"

Michael shrugged. "Don't know. She can watch."

Jody walked to the tack room. "After every weekend when we get some of these asshole horse nuts come out to ride their precious horses, they just toss the crap down when they're done. Expect us to pick it up." He turned to Michael. "Your turn."

"Where's all this go?"

"Hell if I know. I just usually move it around, put some stuff in a pile, hang up other stuff. Treat the saddles good, though. They get particular about their saddles. They go on the saddle stands over there."

Jessie moved to Michael's side. "I'll stay with you."

Michael, however, was looking at the row of horses' asses sticking out of the row of stalls. "So, these aren't his, huh?"

"Nope. Belong to people from all over. Charges up the ass to let the people keep 'em here. Calls the place 'American Boarding'. What a joke. All these people think we have a whole staff looking after 'em. Just me and Flower. But Flower's been gone now two days. Old bull-face says, if we ever let them get loose, they'll wander back to their owners." He addressed Michael. "So, don't untie 'em, hear?"

"Wouldn't think of it. And who's Flower?"

"Some nasty bitch of a sixteen-year-old they had here. Tried to gut the old lady with a pitchfork. Quite the ruckus."

"A real delicate blossom."

Jody laughed. "Yeah." He leaned against the tack room door and ran his hand over one of the saddles. He seemed to be a world away suddenly. He appeared to Michael as if he was about to let some water flow. Instead, Jody wiped his nose. "Been here two months, now. Bout ready to pitchfork somebody myself."

"Bad here?"

"Worse."

Michael was reminded of what his screw-up of a father used to say. Without realizing it, he repeated it out loud. "Beatings will continue…"

Jody shot a look at Jessie, then back up to Michael. "Yeah, pretty much like that."

Michael checked Jessie, but she seemed mesmerized by the shifting line of horse bodies.

"Alright, better get to it.," said Jody, brightening. "When you finish, you can help with horse grooming. It's like the one positive thing we do around here." He gave them both a weak smile, picked up the half-full buckets and sauntered down to the end stall and began kicking dirty straw out into the center of the barn.

Jessie picked up the nearest thing off the tack room floor. "M, what's this?"

Michael wasn't listening. He was trying to connect disparate thoughts and ideas that swirled through him. Most involved escape.

Jessie shoved the item at him to get his attention. "M, do I hang this up and what is it?"

Something, some vague plan was there, but Michael couldn't quite get it. He watched as the horse Jody was brushing stamped impatiently.

Jessie poked him in the stomach.

"What?" Finally giving his sister his attention.

"I said where does this go and what is it, anyway. I'm trying to help you."

Michael took the bridle from her. "It's a bridle." He traced the leather down its length. "See this." He held up the metal bit. It was coppery and worn. "Called a bit. It goes into a horse's mouth."

"What for?"

"It goes in the horse's mouth and you hold the other end of the leather."

"Eww. Why?"

Michael took his time answering. He silently counted the number of horses. There were eighteen.

Perfect.

"You pull left, horse goes left. Right, he goes right. Pull on it, he stops." He smiled at his little sister. "And when you let it go slack and maybe nudge him a little with your heel, that's when he knows to go."

As if in answer, one of the horses snorted followed by a chorus of echoing snorts.

"And where to go."

"And, little sister, where we'll go too."

CHAPTER SIX

It was months ago, and it was yesterday. Or so it seemed to assistant Mallory Dimante since all three of Sacramento's OID team was together. Since she had personally been a one-woman wrecking crew, blowing out the office's glass panels as well as half of Ilsa Pokovich, the resulting investigation had delayed cleaning and repairing everything she had destroyed, making their desks and conference table off-limits as a crime scene. Which is why they had gathered under Sacramento late afternoon sunshine on OID's roof-top 'office'.

The roof-top 'office' was a set of scrounged chairs, courtesy of Mallory and a cobbled together 2x4 and plywood table, thanks to Jake, who also fashioned a lattice-type overhead from some broken pallets, as well as stringing an extension cord for electricity. The final touches were the garage-sale gooseneck lamps Mallory had found.

Mallory stopped tapping her pencil on her yellow legal pad and cringed as she watched Detective, and senior partner, Stan Wyld push open the roof's metal access door. Using his cane and pretending he had never been shot, he made his way over to the small table set up on the tarred roof. He sloughed into one of the rickety wooden chairs. His partner, Detective Jake Steiner, held the back of the chair for him as he settled in.

Stan set his cane aside, leaning it on the table edge and addressed Mallory.

"I'm, fine."

Mallory's eyes widened. "Did I say anything?" Though she wanted to. In just a few days since the shooting, he seemed to have lost twenty pounds and his color had drained to a mottled gray if that was possible.

Stan twisted in the chair toward Jake. "And quit fussing with the chair, Steiner. I sat down didn't I? I made it just fine. And don't you even say anything."

Jake held up his hands in surrender and took his place in the third chair. Still, he tried. "Stan, Bea said-"

"I know what my wife probably said. 'Don't excite him. Don't make him stay too long. Don't let him think he doesn't remember what happened.'"

Jake and Mallory exchanged glances.

"Yeah," answered Jake. "She said she's worried you're rushing back to work and mucking up your recovery. Not in those words, of course."

Stan, shielding his eyes from the setting sun, flipped open one of the four notebooks on the table. "Okay, all right," he admitted, softening. "I'm still a little fuzzy on the edges, my head occasionally explodes, and my heel hurts like hell but please give me a plan to keep this goddamn case from Rodriguez and the other fools in Robbery-Homicide before they completely ball it up."

Stan looked at Jake then to Mallory.

Stan held up a hand. "But first, tell me what the hell happened?"

Mallory sat up. "I'll go. Two days ago, Ilsa Pokovich entered OID, not sure how, and demanded you hand over a bear. A stuffed bear. You remember?"

"Doesn't matter," growled Stan as he waved the question away. "Saw the security tape. Whether I remember all the details or not, it happened."

"Then I shot her," added Mallory as quickly as she could, glossing over what she'd done.

Jake interrupted. "After shooting out the glass on your first shot, which forensics has determined, must've startled Pokovich causing her to fire to the floor which ricocheted into our leader's heel."

"Well, yeah. I guess," smiled Mallory.

Stan shifted in his chair and gave what passed for a genuine smile. "And, I won't say it too many more times," he stated softly. "But, thank you. Wouldn't be sitting here otherwise."

Mallory nodded. She'd heard the accolades all day now that the early preliminary forensics report had circulated through the normal whispered channels of Sacramento PD. Officers she'd never met or heard of, acknowledged her for the first time as she left the Internal Affairs grilling. Stan's wife, Bea, when she'd heard about Mallory's part in killing the crazy woman who wanted to shoot her Stan, bawled her thanks over the phone until Mallory almost had to hang up on her.

It was surreal when Mallory thought about it, which she tried not to do. Now, 48 hours after the shooting, she still twitched with remembered adrenaline; hearing Jake dog being shot, feeling her finger on the trigger, the glass exploding and then all else happening in a slow-motion ooze that still caught her breath up and made her palms sweat.

What made her shake when she remembered was her amazement of how she was able to do what she did. As if Mallory 2.0 had taken over and done exactly what she needed to do. And now, as normal Mallory, she was guiltily taking credit for what some other part of her had accomplished.

"Hey." Jake tapped her arm.

"What?" She jerked her head in his direction.

"Still with us?"

"Sure. Why?"

"We just asked what you thought Stan was doing when you came back from walking Jake."

Mallory sat up straighter. "Okay. Well, when we came back, Jake dog came running in. He needed a bath 'cause he'd rolled in the mud. I took him back-"

Stan interrupted. "Mallory, close your eyes."

"Do what?"

"Close your eyes. Concentrate."

She started to object but closed her eyes, lowered her chin and let out a big breath.

"Where was I when you came in?"

Mallory remembered with a sharper clarity than she had before. She could hear Jake's paws on the floor, dragging the leash as she closed the door. She heard it click.

Her eyes popped open. "I closed the door! Stan, I closed the door. I remember it! I wasn't absolutely sure until just now. Well, not for certain." She continued, excited to confirm a detail she hadn't been sure of before. "The security door was definitely closed, so she didn't slip in behind me or through the door I left open."

Stan looked at Jake. "If she was already in, why did she wait until Mallory came back?"

"She wouldn't," said Jake.

Stan addressed Mallory. "So, if she wasn't already in, she came in behind you. She punched the code. She knew the code to the brand-new security door. How?"

"Maybe she was watching me enter it," offered Mallory.

"That would be tough," responded Stan, dismissing the idea. "She knew the door code."

Neither Stan nor Mallory had anything more to offer. Jake stayed silent.

After a quiet pause, Stan said, "All right, continue."

Mallory settled back and once again closed her eyes.

"I came in, closed the door, started past the office when you called out to me."

"What was I doing? See me."

Mallory took a moment.

She'd paused at the office opening while trying to step on Jake's leash to hold him from wandering. She'd looked up. Stan was...

"At your computer. Staring at the screen. You didn't even turn to me. You just said..."

"What?"

"You said, 'Come here, I have to show you this...' No, first you said, 'Where's Jake?'. I said something like, he'll be here soon. Then you said, something about no calls coming from 911 or dispatch and I don't remember what I said. Then you finished with, 'Come here, I have to show you this.'"

Mallory opened her eyes. "Then I went to bathe Jake dog. Then everything else happened."

Jake continued. "After we replaced your busted monitor, we pulled up what we think you had been looking at that night when Mallory came in. All it was, was the department's roster of personnel."

Stan shook his head. "Why would I be doing that?"

"Maybe you were looking to call someone in the department," suggested Jake.

"Wait!" blurted Mallory. "Something else. You said something about another Pokovich. I remember. You asked me about another Pokovich." She studied Stan. "Another Pokovich?"

"Yeah, there's another." Stan tossed each one a slim folder.

"This one. Nikolai Pokovich. Pokovich number three."

CHAPTER SEVEN

Both Mallory and Jake took less than a minute to scan the single typewritten page in their folders.

"This came by way of our friend Phil Ginger," Stan confirmed.

Jake lifted the single sheet. "This? What is this?"

Stan shifted in his chair, raising his leg so the cast on his left foot rested now on the table. "Yeah. Ginger dug this up."

"How?"

"Doing what we didn't."

"Meaning?"

"He was looking for a story. Something his readers hadn't read, hadn't heard about. Seems he found it.

"How?"

Stan sighed and adjusted his leg. "We made the mistake of thinking that once Ruby Everheart was dead, that was the end of it. That he/she was a one-off. Child predator. No connection to anything else. Ginger, in his own weird way, found another angle to the story.

"He showed up late one night to check out the two Everheart trailers, only to find out they were being removed on two semis. First, he thought they were going to the dump. Made sense that the owner of the Sunshine Vista wanted them out as fast as possible. No need for a reminder of what had happened."

"I don't suppose he followed them," Jake asked, knowing the answer.

"Security guards dressed like cops he said. He could tell they were rent-a-cops, not official. But they discouraged him at gunpoint from doing any following by pretending to check his I.D. and his press credentials and his registration and his insurance. Just long enough for Phil to lose the trail."

"They had guns?" asked Jake.

"That's when he knew he was onto something. That's when he discovered that even though Ruby Everheart was dead, he/she wasn't buried at all."

"I don't get it," said Mallory.

"Not following either," added Jake. "Body was cremated, yes? That gets close to done in my book."

"Well done," chimed Mallory.

Stan shook his head. "We never followed up. We were consumed with Marston. Never looked back. And, no. Ruby Everheart was never cremated. Supposed to be. While we weren't looking, the remains were quietly claimed."

"By who?" asked Jake and Mallory simultaneously. Then Jake added. "Do not say Ilsa Pokovich?"

"Bingo," sighed Stan. "Ilsa Pokovich late one afternoon, after most of Danni's staff had left, she appeared with a formal paper, a will or power of attorney, that gave her jurisdiction over the body. Whoever was on duty didn't question it or didn't care. Danni had already done an autopsy. The body had been sitting bagged up for three days and was just about to be taken and burned when our friend Ilsa showed up."

"No way," exclaimed Mallory.

"It gets better," smiled Stan. "This is what Ginger discovered. He knew he was on to something. Just wasn't sure what. So, according to him, he traced the logistics of how one woman could physically claim the body. There must've been a vehicle. And she probably had help."

Both Jake and Mallory sat forward, anxious to hear the rest.

"And, turns out she had a specific vehicle and she did have help. Here's how we know."

Stan tossed five 8x10 photos on the table. Both Mallory and Jake grabbed for them. Jake won so Mallory moved closer to look over his shoulder.

"How did Phil get these?" asked Jake.

"How does any reporter get stuff? He cajoles, flatters, lies, pays, I'm not sure. But he was able to get a copy of the security tape. Had these printed and delivered to me yesterday. Then, of course, Danni made a copy of the whole tape and sent it to me, but these are the best views."

Jake held screenshots from the security camera at the back of the SacPD basement loading dock where bodies come and go. The first showed what was obviously Ilsa Pokovich standing next to a gurney on which was a black body bag. Next to her was a short brown man. The second photo was a closeup of the brown man.

"Wait," said Mallory. "Let me see that."

"You know who it is?" Stan asked.

"I'm... not sure. Those kids, the Cooper kids. The boy said he'd been followed by a man just like this. Said he had to fight him off at the church where I found them. If it's the same guy Michael Cooper was talking about then maybe Carruthers was right and I take it all back. Maybe the Captain is on to something. Maybe that's why he was insistent on finding those kids. Maybe that's why he wanted to shoehorn himself into this investigation."

Jake and Stan exchanged glances. They both knew Carruthers was a dimwit investigator, had been back in the days of the original Olive Park investigation and in the years since then. The only reason he rose in the ranks to become Captain was that he seemed to have a knack for being in the right place and administrative positions above him opened up at the right time. His involvement in their case was only going to be a nuisance.

Finally, Jake pulled out the third photo and put it on top. It showed the back of a limousine, trunk open.

"They were just going to dump the body in the trunk?" Mallory asked, incredulous.

"Evidently not, according to Phil. They just retrieved a few blankets. The next picture shows the body bag being loaded into the back seat."

"Damn," exclaimed Mallory. "Don't know what's worse, putting old Ruby in the trunk like a spare tire or making that sad sack of decomposition comfortable in the back seat."

The picture showed the body bag half in the back seat with Ilsa and the brown man holding on one end of the bag. The intriguing part of the picture was the two arms extending from the interior of the car guiding the other end.

"Who is in the car?"

"I'll get to that," said Stan. "Notice the license plate. You can just see it at that angle."

"And we traced it?" asked Mallory.

"Not us. Again, Phil did the work for us. It was registered to this man, sort of."

Stan held out a final photo. Both Jake and Mallory reached for it together. It showed the front of the car and half a figure through the windshield sitting in the driver's seat. It was blurry from enlarging but revealed a large man, balding, heavy facial features. He was lit from only a garish overhead fluorescent as the car was leaving. It was not enough to even begin to build a facial match with any system SacPD at their disposal.

"According to the trace, it was registered to a corporation."

"Of course," chimed Mallory.

"Through a week of digging, Phil found out the owner of both the corporation and the car was none other than our ghost. Nikolai Pokovich."

"And there must be a reason why you didn't send the cavalry to the address."

"Couldn't. Corporation registered in Delaware. Some lawyer's office. A lawyer that doesn't want to be found, it seems. Or doesn't exist."

All three were silent, trying to connect the seemingly unconnectable.

Jake stirred. "Umm, yeah but now there's another Pokovich cooling her heels in cold storage, or has somebody already collected her too?"

Stan sighed. "Still there. Danni has orders to keep her until someone comes for her. We have two extra security cameras ready to capture the Kodak moment. So far, nothing."

"Wait a minute," said Mallory excited. She took the photo from Jake and tilted it so it was in a better light from the table lamp. She looked up to them both.

"There's a gun on the dashboard. And something else. Can't quite make it out."

"Yes," agreed Stan. "This Nikolai is either expecting trouble or ready to make it. Not sure myself what the other thing is."

Jake took the picture back. Whatever the thing was, it picked up the light from overhead and shimmered back in a chain of small, bright reflections. He turned the photo sideways then back straight up. Even though he'd never seen one before, small hairs rose when he realized what it was. The sharp diamond teeth, welded to a wire strong enough to slice through bone and gristle and nerves and muscle with savage impunity, convinced him.

Jake Steiner was staring at a daiishka.

He handed the photo back to Stan. "It's a daiishka, Stan. Probably the one that took care of Marston." Jake blew out a big breath remembering the day so long ago that the severed head of film director James Marston Junior fell at his feet when he opened Marston's car door.

Stan was about to respond when his phone buzzed. He checked the text.

"Okay look, Bea is downstairs waiting for me. One more thing. No, two more." He addressed Mallory.

"Your theory is Pokovich was after the stuffed bear that the little girl was dragging around. The Cooper girl?

"Yeah, the kids' bear."

"You're sure that's what Pokovich said before she shot the dog? Both Jake and I ran the security tape more than once. The audio wasn't clear, but you heard that? For sure?"

"We played around with the audio. We all heard it. Susan, myself and the IT techs. She said, 'Give me the fucking bear'."

Jake shook his head, disbelieving. "She shot my dog. Was willing to shoot Stan. And she died for a stuffed animal." He looked hard at Mallory. "You tell me what could be in a simple stuffed animal that's so important?"

"I don't know," answered Mallory.

"That's your priority," said Stan. "Find those kids. Lean on CPS. Use the IT group. Whatever. Use that pal of yours-"

"Susan."

"Yeah. Her. Maybe even Phil Ginger."

Then he handed Jake a manila envelope.

"Second, this Anna Chase. Danni triple checked the fingerprint she found in Marston's car. As unbelievable as it is, they really belong to this young girl in Jersey. This is too important to do long distance, so you're elected. I can't go and Mallory's not eligible."

Jake undid the little string that held the envelope closed. The first item he removed was a picture. It was an 8x10. He held it up.

"That's her," said Stan. "Danni tracked down her school picture."

Eleven-year-old Anna Chase of Plainfield, New Jersey. To Jake, she seemed slightly lost. As if she normally wore glasses and somebody had made her remove them before the picture. Still, there was a studiousness about her whole persona. She sat straight and seemed older than eleven, at least to Jake, who didn't call himself an expert in judging a girl's ages.

The camera liked her though, he thought. Blond hair and blue-gray eyes would serve her well in the future.

Also, in the envelope was a single piece of paper that contained everything they knew about the young girl. It was a skinny paragraph and covered meager information about the family; father and mother's employment, the address of every home the family had occupied, and very little background on Anna herself, only that she had participated in some sort of beauty pageants. It was all Danni and her crew could glean in so short amount of time.

"Soon as you can arrange it, get out there. See if you... uh." Stan hesitated. "Look. Let's keep this to ourselves if you get my meaning."

"Rodriguez," said both Jake and Mallory at the same time.

"Correct. He and Carruthers would never authorize a fishing expedition such as this. Still, I have a feeling. Anyway, I'll authorize it through channels later. Just get back soon as you can."

Stan started to rise and both Jake and Mallory moved to help him, but he waved them away.

"I can do it," he said more sharply than he intended. He addressed Jake. "Find out what a little kid in New Jersey has to do with our headless director."

Pointing at Mallory. "No more half-brained, middle-of-the-night scavenger hunts, okay? Not without backup. And I don't mean office staff. Clear?"

Mallory nodded.

When he arrived at the door to the lower level of the OID offices, he paused. "And you two... work together. For a change."

With a scrape of the metal door on a metal threshold, he was gone.

CHAPTER EIGHT

Mallory and Jake self-consciously watched as Stan exited the roof. The security door swung shut with a rattly metallic clang. Thanks to Jake's previous handiwork, it didn't lock but bounced back open a few inches. Permanent protection against being locked out on the roof.

Jake went to the small table and switched off the table lamp. "Seems like weeks since the three of us have been up here, drinking beer, figuring out... everything," he said.

"Yes."

The wind picked up and Mallory tried to fill the awkward silence.

"They're doing a good job on fixing the office," she said brightly.

"I saw."

Music from somewhere drifted up from the street.

"Don't you think Stan's pretty much back to his old self?" she continued.

"His old self, sure. Except for the limp. And the fact he can't remember what happened two days ago. But, sure."

They stood facing each other on either side of the table. They could almost make out the other's faces in the dark.

Mallory smiled.

Jake smiled.

"You hear that?" asked Mallory, again with more eagerness than she intended.

"Hear what?"

Mallory left the table and moved to the parapet edge of the roof. The music that drifted up was louder, clearer. Jake came and joined her.

She turned and faced him.

"Steiner, do you dance?"

It was hard for Mallory to tell, but Jake appeared unable to speak.

"Well?" she pressed.

"Dance?"

"Dance. I know you've heard of it. Moving with music. It was in all the papers."

"You want to dance?" stalled Jake.

"I want you to dance with me."

"Now?"

"It's required. You hear this? It's Unchained Melody. When you hear this, it is required that one, or two, in this case, dance."

When Jake hesitated, Mallory insisted. "C'mon. You must know how."

"My grandmother taught me the box-step." Jake smiled.

"The box-step? The box step! Okay. Well, one works with what one has. I promise to tell you your box-step is the best thing ever. Now, give it up."

Mallory held out both arms.

Mallory felt his hand in hers. Rough, dry, firm. Around her waist, he gripped with assurance and pulled her closer than she expected.

Though he stared at her, she avoided his gaze and realized that if they even listened to the words, she would be embarrassed. 'I need your love. God speed your love.' What the hell was she thinking?

Instead of being the dance master, lightly guiding Jake around the roof, Mallory found herself being shepherded expertly, effortlessly, her feet, her whole body, mating to his moves.

"Jake, this is no box-step. You're a great dancer."

"My grandmother had a lot of time on her hands."

Mallory went to pinch his arm for once again sandbagging her expectations of the real Jake Steiner, but something had changed.

When the music stopped, when the Righteous Brothers stopped singing 'I need your love', Mallory held Jake at arm's length and held his gaze.

"That was nice Jake."

Mallory wanted, needed to say more but nothing came out of her mouth. Not even, 'We should do this again sometime.'

Just. Nothing.

Jake smiled. "I need a favor."

Mallory shivered. Here it comes.

"You know me. What is it?"

"I need you to look after Jake while I'm gone."

"What?"

"I mean, if you can't do it Mal, I can find someone else."

"No, no. I can."

"I picked him up from the animal hospital this morning. He had a slight setback, just a fever, but he's fine now. Limps like the invalid he pretends to be and goofy with the drugs they've given him, so I have him resting at my place. He could use being with a friendly face."

"I can take him."

"Thanks. I'll drop him by in a few hours on my way to the airport."

Mallory hesitated. "You, uh… mean there isn't anyone else at your place to watch him?"

"No," replied Jake, avoiding Mallory's stare. "Besides, you know him, and he likes you."

Mallory did a small, internal fist pump. A personal acknowledgment that there was no one at Jake's to look after the dog,

Mallory studied Jake. "Okay."

Jake did a quick agreeing smile, hesitated, as if he was supposed to say something else, then smiled again.

It was so cute that Mallory almost laughed. As if they had just agreed to go out on a date and he was surprised she said yes.

Jake cleared his throat. "Now I better call New Jersey and make a date with an eleven-year-old."

"Sure." She turned and listened for the next tune to come floating up. It was something gangsta.

And the mood was gone.

CHAPTER NINE

It wasn't a school night for Middle Schoolers in Plainfield, New Jersey, so eleven-year-old Anna Chase was allowed to move the family's laptop computer up to her room. She set it up on her desk, plugged it in, adjusted the mouse, pushed back her long blonde hair and plowed into the internet.

"No dirty stuff" was her mother's admonition. Her mother had said it with a knowing understanding that there was nothing she could do if Anna ended up on some porn site. Sure, the guy at the computer store had shown her how to install the block that limits internet searches, so theoretically Anna, or Anna's father for that matter, couldn't come anywhere near the sites showing male-male-female swinging threesomes exploring each other. Still, she knew her daughter knew much more about electronic circumvention than she did. She just hoped she and Johnson had raised Anna with strong moral values.

Or the threat of removal of anything Anna held as holy.

Still, curiosity was curiosity. And pre-teens are the most driven to explore.

Anna turned off the lights. She liked to work in the dark, lit only by the light from the screen.

After logging on, she skipped the private messages from her friends. She actually called up her email. She never really used it anymore. Texting was faster and less cumbersome. But she was waiting for a special email. She had checked every weekend for the last few weeks, positive that a copy of her TV commercial would come from Cassie, the producer.

She hadn't really expected it to hit the TV. After all, Cassie had told her and her mother when they shot it that it was just a test commercial for OrangeSquish juice. The marketing people would use it somehow, she said, testing it against other commercials. There was still a chance it might appear some night when she least expected it. But it had been weeks and weeks and weeks now and nothing.

And no email with a cheerful greeting and Thank You from Cassie telling her what a great job she did and by-the-way, here's a copy of the finished commercial for you.

She scanned the emails again. Nothing.

Then she had a thought.

She typed in the name of the juice. She still had the script. She'd put it in a frame and tacked it to one of her slanted ceilings.

'OrangeSquish Juice.'

The only thing that was remotely close was some sugar-free Japanese drink that managed to have 'squish' in the name.

She typed Cassie's name with 'TV producer' added on.

Lots of Cassies, but not her producer Cassie.

She didn't understand. Maybe the TV production company Cassie worked for was too new.

But she knew they existed. For sure, they had money to pay people. She and her mother had driven straight to the bank after the shoot and popped it into Anna's account.

As her mother said a few days later when she had examined the account, 'Looks like it went through. What d'ya know.'

Anna took that to mean it was okay. So, they must be true. They must exist.

Why else would someone pretend something like that? It would be cruel to fool kids.

Her father knocked on her door and told her it was late and to shut it down. Anna closed the laptop and brought it back downstairs for her parents to use.

After setting the computer on the kitchen table, she remained slouched in the kitchen doorway.

"I need my own computer," she stated. She tried to keep desperate defiance out of her voice, knowing the only thing that would work was logic. Or not.

"I'm old enough. I have saved some money, you know."

Katherine gave her daughter the smile that always preceded a 'No' when the phone rang.

Anna remained in the doorway, tapping her fingernail on the door jamb, attempting annoying threshold level 2.

"Don't answer it, mom. Let voicemail get it. Please! I need a computer! My own!"   ,

Her mother held up a hand.

"We'll talk about it, your father and I," as she reached for the phone. "Later."

Anna rolled her eyes and continued tapping her fingernail.

She couldn't tell her mother how much she needed one, but she'd just had to erase three Private Messages from friends because she didn't think her parents would understand why her friends were using swear words.

With her own laptop, she could do what she liked.

"Stop with the tapping," scolded her mother. "The tapping with your fingernails. We'll talk later."

Anna's mother checked her phone's screen. The area code was from somewhere in California. California! Anna's mother didn't have all the area codes memorized, but the call was definitely originating from the West Coast.

"Sweet Jesus. California!"

Anna's mother saw her daughter stop tapping and straighten up out of her slouch.

Anna's mother reached for the phone. Images of some Hollywood producer so moved by Anna's audition tape that he had to call and invite them out for an audition or better yet, for a part. Maybe he'd seen the test commercial for the OrangeSquish juice. Maybe. Maybe. Maybe that Cassie woman was right. Maybe this was how it worked.

Anna's mother looked at her daughter as she picked up the receiver. Visions spun and escalated.

She took a deep breath.

"Hello."

"Is this the Chase residence?"

She nearly wilted. "Yes. Yes, it is. How can I help you?"

"Detective Steiner with the Sacramento Police. Is there an Anna Chase there?"

Anna's mother held the phone out away from her and regarded it as if she was holding a cucumber and it had just spoken to her.

"Goddamn scammers."

She hung up.

When it rang again three more times, she finally turned it off.

"Bastards."

It wasn't until the morning she checked her messages.

CHAPTER 10

Jake was awakened by the flight attendant just as they began their descent.

For a moment, he forgot where he was and what he was doing. After three hours of trying to sleep, he'd sunk into a fitful dream. The dream had involved his dog, Jake. They were running up and down multi-colored hills of some endless park and the dog was wearing him out. Which is just how he felt when he woke with a start.

God, he hated red-eye flights. Long ago vowed he would never take another one. But this red-eye was the first flight that wouldn't have him losing a whole day flying, the time change notwithstanding. It was also the quickest way to get to Plainfield to track down Anna Chase and discover how the hell an eleven-year-old New Jersey elementary school girl was connected to the decaying head of Hollywood film director James Marston, currently residing on the second shelf in the fridge at Sacramento Forensics.

He struggled to clear the fog from his head, get some feeling back in his legs. Thankfully, he had the window seat and had remembered his blow-up neck pillow, so he had room to contort himself into something resembling a tortured cripple, which was as good as he could expect.

Jake had made a strong case for First Class but by the time he had approval for the flight, they were all taken.

He glanced at the person next to him in the center seat. She was twenty-ish. To Jake, at thirty-eight, everyone younger seemed twentyish. White earbuds snaked up from somewhere in her lap and disappeared in her curly brown hair. She looked over at Jake with sparkling green eyes when he stirred. She seemed relieved to see he wasn't dead.

"Did I snore?" he asked.

She pulled the earbuds from her ears and turned to him.

"Define snore."

"Yeah. Sorry."

The girl shrugged. It wrinkled her nose when she did. It made her alarmingly cute, in a kind of I've-been-up-all-night kind of way.

"You were fine," she said. "You were pretty out of it."

Jake tried not to stare so he pulled the plug on his pillow and squeezed it to deflate it.

The engines changed their pitch and he could feel the autopilot cut off and the plane begin to drop. He knew they were about twenty minutes out.

"You live here?" He indicated New Jersey slipping below them.

She glanced past him out the window, smiled, then busied herself gathering her iPod and earbuds and replacing them in her carryon.

"L.A."

"Visiting family?"

"Work. Just in for a day. Headed back tonight."

Jake looked closer. Too young to be a jet-setting CEO. Besides, she was in coach instead of first class. She was dressed in jeans and a coral turtleneck sweater. Her brown hair was simply pulled back and she appeared more awake than anyone he had ever seen after flying all night.

He turned toward her. "Tonight? You're just here for a day?"

She nodded. "Just an audition."

"Ahh," Jake said. He turned back to his own seat and resumed gathering everything he had spread around him.

"Ahh?" There was an accusatory tone in her voice.

Jake turned back. Her eyes were narrowed, offset by a slight smile. She was an actress. He couldn't tell if he offended her or not. She was an actress. Nothing they did was real.

"You're an actress," Jake said stating the obvious.

"Ahh?" she repeated Jake's response perfectly.

"Nothing." He shrugged. "A noble profession, they say." He turned back to the window, but he could feel her stare. Again, he had no clue whether she was faking her indignation or just playing the insulted.

After a moment, she started up again. There was no rancor in her voice.

"Sounds like you have issues. Maybe some unfortunate experience in the past?"

Jake smiled to himself. He had never dated anyone that called themselves an actor, but he had seen plenty of them. They carpeted California. Most were narcistically obnoxious, singularly concerned with themselves and living their life as a stage play in which they were handed a new scene every day. And yet, despite their lack of success, they were shockingly optimistic about their chances of ever succeeding in their 'profession.'

And California was headquarters for them all. Picture resumes were more available on the streets of L.A. than the porn cards handed out in Vegas by the flicker guys.

Still, she appeared to be marginally more successful than most actors. At least she could afford a plane ticket.

"What's your audition for?" asked Jake, realizing he still had ten minutes before they landed.

The girl studied him for a few seconds but succumbed to the temptation to talk about herself.

"Rosie Pilkington."

When Jake didn't respond, she continued.

"Rosie Pilkington. Female lead in 'How to Succeed'. You know?"

"New York?"

She smiled. "Not much theater in Jersey. Here, listen."

She handed him one of her earbuds. It was still warm. She kept the other in her other ear, pressed play, and leaned closer to Jake.

They listened to a song about keeping someone's dinner warm. When it was over, he handed the earbud back to her.

"You'll do well." He meant it. Suddenly, he found himself rooting for her.

"Thanks."

Jake expected the self-deprecating monolog that usually accompanied any talk of trying out for a role. He'd heard it too many times. 'Oh, I'm probably not right for it, you know. Oh, it's a long shot. Oh, there are a lot of better actors up for it. Oh, I'll probably not get it.' Then a pause, during which Jake was supposed to jump in and support the effort, offer encouragement that their talent would shine through, and give assurance that they would, in fact, secure the role because they deserved it. California ego hash.

But she surprised him.

"I should have it. Hell, it's my third time out here. They even paid for the ticket this time."

Jake smiled. "Yeah, but they only paid for a coach seat. I don't see you sitting in first class."

She laughed. "Not yet. You know they don't call it coach anymore. It's economy. They did a study years ago. Thought coach sounded too much like old people. Too much associated with trains and baggage. Something like that."

She held out her hand. "Amy."

Jake took it. Her grip was firm and confident.

"Jake."

"What do you do?"

"Sales. Steel shelving," he said without pause.

Her eyes narrowed again, and that slow smile appeared at the corner of her mouth. She wasn't certain if he was kidding or not.

"When is the audition?"

"After lunch."

"I hope they're paying for lunch."

She turned away embarrassed. "They're even sending a limo, they said."

"You mean a guy in a black suit and a little cap with your name on a little sign standing at baggage claim? That kind of limo?"

She laughed and pretended to be busy putting the stuff away she'd already put away.

"I guess."

"Have you been up all night?"

She turned to him quickly. "God, do I look that bad? I meant to sleep, but I just couldn't. Kept listening to the first act over and over. Shit, I knew I should've slept." The concern was real.

Jake couldn't help laughing at her. She was the best-looking person who'd stayed up on a red-eye flight he'd ever seen.

"You look fine. Really." He hoped his sincerity seemed genuine. "Actually, better."

One could stay up all night on a plane when you were in your twenties and then go have lunch and audition for a Broadway play. On the other hand, he felt like maggot meat. He imagined all his thirty-eight years were crammed into the bags under his eyes.

She pulled out a small mirror to check for damage, then began digging in her bag.

Out of habit or politeness, or something else, he wanted to ask for her number. But they'd only shared an airplane flight and ten minutes' conversation and he was a decade and a half older, so he kept quiet. But again, she surprised him.

"Here." She held out a card that resembled a large business card. On the front was a name, Chris Barker. On the back were a series of phone numbers and emails and twitter ids and Facebook contact information, all in a stack and all the numbers crossed out with a single line through each. At the bottom of the stack was a number with an area code Jake recognized as an L.A. prefix. There was no line through it.

"Here. I may need some steel shelving. You could try and sell me some sometime. If you feel like it."

"Looks like you've moved around a bit."

She smiled. "This was my idea. The card. Sometimes I get guys trying to hit on me. Happens sometimes."

"I was just going to do that," he said.

She looked at him. "No. You weren't. You're too shy, I think. Maybe too polite. Or you believe yourself too old. I don't know. Anyway. Do not call that last number, the one at the bottom without the line through it. Don't call it unless you need to be put in touch with L.A.s premier escort service. My number is the first one that's crossed out. The first number."

"Clever."

"Thanks. And my name really is Amy not Chris. Amy Champion. I know, too pretentious."

"Maybe not. Listen…" Jake hated people who promised to call and never did. He promised himself never to do that.

"I'll…"

"Probably never call." She shrugged. "That's okay. Just nice to meet someone polite who isn't in the biz."

Jake put the card away in his inside pocket. He didn't offer one of his own.

"I know you're probably thirty or something, but you seem nice and trustworthy," she said. "Are you?"

"So far."

She read his face, trying to detect deceit or sarcasm or false anything.

"Not married, right? No wife?"

Jake unconsciously sat up straighter. "No wife. A dog. I have a dog."

"Ahh," she smiled. "Second stage, then."

"Yes. Second stage," Jake said, surprised again. "What about you?"

She looked away, then back to Jake.

"Okay. Cactus. I'm up to cactus," she admitted.

"Cactus?" nodded Jake. "Bold."

She shrugged. "Limited water. Limited attention. It's like a plant on autopilot. 'Bout as much as I can handle."

She touched his arm. "Nice to meet you, Jake. You know, even if you are a cop..."

She glanced down at the Marston folder on his tray table.

"Even if you are, I'd think you were still nice. Good luck with those shelves."

She smiled, slipped out of her seat, grabbed her bag from the overhead and was gone.

Jake wondered if he should feel some semblance of guilt. She was only twenty-four. When did age difference become obscene he wondered. He decided not to worry about. It wouldn't be an issue. No call would be made.

And that made him think about Mallory. Maybe he should check in. Instead, he made sure his phone was off. He didn't need to hear her voice.

He gathered his bag and as he exited the jetway he looked up at the gate number, their arrival gate and he stopped.

Gate A17. Newark.

Jake set his bag down and watched the opening to the jetway until the last of the passengers had exited and the flight attendant came and shut the metal door.

Gate A17.

He picked up his bag and tightened his grip.

Flight 93 had pushed back from this gate in the Newark airport on September 11, 2001. Headed to San Francisco. It made it to Shanksville, Pennsylvania.

Jake turned and headed to baggage claim. Not being a praying man, vowing never to forget was the best he could do.

CHAPTER 11

The only reason he was sure he had entered Plainfield was because the green road sign welcomed him to Plainfield. Below the Welcome sign in small script was the line, 'Founded by the Quakers, 1684'. Oh, if thee could only see it now.

Arbitrary political demarcations divided what seemed to Jake to be a flowing mass of people and homes and fast food and factories. There was Plainfield as well as a North and South version. All of which glommed together seamlessly.

It had always seemed to Jake that Newark and surrounds were the lahars to New York City's eruption. Communities that suckled at the tit of the Big Apple and would be the first to go when the shit hit the fan.

Before he endeavored to find Anna Chase's house, he swung into Plainfield police headquarters and showed some respect. Always a good idea to register your presence when you drop into somebody else's jurisdiction.

Warren Deitcher, the only detective around, appeared to be nearly napping at his desk but perked up when he heard that Jake was from California. California, magic words to anyone not living in California. Grass is always greener.

"Hey, so what you doin' out this way?"

Jake settled into a hardback chair hard up against the detective's desk.

"Slummin'."

"Ain't that the truth," replied Deitcher. "Coffee?"

"I'm good," Jake said.

"I'm on for another two hours and I've been up all night helping Newark deal with some of their shit," sighed Deitcher as he stirred more sugar into the steaming cup before him. He looked concerned. "You're not gonna need any help, are you? With what you're doin?"

To Jake, it didn't look like the man had the energy to lift his spoon, let alone get out of the chair and tag along.

"Nah," Jake said. "Just trying to track down a lead in a missing person that's turned into a bigger mess."

"Good. Where you out of?"

"Sacramento."

"Sacramento!" Deitcher leaned forward. "Anna Chase, right?"

Jake couldn't have been more floored.

"What? Yeah. But how did you know that? How do you know about Anna Chase?"

Deitcher was all energy now. "What're you doin' here with me? You should be over there, man. We should go."

Jake wanted to grab the man and ask him what the hell was going on but Deitcher had already snatched his jacket and keys and was headed for the door.

"Where?"

"To Anna Chase's. I'll drive."

"I have a rental," was all Jake could add.

Deitcher held the door for him. "Hah! That ain't gonna do you any good today. C'mon man."

Jake slid into the passenger seat of Deitcher's dirty Chevy. Deitcher accelerated as soon as Jake's door closed.

"You know when I heard you were from California, I thought you might be from L.A. We get some L.A. guys here now and then. Pokin' around. Usually drug connections, you know."

Jake had had enough. "Detective, how the hell do you know about Anna Chase?"

Deitcher glanced at him as if he was kidding. "Huh? Don't your people keep you informed? Everybody's heard about Anna Chase this morning."

Jake thought for a moment they must be talking about two different Anna Chases.

"Shit!" He realized, as he pulled out his phone, that it was still set to 'airplane mode'. His people had probably been doing their best to keep him informed.

"Shit!" He stabbed the screen activating the phone portion. It took only a few seconds for it to start to vibrate and ding with pissed-off notices of over thirty unanswered messages and texts.

Deitcher couldn't help but smile as Jake combed his phone to catch up. "And I thought we were the leakiest department on the face of the Earth. You got us beat, seems."

Most of the messages ranged from 'Call me right away' degenerating to 'Where the hell are you?' This last was from Stan.

Jake texted back a short, innocuous text. 'I'm on it.'

When he finished, he turned to Deitcher. "So, what the hell happened here?"

"Somebody out your way leaked to the press that the only suspect to some guy getting his head chopped off was a little girl from right here in Plainfield. Eleven years old. It was so weird the media jumped all over it. That's why I was the only one in the building when you got there. We had no idea what the hell was going on, but when the TV trucks started to try battering down the girl's door this morning, we sent a couple squads and two of our detectives over there to try to make some sense of it.

"Our Captain has already had a few back and forths with yours…"

He looked at Jake. "Don't think either of 'em are very happy. Blindsided was a word I heard thrown around."

"Shit!" Jake said, mad at himself for falling out of the loop for so long. Mad at a press leak that was going to cause all kind of problems. Mad at having this case dumped on OID.

He hated the feeling of running to catch up.

"So, fill me in," said Deitcher. "What's the deal?"

"This is ridiculous. I'm just out here to talk to the girl. Following up on a lead in what was a missing person case."

"Flew across country just to talk?" asked Deitcher, waiting for more.

When he didn't get it, he continued. "This is a missing person or a homicide?"

"Both," sighed Jake. He didn't really want to get into it with Deitcher, but he could see the detective had his radar spinning.

"Okay, Forensics found this girl's fingerprint on the inside of the car of our MP. Just one print. Could be a fluke, but we only found it because she had been registered by her mother in that National Child Registry. As I say, we first thought it could be a fluke. Now, we're sure it's a plant. Just don't know how the kid fits in."

"Yeah. Well, what's this have to do with a missing person?" queried Deitcher as he honked his way through traffic. "I mean, it must be California royalty that's missing to have you fly over here for this? Who is it?"

Jake shook his head, trying to underplay Marston. "Just some old film producer."

"And you haven't found him?"

Jake sighed. Shit, here we go.

"Oh, we found him all right. He was in the car. Been baked in the sun for about two months."

"In the car? Same car as the fingerprint?"

"Same."

"And head chopped?"

Jake nodded.

"Okay. Now I see," said Deitcher, swinging his head back and forth as if he was listening to unheard music. Jake could tell this Anna Chase-Marston fiasco was way more interesting than most of the stuff that came across Deitcher's desk. Typical detective. Anything new, out of the ordinary, was good. But Jake was damned if he was going to throw combustibles on an already growing fire and try and explain the extra body in the backseat.

They crossed Cleveland and Mercer street. Deitcher had the gumball working on the dash but most of the traffic ahead of them ignored it.

"Child Registry? That's how you found her?"

Jake nodded. "Luck. Just luck."

"Funny thing," he said. "You got parents registering their kid's prints and pictures and stuff, case they get taken. Then you got parents suing the crap out of some school for taking their kid's prints without permission. Crazy world."

Deitcher started tapping on the steering wheel, frustrated with the pace of traffic flow. "So, what d'ya know about the girl, this Chase?"

"Not much. The kid has her own website. I can tell you she was in one of those little girl pageants here. More than one it looked like. Came in second. You know the kiddie beauty pageant where mothers dress their kids up, makeup and shit and makin' 'em dance around."

Jake remembered seeing Anna Chase's own web page just before he left. She was cute. Blond. Probably hair dyed by her mother. Ringlets, like a blond Shirley Temple. Outfitted in a frou-frou dress with some sort of tiara and sparkly crap in her hair. Even so, her eyes and her smile seemed genuine and shone through the bullshit of having to prance around on stage while, Jake imagined, mothers nudged each other in the audience, and oohed and aahed.

"Kinda sickening isn't it," stated Deitcher. "I mean making kids do all that just so the mothers can get their rocks off. Crazy world, my friend. I didn't know we had contests like that in Jersey."

"I think they're everywhere," sighed Jake. "Like a sick scam for mothers who couldn't make it. Now they make every kid a winner and suck more dough out of the parents."

"What about the girl's parents? So, what's the mother like?"

Jake had noticed a few family pictures at the bottom of Anna's web page. Anna's mother was hippo-fat. Rolls of extra helpings spilling out of her clothes. Made you want to start a diet.

"The mother?"

"Yeah," said Deitcher. "What's she like?"

"She'd take us in a fair fight."

"Really? Didn't know that. Okay. I did overhear the guys this morning. Someone checked on this Anna and found no wants or warrants."

"She's only eleven."

"Yeah. Even so, we get some pretty damn aggressive little shits growin' up here." Deitcher was all smiles now. Energy restored, ready to cuff up some of those little bitches and drag their butts to holding cell heaven.

"Listen I can go in with you when we get there..." continued Deitcher. The desperation to be doing something, anything different with someone different was showing through.

Jake put on his best smile. "Not necessary. Don't want to scare her and her mother with a lot of us showing up."

Deitcher snorted. "This is Jersey. The general populace is used to seeing us flying into somebody's home. Wouldn't be a day in good old Plainfield without us beatin' down someone's door. Besides, you said the mother could take us both on. You may need help." Deitcher looked sincere as if Jake's safety was paramount.

"Thanks anyway, but this won't take long. And I gotta head back this afternoon." He felt his words echoed what his seatmate had said. Idly, he wondered if they'd be on the same flight back.

"Back today?" asked Deitcher as he tried one more time. "Stay over why dontcha. We could hit the big city. I could show you parts of NYC you'd never see. Curl your California hair."

This whole business had jumpstarted old Deitcher, thought Jake. He checked his watch. "This thing is a goose chase as far as I'm concerned."

"Funny," said Deitcher. "Goose chase. Anna Chase."

"Yeah." Jake was already tired of Detective Deitcher.

A sharp turn put them on Naamans street. It seemed to run for miles and most of it was lined with row houses that were tight up against sidewalks that squeezed the street so that cars had to jiggy jog left and right to avoid all the 'previous owned' vehicles parked on both sides.

There were no trees, just a hard front line of buildings that appeared to be covered with many hues of beige asphalt shingles. Every house had two or three concrete steps leading up to it and identical iron railings down one side.

Kids swung on the railings or played on the steps. A few were running in the street. There was a boxy claustrophobia to the whole street. Only two ways out, coming and going, assuming you had the wherewithal to leave.

They only had to park about a half block away, but Jake noted that Deitcher made sure to hear the click of the remote lock before he left it.

There was no question as to where Anna Chase lived. The place was swarming with people. Mostly neighbors, Jake figured. But all it took was a TV truck and a few cop cars to bring out the populace.

Three TV crews, Jake could see. And four patrolmen guarding the steps leading up to the Chase residence. Two more suits lingered nearby.

So much for sitting down and having a nice little afternoon tea chat with Anna and her mother.

"Hey, Joseph. Nelson." Deitcher greeted the two other detectives who looked like they were ready to boil over.

"This here's the California guy. He's responsible for all this."

Deitcher waved his arm around, meaning the circus that was now Naamans street. Both detectives glared at him. Outsider. Troublemaker.

Jake extended his hand. "Detective Steiner, OID division of Sac PD." He guided them away from the TV cameras.

"Look, sorry about all this, but it appears we have a bunny in the woodpile that can't keep her mouth shut."

Nelson spoke up. "Yeah, well this is one group grope you people caused. Nobody knows what's going on. Press all over the place. What ya gonna do? Arrest the kid?"

He looked at his partner then hard at Jake. "He's just here to talk to the kid," butted in Deitcher.

This obviously made no sense to either Nelson or Joseph.

"Mother Mary!" exclaimed Joseph. "What's all this shit for then?" He meant the press. He meant the squads called out to keep the people away. He meant Jake showing up in their territory and maybe, just maybe making them look like fools in their own city.

Jake decided to throw his lot with Nelson and Joseph and Deitcher.

"Look detectives, we got sandbagged. All of us. You guys, me, Sacramento, Plainfield. All of us. Some attention-seeking asshole somewhere in Sacramento screwed me and you guys by releasing privileged information to the dogs. This is the result." Jake feigned exasperation.

"I spent six hours on a goddamn redeye to be greeted with this crap. And you guys. You guys had no idea what the hell was going on, so I feel for you guys."

Nelson and Joseph accepted the acknowledgment that they'd all been played. They were all on a similar, if not the same, team.

"Dunno," volunteered Nelson. "Guess we could help. Neighbors are gonna be pissed, though, when they see you drag the kid out. 'Spose we could run interference."

"That's just it. No arrest. We're sure the kid is innocent. I mean, hell, she's eleven. Somebody somehow got her prints and planted them at the scene. I'm just here to find out how the asshole did it."

"No shit," said Nelson.

"So, no arrest then?" asked Joseph.

"Sorry," said Jake.

"Well, damn. We're outta here then. What about them?" Nelson hooked a thumb over his shoulder toward the TV.

"I don't know how you guys usually do it, but in California, we just usually stand down and let 'em get bored. You try and talk to 'em and they get all excited. Better they should just get bored and leave."

"Okay," agreed Nelson. "We'll pull all but one squad guy and Joseph and I will make a big show of leaving."

Whatever thought Jake.

"I'll stay. Gotta stay and give you a ride back, right?" asked Deitcher.

Fine, thought Jake. Just let me get on with it.

Nelson and Joseph shook hands with Jake, their new fellow laborer.

Jake showed them some white California teeth as he extended his card. "Thanks, Detectives. When you decide to get rid of that pasty look and come out and get some sun, look me up."

"Will do. Take care," came the obligatory response.

But Jake knew they'd never venture out of Jersey and if they ever did, maybe Miami on a vacation with the wife and kids, they'd feel uncomfortable being away from the East, venturing as far as the wacky, crazy, screwed up, liberal hotbed that was the West Coast.

The job, this job, was a soulless magnet that never let go.

CHAPTER 12

Jake propped open the white aluminum screen door of number 3268 and knocked. It was unbolted to a chained distance by a man with glasses wearing a Bulls T-shirt.

"What?"

"I'm Detective Steiner from Sacramento. I called."

The man turned and spoke over his shoulder, "He's here."

Jake heard a mumbled voice from somewhere inside give an "Okay."

The man closed the door, unchained it, finally opened it, but quickly brought it nearly closed again. "Sorry. I.D. please."

He looked pleased to have remembered.

Jake produced his I.D. and handed the man a card. Like most citizens, this guy had no idea what a real I.D. looked like and wouldn't know what to look for on an I.D. anyway. It's just they always had to ask to see the I.D. Thanks, CSI.

"C'mon in." He stepped aside, and Jake entered with his briefcase. He was faced with three more adults. He recognized Anna's mother. She was flanked, if that was possible, by two other men of similar size.

Anna was nowhere to be seen.

The man with the Bulls shirt closed the door. "Okay. Well, I guess I can introduce…" He checked the card he held in his hand. "Detective…"

"Steiner," finished Jake. He extended his hand first to Mrs. Chase. She was surprised as if she didn't expect to have to touch him. Her grip was weak and wet.

"That there is Anna's mother. There's her brother, Ralph and our attorney Anthony Shapiro."

Jake acknowledged the two men.

"I'm Johnson. Anna's father."

"Glad to meet you all," Jake said with as much sincerity as he could muster. "I'm sorry about all this, he said turning to indicate the TV hounds. I'm not sure what happened. I think it's a case of someone told someone in the press something that wasn't true, and you know how they can be."

Anna's mother looked out the window. "There's Channel 11, 6 and even 3." It was obvious she was not miffed, but rather excited at the attention.

The attention-whoring was well instilled from mother to daughter because at this moment Anna was standing at her upstairs bedroom window, excited about being videotaped by all three news crews.

"Now, what's this about Anna?" asked Anna's father as he looked serious.

No one sat and no one offered Jake a seat. He smiled again. He didn't blame them. A policeman flies across country to grill your eleven-year-old girl. Clogs the street with media. Riles the neighbors. Guess he'd be pissed too and round up the troops for protection.

"May I sit?" asked Jake. And sat anyway.

They all looked to attorney Shapiro for advice. Evidently, it was possibly an admission of guilt if they sat as well.

"Yes, please sit Detective," said Shapiro. They followed Shapiro's lead, and all settled themselves; Katherine's brother on the couch, Shapiro perched on the front of a straight-backed chair. Anna's father sat in a kitchen chair that had been brought into the tiny living room just for that purpose, Katherine lording over the group from her throne in an over-stuffed armchair.

"By the way," asked Jake. "Is Anna here?"

Once again, everyone looked to the attorney for advice. Jake sighed. This was going to be a long day.

Shapiro cleared his throat. "We'd like to know what this is about first, detective, if you don't mind." He smiled to show he was just being the attorney and not a real obstructionist asshole.

"Of course. Sure," Jake said. "It is complicated but just to let you know, the real reason I'm here is I need your help. Before I get into it, I have to say this is an ongoing investigation and I won't be able to reveal all that we're working on."

"I understand," nodded Shapiro.

"In addition, I'd ask that whatever we discuss stay with us and that you make no statement to the press."

Anna's mother spoke up. "What about the neighbors? They have to know somethin'."

"I think they'll be fine not knowing," Jake said, though he had no illusions as to the privacy of what they would be discussing. The neighbors were owed allegiance. He was just carpetbagging.

"As I say, I just need your help."

They all looked from one to the other. This is not what they expected.

"So," drawled the attorney. "Neither Anna nor Johnson or Katherine here are in any trouble?"

Jake pretended to be surprised. "What? No. As I said, we have an unusual situation in Sacramento that may require some answers from you all. And Anna."

"What about all them press out there? Did you send 'em?" Johnson had a bullying tone. People had invaded his street, pissed off the neighbors.

"I mean Christ," he continued. "Makes it look like there's some sort of cop activity here. Like they're gonna bust down my door and arrest me for drugs or somethin'."

The group waited for Jake's answer.

Jake lowered his eyes and addressed the group. "I don't know what happened there. Someone, probably someone out our way in one of our departments thought they were being cute and leaked Anna's name to the press as someone who was a suspect in our investigation."

Jake held up his hand. "But, as I said, I'm just here for your help. Neither Anna nor any of you are suspected of anything, except possibly being duped in some way."

"What situation is that?" asked Johnson.

Jake smiled his 'God, I'm overworked' smile and sighed as if the burden of following up on this case was damn near killing him.

"While I don't believe there is any credence to it, I have to tell you that we have a murder in Sacramento. A film producer. Former film producer."

Jake saw Katherine's eyes widen.

"Hollywood?"

"Used to be."

He paused.

"And the reason I'm here, the reason I've flown cross country, is that the only set of fingerprints found near the body of the murdered man were those of Anna P. Chase. Your daughter."

In the silence that ensued after Jake spoke came the intrusion of the brain-pounding thump of a car stereo pumping out crap rap as it sat down the middle of the block.

Katherine's brother who had looked ready to fall fast asleep before was now wide awake.

Katherine's mouth hung open. Shapiro moved further to the edge of his chair. Johnson was the first to utter a word.

"What the hell?"

No one admonished him for his cursing.

"Just what the hell are you talking about?" Johnson persisted.

Shapiro, the cooler head glanced around at everyone before he restated the same sentiments in a more restrained tone.

"Detective, obviously this is a mistake. It must be one of those one in a million shots where two people have the same fingerprints. Anna's must match someone else's."

Shapiro looked to reassure the assemblage.

"Mr. Shapiro, that chance is about one in at least 100 billion, not millions. In fact, no one has ever found two identical prints. Even twins are slightly different. So, we're rather confident that the fingerprints are Anna's."

"That can't be," insisted her father. "The girl's not a criminal! She's never had her fingerprints taken. Right?" He looked at his wife for confirmation.

Katherine's mouth opened but she didn't speak.

Jake spoke up, looking at Katherine. "Mrs. Chase, five years ago, didn't you have Anna registered with the Child Registry for Missing Children?"

Katherine went blank, then she covered her mouth with her hands.

"And didn't they take her picture and her fingerprints?"

She nodded in slow motion. "God, yes, I forgot. Remember John, we took her down to the fire station on Aricola?"

Johnson looked mildly disgusted, now sure that his wife was to blame for all this hoopla. "You took her. I didn't."

Katherine turned from Shapiro to Jake.

"I got her all registered. They did, anyway. They took her picture and they made her fingerprints. You know with ink and all. Had a great time. They made a big fuss over Anna and the kids. Had fun getting the ink off. Had a washtub where they had a clown washing their hands..."

She stopped, realizing she'd been jabbering.

"I remember that," she added with an affirming nod to Jake. "I do."

Shapiro continued with the cross-examination. "I still don't understand, detective. I mean I see how you got a copy of Anna's prints from the Registry, but what made you think they were also in the car where this man was found?"

"Our Forensic team lifted them from the car hours before we found Anna's prints in the Registry database," answered Jake.

"So how did they get in the car?"

Jake didn't answer directly. "Let me ask Mr. and Mrs. Chase if Anna has ever been to California or Arizona?"

Johnson looked to his wife for confirmation at the same time he answered. "She ain't never been outta state, right? She went to the shore, Ocean City, couple a years ago with a friend, but she ain't traveled anywhere else."

Katherine nodded.

"Why Arizona?" asked Shapiro. "Thought this was just California?"

"We need to eliminate the possibility that Anna was ever in that car. That car ended up in California but was originally sold by a dealer in Phoenix."

"Nope. Never been there," replied Johnson with confidence. "Either place."

Jake nodded. "And, unless the owner of the car drove it out here to Plainfield, New Jersey, which is unlikely, it means Anna's prints were planted in the car," Jake said.

"How do you do that?" asked Johnson.

"It's sadly very easy to lift prints off of something and reset them on an appropriate surface."

"So, you're saying someone… stole Anna's prints and placed them in this car?"

"We believe that."

"Why?"

"Our guess is to throw us off with prints that couldn't be identified. They didn't expect that Katherine had had the foresight to have Anna registered."

Katherine sat up straighter and looked to the men for a bit of approbation. Nothing.

"But, because whoever it was chose Anna, we now have a lead to whoever did this. We hope."

Jake stared at Anna's mother.

"What?" she asked.

"We believe, Mrs. Chase, that you and Anna, or maybe just Anna herself, came into contact with the person who stole Anna's prints."

"I have no idea who that could be," said Katherine Chase, appearing both guilty and bewildered.

Jake knew it was a stretch. If whoever did this was skilled enough to plant the prints, they would be subtle enough to avoid suspicion.

"Mrs. Chase, while you're thinking, I'd like to speak with Anna. And I'd also like to take her fingerprints." Jake attempted to slip in the last bit of information matter-of-factly. Didn't work.

"What?" shouted an excited Johnson. "No way! No damn way."

Surprisingly, Shapiro came to Jake's rescue.

"Johnson, listen," soothed Shapiro. "It's for Anna's protection. Besides, it seems she's already been printed once. And it may help this detective who's flown all the way out here to possibly solve his case."

It was a simplistic statement, but Jake let it stand.

Katherine spoke up. "I'll go get Anna."

"I don't know…" mumbled Johnson. "I don't get it."

"It's fine Johnson. It'll help him," stated Shapiro.

"He's right," added Jake as he readied the fingerprint scanner.

"What's that?" asked Johnson, trying to muster some authority in his own home.

Jake held up the scanner which was as small as a TV remote. It had a small screen on which each finger of the subject was placed and scanned and recorded.

"Scanner," was all Jake said.

He looked up as Katherine entered the room.

She brought her hand around and introduced a stunning little girl with blond hair and blue eyes dressed in a blue jumper.

Anna P. Chase, person of interest in the murder of James Marston, Junior, looked to her mother before sitting across from Jake.

"Detective Steiner. This is my daughter, Anna."

Jake laughed to himself because his one thought was this cute little girl had a killer smile.

CHAPTER 13

Jake smiled his best welcoming smile. He wasn't skilled at interviewing kids. He had little practice, and he tried to hide his discomfort by smiling. It hurt his face.

"Good morning Anna."

The girl's eyes were bright with undisguised interest but there was a reserve that came with a poise that belied her eleven years.

"Hello."

Katherine Chase put her hand on her daughter's back and leaned over her.

"Detective Steiner needs to ask you a few questions, dear."

Anna looked at her mother, then swept the room, glancing at her father, her uncle and lawyer Shapiro. Finally, back on Jake.

"Are you a real detective?"

"I am."

"From California?"

"Sacramento. Yes. That's the capital of California," he added lamely.

"I know," said Anna. "There are a lot of people in front of the house. I see TV cameras. Did you bring those?"

Jake looked down, so regretting the leak that had spawned the circus outside.

"No Anna. I had nothing to do with those." Sort of.

"Am I in trouble?" She looked at her mother.

"No dear. The nice detective came all the way from California just to ask you a few questions." She spoke of California as if it was located just a little south of heaven.

Anna returned her attention to Jake. "I don't understand. Not really."

Jake smiled again. "I'll do my best to explain it, Anna. We, in California, are investigating a case. A missing person's case. Well, it was a missing person case until the other day when we located the gentleman. He was found deceased in his vehicle."

Jake could see that while Anna was listening, it was so far out of her purview that what he was saying was washing over her like an inconsequential breeze.

He brought it to her level. "You watch TV? Detective shows?"

Anna shrugged. "Sometimes."

"You know about fingerprints, of course, and how they're used to identify people I'm sure."

Anna didn't nod, just waited for more.

Jake shifted in his chair. God kids were tough. His face hurt from smiling.

"The thing is," he went on. "We found your fingerprints inside the vehicle of the man who was... is deceased.

Jake saw little Anna Chase pale.

"M-Mine?" she stuttered.

Shapiro leaned further forward on his chair. "Don't worry my dear. It's a mistake."

But Anna's eyes didn't leave Jake.

"What do you mean? I didn't do anything."

The girl's tension only reflected what everyone else was thinking and feeling. He wished he had her alone without three other sets of eyes.

Jake kept up with the smile.

"Mr. Shapiro's correct. It is a mistake, Anna. And you didn't do anything wrong. I'm only here because I need your help."

Anna's face softened slightly. Jake noticed she resumed breathing.

"What we believe happened is someone stole your fingerprints and planted them in the man's car."

"Stole? How? How can someone do that?" Anna glanced at her hands.

Jake wanted to avoid getting mired in fingerprint details.

"It is easier than you might imagine. So, I need your help because we believe the person who stole them from you is involved in the man's death. You understand?"

Anna swallowed hard. And nodded. Then she shook her head.

"I didn't do anything wrong. I don't talk to anyone I don't know." Then, "He stole me? In California? My fingerprints? And killed someone. I don't..."

She turned and looked at her mother and father. Her bottom lip fluttered as she turned back to Jake.

"I didn't do anything. Honest."

Jake wanted to reach out to her and tell her he knew. He wanted to reassure her that it wasn't anything she did. But most of all he wanted to try to bridge the gap between his reality and hers.

"Anna," Jake said as softly as he could. He kept the smile plastered on.

"Just like on some crime shows on TV you've seen it is possible to take someone's fingerprints and transfer them to somewhere else. And that's what happened to yours. Someone got hold of your prints and saved them and planted them in the car. Sort of like what might happen on TV. Understand?"

"Okay."

"So, I've flown out here from California to talk to you and your mother and father and try to figure out where someone could have gotten your fingerprints. Especially you."

He reached out with an affirming grip on her hands.

"You, Anna, are maybe the key to helping me solve this case."

Anna cleared her throat. "Why is it me?"

Jake studied her wondering face. "I don't know Anna. You know what random means, right?"

She shrugged. "Means... random."

"Right. We believe your fingerprints were picked out at random and were meant to confuse us. We think we were never meant to find out who belonged to the prints. But we did because your mother registered your picture and your prints with a child registration site when you were younger. And we matched you. And whoever did this, whoever killed the man, didn't think we'd ever find you. Now we have and now your job and mine and your mother's and father's job is to figure out who they are. We need to figure out your connection to someone in California…"

Anna brightened and turned to her mother then to Jake.

"I know," she beamed.

"You know what?"

"My connection to California."

CHAPTER 14

Danni Harness stubbed out her home-rolled cigarette into the ashtray commemorating her ten years as medical examiner as a new candidate for autopsy was wheeled in by her assistant, Jeff.

"Here you go," he said.

As he unzipped the body bag. "I'm going to lunch," he announced.

"Sure," said Danni. "Go ahead but help me with this first."

With gloved hands and masks and face shields in place, they lifted the body out and placed it on the autopsy table. Under the bright lights, they observed the gross trauma that was easily seen. He was an average man, the only thing that was of note was his red hair.

His back and left side were burned. Skin blistered, some curled and sloughing off where his left arm used to be. When she saw the condition of the body, she flipped on the exhaust fan to high.

"Where'd they find this dude?"

Jeff unfolded the paperwork on the clipboard. "This druggie was sprawled on his back on a pile of pallets over in East Sacramento. Near Orleta."

"Like this?"

"Evidently just like that. Clothes were in a pile next to the body. They brought 'em in. I went through them," stated Jeff. "Nothing in pockets. No I.D."

The gasoline smell coming off the body was mixed with the cachet of decay.

Jeff shrugged. "Someone stripped him and tried for well-done."

"Well, he didn't burn so well. Though somebody gave it a good go," mused Danni.

"I'm back in an hour, okay?" With that, Jeff pushed open the door and turned on the light outside the room that stated innocently, 'Room In Use'.

But Danni never heard him as something had caught her attention. Her assistant had called him a druggie. And it was true, he was found in an area rife with human detritus from drug deals gone awry, but this was different. She realized what it was that got to her. This guy wasn't an addict, she thought, though she'd confirm that shortly. No, he looked like a professional man. One that could probably never even find his way to the armpit of Sacramento to pick up a bunch of coke or a few needles full of heroin.

She grasped his right hand and turned it over. It was relatively unburnt. Though it was encrusted with dried ash and mud, when she wiped all that away, what she saw confirmed what she felt. This guy had soft hands, maybe even a manicure.

She straightened the right arm with some difficulty. Between rigor and the damage, the fire had done, the skin was stretched tight, where it still existed. By gently working the arm, she was able to reveal the area where the most common injection sites were - the basilic or the median cubital vein on the inside crook of the elbow.

There was nothing that Danni could see. Even with all the trauma to the body, she could see there was no subdermal bruising, no obvious track marks in the veins.

"Okay, my friend, I apologize for my stupid assistant. Just because you were found there doesn't mean we will lump you in with those poor sots. Location isn't everything. Least not when you're dead. But you surely must've pissed off somebody."

She stepped back and checked that uneasy feeling in her gut. She turned the man's head so she could look into the face of what used to be an average white guy. For some reason, she figured him to be a suburbs type of guy.

"Just what kind of shit have you been up to?"

But the man didn't answer.

As she did through most of her autopsies, she conversed with the dead, asking pertinent questions, suggesting ways that death may have happened. The only answers she received were the ones she supplied herself. Since there was no identification on the body when it arrived, she went ahead and named him. A name close to his suspected origin often helped her figure out what the guy had been up to and maybe who he had jacked around because, she guessed, he'd had little to do with agreeing to set himself on fire after he was killed.

She started her digital recorder.

"Okay Red, tell me about yourself."

It took nearly twenty minutes for her to examine all the scorched areas of the body. Though she quickly determined the damage had all been done post-mortem, and except for two scarred-over bullet entry wounds, she saw no other areas of trauma that would indicate how Redhead had met his fate.

"All right," she said. "If you're not going to help me, I'll have to do a little exploring on my own."

Using the magnifying glass, she started with his feet, separating his toes, which were all intact. No needle marks between the toes, a popular fall back when arm veins gave way, or when it was important to hide all evidence of illicit drug use.

The bottoms of his feet were also unremarkable.

Working up each leg, she identified several deep ring-shaped bruises, as if his shins had connected with a table leg or the other way around.

"Genitalia intact and also unremarkable. Sorry, Redhead."

She made it to the torso. "What have we here Mr. It-Looks-Like-I've-Been-Shot? Shot several times it appears."

She ran her glove over what she believed to be gunshot entry wounds on the left side of the chest. "Good news, Redhead. These aren't recent, and they obviously didn't kill you."

She stood up and stretched her back and considered what she'd found so far. Burned. Shot. Bruised. Not a druggie.

"Who are you?" she asked. "I'm going with accounting, sales or any desk job for you, though it's not easy to pick up a few 45 holes when you're sitting at a computer screen. So, maybe you were-"

And that's when she noticed his left arm.

She swung the magnifying glass into position though what was on his arm was easily seen without it.

Just below the right wrist was a series of faded numbers. It appeared they'd been written in a permanent marker, though nothing is permanent on the skin she knew. Everything will eventually wear or wash off. And in this case, was spared the flames.

She moved around so she was looking at them the way Redhead would've seen them.

Ten numbers. Phone number.

Procedure deemed she needed to report it to somebody in Robbery-Homicide.

"And report it I will. Just as soon as I try it myself."

She switched off the recorder, removed her face shield and mask and pulled out her cell.

She punched in the number.

It rang six times.

She held her breath, finger poised, ready to end the call.

The phone clicked as someone answered. Danni pressed her ear tight to the phone waiting to hear how the person answered, but she was unprepared for what she heard.

"Hey, Danni, what's up?"

She snatched the phone away and looked at it, then to the dead man, who while he wasn't smiling, seemed to be enjoying this.

She hesitated because she didn't believe the name that came up. "Who... who is this?"

"What do you mean Danni? You called me. It's Mallory. Mallory Dimante. What do you need?"

It took a moment, and she didn't mean to, but she laughed. "What do I need? What do I need? I need you to tell me why the assistant to the On-Going Investigation Division's phone number is on my dead friend Redhead's arm."

"Redhead?"

"Yeah.

"He has red hair?"

"Yeah."

"He's dead?"

"Melanie, most of my clients don't drop in for a chat," she intoned. "I don't get many live ones here for an autopsy, you know. So yeah, dead, like he's no longer with us. But, his body is right here, and it has you written all over him. Maybe you can explain"-

Mallory had already hung up.

Mallory was able to get Stan on the first ring.

"What?"

"Uhh, how are you feeling?"

"Just tell me. No one calls about anything anymore. They all think I've been moved to a nursing home. What's up?"

"Did Phil Ginger have red hair?"

"Did?"

Mallory paused. "We should meet at Danni's. Soon as you can."

CHAPTER 15

Danni hadn't waited for Mallory but had examined Redhead's posterior since it needed to be done. With Jeff's help, she'd flipped Redhead over and done a thorough exam of the entire backside, again starting with the feet and working upwards.

Not pristine, but there was no sign of anything untoward that would cause his demise.

Leaning up against the outer autopsy door, she idly considered resurrecting her stubbed out butt in the ashtray but opted for a fresh one.

Frustrated, she would usually have a good idea of what killed one of her clients before she cracked them open to poke around and take tissue samples. Unless this was poison, and Danni considered it unlikely given the mild history of the guy, whatever got to him she'd have to discover when she opened him up.

She gave Mallory one more minute and when she didn't appear, she pushed off the wall, flicked out her cigarette added it to the ashtray's growing collection.

Danni had saved the head for when Mallory arrived, but now she couldn't wait. She leaned over and used the magnifying glass to probe through all the matted hair. It took her ten minutes examining every inch.

Nada.

"Come on buddy, talk to me."

She stared straight into his face.

His tongue was lolled out of the side of the mouth. Dried blood, probably from biting the tongue she surmised, dotted one side of the cheek.

Using two pairs of forceps she pried open the jaws. She pushed the tongue further to the side.

"What the...?" She positioned the LED light so it rested next to her head. It lit up the interior of the mouth like the sun. She probed with the forceps, pushing aside a cheek, checking the left side, then the right.

The interior of the mouth as well as the back of the tongue was decorated with hundreds of tiny cuts. Slits a half inch long from which blood had oozed and coagulated at the back of the throat and further. She tried to push the tongue to get a better view of the back of the throat, but it was clogged with dried blood.

Danni Harness straightened up. Now she knew how Redhead had died. He'd drowned in his own blood.

She needed a cigarette but instead roughly pushed aside a cheek and used the smallest forceps she had to explore along one of the cuts until she found it.

She extracted it from the cheek's flesh and deposited it on a sanitary tray.

She dove in again to the next cut and the next, extracting something from each. It took nearly a half hour to pull out over a hundred pieces.

Using the lighted magnifier, she rearranged them until the pattern became clear. And when it was, she shivered like she hadn't in years.

She backed away from the tray as if it was death incarnate.

CHAPTER 16

Stan watched as Mallory adjusted then readjusted her paper mask so it completely covered her nose and mouth. He had no idea how many autopsies she had been to, but he guessed since she was almost as white as the walls of the autopsy room, that it hadn't been many.

She seemed to regard the burned body with solemn alarm and he was just about sorry he'd let her stay when he optimistically thought it would be a break from continually trying to contact Jake in New Jersey or trying to find two kids lost in the quagmire of the Child Protective System. Maybe he was wrong. On the other hand, according to Danni's call, the guy had Mallory's number with him.

Burned bodies were always of a dissociative nature. Stan never knew who they were. Had never spoken to them. Didn't know their life story. Didn't know what they cared about. Had never had a drink, or four with them.

Not so with Phil Ginger.

Stan turned to Danni. "His name's Phil Ginger. Used to be a reporter with the Bee," said Stan with more strength in his voice than what was really there. "He was following up on bodies that came out of here. Out of the morgue."

"Him?" asked Danni, now alert. "I thought it was you guys who were watching the body flow out of here." She came to stand next to the autopsy table. "Why him?"

"He was following a hunch," said Stan. "Found out someone had claimed Ruby Everheart's body when it was supposed to be cremated."

"Yeah. Okay, sure. I remember talking to him on the phone," said Danni, finding her voice. "I told him some relative had claimed the body. Made a copy of the power of attorney and left it for him. That was the last I heard. Until someone told me you were waiting to see who would claim the torn-up carcass of the lady your Melanie shot up."

"Mallory," corrected Mallory.

"Whatever."

Stan surveyed the remains of Phil Ginger. He turned to Danni. "You waiting for us to get here to cut him open? Find out how he died?"

"No need. I know why or at least how he died." Danni glanced at the metal tray that sat alongside the autopsy table. It was covered with a clean white cloth.

"And where was he found?"

"Drug heaven. Orleta."

"He wasn't an addict Danni." Stan reconsidered. "Least, I didn't think he was."

"You are correct. No track marks, no evidence elsewhere. Course toxicology will show if he really was."

Stan shook his head. "He wasn't, I'm sure. Maybe two-thirds the way to becoming a professional alcoholic, mostly a functional drinker. Could always do his job."

"What was he working on?"

"You mean besides tracking dead bodies? I don't know."

"Well, one thing for sure, it appears he found out what he was looking for. Especially if it involved him being tortured."

"You say he had my phone number on him?" asked Mallory, finally getting a question in. She moved a step closer to Ginger's body.

"Not just on him, like in his shirt pocket. I mean, 'on him'."

Danni once again stretched out his right arm. "I mean on him. There."

Mallory saw her phone number in permanent marker upside down.

"And your address."

Stan had to twist around to accurately read the address. It was a street address with six numbers below it.

"That's not my address," said Mallory. She crossed her arms and tried to look dispassionate as if this was just another day giving her professional opinion on the latest fatality to come across the threshold.

Danni joined them and twisted the arm around so she could also read it.

"Whose is it?"

"No clue," said Stan. "Not mine or Mallory's. Not his either. He lived out toward Antelope if I remember. Had a gentleman farm, he liked to say."

Stan pulled out his phone and took two pictures of what was written on Ginger's arm. Close enough so he'd be able to see it on his phone's screen.

"So, you said he was shot?" asked Stan.

Danni waved the idea away. "Long time ago, I think. Wasn't the cause of death. Had two holes in him that I could find. Scarred over years ago. Shoulder and upper chest. Seemed to have missed anything important."

"He was a former paratrooper. Air Force, I think. Though he didn't like to talk about it."

"Well, they were old wounds."

"Danni don't tell me he was burned alive, please," murmured Mallory.

Danni seemed to be in a sort of trance. "No, they, whoever they are, tried to burn the body after he was dead. Gasoline. You can smell it if you get close. But they weren't very successful."

Danni probed a few of the burnt areas with her gloved hands then they came to rest on either side of his mouth.

"He suffered. He did. The inside of his mouth was cut with a million tiny cuts."

"Shit," whispered Stan. "You saying they cut the inside of his mouth?"

"Not exactly."

She moved to the small tray with the white linen covering it. Her finger started to lift the edge of the linen.

"I believe they made him drink something. He ended up choking on it because of what was in it."

"What?"

She pulled back the linen.

Neatly arranged on the white cloth were hundreds of metal pieces.

"Stan, someone cut up razor blades and forced him to swallow. They stuck. In his mouth. Down his throat. They dug in. The more he choked and swallowed the more they cut into him. He bled to death at the same time he died drowning in his own blood."

Stan and Mallory stared at the pattern that Danni had displayed. The glinting blue shape was distinctive. And deadly sharp.

"I think…" began Danni.

"What?" Stan managed as he swallowed hard. "What?"

"I think they didn't want him to talk. To tell what he knew."

"Or," said Stan. "Punishing him because he did."

They were all silent as the razor bits shimmered in place.

"I need a drink," whispered Mallory. "Many."

CHAPTER 17

"They said I'd find you here." Susan slid into the booth opposite Mallory.

"Who's they?"

"You know. They. Them. Others. Anyone who knows where you might be."

"Well," sighed Mallory. "I guess they were right, 'cause here you are and here I am."

With two fingers Susan pushed away the empty glasses that sat before Mallory and replaced them with a small stack of file folders.

"This?" asked Mallory.

"This, my good girlfriend, is all the stuff you asked for. All the dirty dirt on your Mr. Marston and his ill-fated love affairs, shady business dealings and other assorted activities that one does when one is pretending to be straight but is, in fact, gay as a very happy clown. If you get my drift."

"I'm getting your drift, girlfriend."

The waiter appeared at their table. "Ma'am?"

Susan checked the disarray in front of Mallory. "I'll have just one of what she was having."

"I'm still having," answered Mallory.

Susan held up one finger and mouthed 'One'.

The waiter gave Mallory a quick glance, nodded to Susan and left.

"Did he get my order, you think?"

"He's on top of things, I'm sure," answered Susan. "Listen, also in that pile before you, all mostly neatly typed I might add, is what I could find on any and all Pokovichs, which is pretty much zip.

Mallory raised an empty glass. "Well done, girl." Noticing the empty glass. "Oops. We'll have to wait until my friend Henry comes back with refills.

"It may take a while," smirked Susan. "Henry?"

"In France, it's pronounced Henri," Mallory declared, letting the 'R' rattle around more than the cubes in her most recently empty glass.

"With a little accent mark over the last 'i'."

"How long have you been here?" asked Susan, with some mock concern.

"What's today?"

"Funny."

Mallory settled back and started scraping the little wet white doilies that had adhered to her martini glasses. "I'm fine. Just don't need to see any more of Danni's handiwork. Not anytime soon. Or ever."

"Bad?"

"Poor Stan. He knew the guy."

"Stan's up and running?"

Mallory shrugged. "Running when Bea tells him to run I guess. Still, he knew this guy. They shared secrets for years. Back and forth. Stan would feed him the shits that were happening with some investigation and this guy would come up with gems, as Stan called them, on his own. Tit for tat arrangement."

"What happened to him?"

"Oh, nothing much. Someone decided to shove razor blades down his throat until he choked on his own blood. Then they tried to burn him. All that was after they beat him."

"Bloody hell." Susan took a moment to absorb that. "But it's not related to what you guys are working on, right?"

Mallory held up a finger. "Wrong, my dear. Very, very wrong. Seems this guy, the name was Ginger, by the way, red hair, had met with Stan a few days ago and was hot on the story of missing bodies."

"Who's missing?"

"Let me take you back in the WayBack machine. You happen to recall the infamous tale of Ruby Everheart and her... I mean his, demise?"

"I don't care what they say about me, I'm not senile. What about her... him... it?"

"Body's missing."

"Missing? Really? Did somebody dig it up? I thought they cremated that pervert."

"Hah! Wrong again. So, a car pulls up about quitting time at Danni's crypt with an official paper and spirited good ol' Ruby away. No cremation. No burial. Nothing to dig up, 'cause Ruby is long gone. Poof!"

"Don't you guys keep track of things like that?"

"We were too busy finding Mr. Marston's head and thanks to you, the rest of him."

"Welcome."

"No, it was this Ginger guy who found out Ruby was spirited away. He did our job for us. I mean we can't be in two places at once, can we?"

Before Susan could respond, Mallory continued. "Here's the kicker. Mr. Ginger discovered who took it. Seems it was our friend, now blown to shit thanks to me, Ilsa Pokovich, and some little shit of a man and some person used to be unknown, now known. Took it God knows where."

"What the hell. What connection did they have with Ruby Everheart? They family or what?"

Mallory tapped the folders before her. "You tell me. The only thing Ginger could find out was if there is another Pokovich. It's like they're cockroaches and when you run one through with a garden rake, another one appears."

"So, they're related? Pokovich and Everheart? I thought Everheart was this Rendell character. From Florida."

"The paper they delivered to spring old Ruby stated they were family or legal conservators. Something like that. And really, who knows who Everheart was. Supposed to be this guy, Rendell. Anyway, the missing Pokovich is one Nikolai Pokovich. According to Ginger."

Susan shook her head. "Where's my drink?"

"Where's my drink?" echoed Mallory.

"Speaking of tasty drinks that neither of us is enjoying right now, where's Detective Steiner?"

Mallory just shook her head. "Not available. On a date with an eleven-year-old."

"I don't want to know."

Susan regarded Mallory and the reports before her and decided.

"Listen, just so you don't have to strain your eyes reading my perfectly typed reports, I'll summarize for you.

"Probably wise. Go for it."

"Lot of it you know but here's something interesting. After Ilsa Pokovich was carted off to jail after trying to maim Mr. James Marston, Marston never divorced her. It was as if he just forgot about her. Maybe he thought she'd be in prison forever. In any case, he kept busy with a series of male persons. Then, a few months before Ms. Pokovich gets out of prison, he changes his will. Actually, there seem to be a couple un-signed versions that this attorney… uh"

"Saunders, I think," volunteered Mallory.

"Yeah. Him. Anyway, Pokovich is gone inheritance-wise. Finally, leaves much of what he owns to a charity. Don't remember the exact name, it's in there. Anyway, it's something like Charity of Aged Retired Actors. Something like that."

Mallory considered, then nodded. "A noble cause."

"Would be. If it existed."

"It's a fake?"

"Oh, there is a name. And a post office box in Delaware. That's it. No record of any charity work."

"That it?"

Susan smiled. "You'll love it. The only name, buried under a sea of paper flotsam, was one Nikolai Pokovich."

Mallory took a moment to connect things.

"So, Marston leaves his property and stuff-"

"Practically all of it."

"Yeah. Leaves his stuff to this Pokovich with a fake charity. And poor Phil Ginger finds out that there is a Nikolai Pokovich who claimed to be family to Ruby Everheart and takes the body to God knows where. Ginger finds out and he's-"

"Killed." Added Susan.

"No," contradicted Mallory. "Not killed. Beat to shit, made to eat razors and set on fire on a pallet in slum town."

"Mal."

"What?"

"You guys need to be careful."

Mallory looked away. "Tell that to the two Musketeers."

"Mal. I'm serious. I have a bad feeling." She reached out and took Mallory's hands. "And all this for a kid's bear that the crazy bitch you shot demanded from Stan?"

"Crazy, huh?"

Mallory seemed to consider whether to say more. Then did. "There's something else I didn't tell you."

"Dear God, now what?"

"Phil Ginger had my phone number on him."

"Your card? Holy shit, he had your card?"

"No. Not my card. He had my number, my phone number, written on his arm. In ink or marker."

"Mallory? Why?"

"We don't know. I don't know."

"Mal, that means... damn. Whoever did that to him saw your number. They know you must've talked to him."

"But I didn't."

"They'll think you know what he knew."

"But I don't. He only communicated with Stan."

"You need to be more than careful, girl. Like, hyper careful."

Mallory tried to block out the last sight she had of Phil Ginger lying on Danni's gleaming autopsy table. Head to the side. Mouth clipped open with forceps that peeled back his lips. Danni rooting for more pieces.

And the shimmering display of blue death razor bits, haphazardly decorated with dried blood and bits of Phil Ginger's throat.

She looked up at Susan. "Careful. Sure. No problem."

CHAPTER 18

"It won't work," affirmed Jody. "It just won't." But his eyes said something different.

It had only been a day doing hard labor at McCardle's stockade as Jody liked to call it and now Michael had cornered Jody and told how all three of them were going to take their leave of the McCardle's hospitality.

Michael could see the kid was both excited and mildly terrified, especially since Michael was asking him to be instrumental in their escape plan.

"It will though, I know it. Well? What do you say?"

"What about your sister?" Jody asked, delaying any answer he had to give.

"She can't wait," lied Michael. In fact, Jessie, much to Michael's dismay, had done her best to settle in. She had taken to helping the old lady with household stuff, like dishes and laundry. When Michael had told her he had a plan for them to escape, she'd begun to cry.

"I don't want to go," she'd said.

"You don't like it here," Michael had challenged her. "You said so."

Jessie had turned away. "It's okay, I guess. It's not too bad."

"Yet," Jody said. "Sometimes things get ugly. Like physical ugly. Beatings ugly."

"But it seems okay here." Jessie had looked from Jody to her brother. "Maybe you should go."

"And leave you here? Are you nuts?"

He knew he had her convinced when she'd finally asked, "Where would we go?"

"Where we'd always planned. Arizona."

"How? You have money?"

Michael had brushed off the question with an 'It's all taken care of' smile.

There was no money, or very little. When the CPS gendarmes had come to escort them to the hinterlands, things like money and belongings were misplaced. They still had their backpack, and Michael had even managed to throw a thrift store pair of jeans for himself and a shirt for Jessie into it, but his stash of dinero he'd secured from his aunt's situation had somehow found its way elsewhere. Just another shining example of government workers taking what doesn't belong to them.

Sure, there was precious little scratch on hand, but he had a plan. And, unlike most Michael Cooper plans, this one came with a backup. He hoped.

"Yeah, we're both good, Jess and me," he confirmed to Jody. "So?"

"I don't know…" Jody drawled.

"You've stashed some food for yourself the last few meals, haven't you?"

Jody's nod was good enough for Michael. Not the ringing endorsement of his plan he had hoped for, but it would have to do.

"It's almost a full moon tonight. It'll last until sunup, give us the light we need. We'll be fine. It's a stealth mission. Commando. It's solid and you know it."

Jody smirked. "Maybe. Either way, it'll be good to get on the road again."

"Hey, I never asked where you're from."

"Just outside L.A."

Michael was surprised. "How d'you get a way out here in the middle of wherever we are?"

"CPS passed me around. I did... something to one of my uncles a year ago. Said I was a danger. One night the parents up and moved without me. They couldn't handle me."

Michael looked at the scrawny kid in front of him. The kid who kept pushing his glasses back up on his nose and his hair back away from his face looked like something anyone could handle.

"Your uncle okay?"

"Don't think so."

Michael tried to think of something to say. He thought back to his own situation, with his shit of a father and what he did to Michael and what Michael had had to do to him.

"You did what you had to," offered Michael, wondering though if he was seeing the gestation of someone with a darker soul in this quiet, seemingly ineffectual boy. If so, it was good he had the plan drawn out the way he did. They would be going their separate ways.

"Three sharp. Got it?"

Jody nodded.

After dinner, Michael lay in bed thinking how proud he was of his preparation. Sure, stuff could still go sideways. If his life up to this point was any indication, there would be some aspect of this whole adventure that would sour. But, even so. They were what his mother used to call, 'being proactive'. Doing something about something. Not just lying around waiting for the walls to cave in.

Once they hit Arizona and had all this crap behind them, then life would start over. It was true because he'd been without access to a phone or computer or even able to mail a letter, that he hadn't been able to re-establish contact with Shippen Travers, his mother's cousin, who had reluctantly agreed to take them in. But he believed with all the hope he had left that good old cowboy Travers hadn't abandoned them, that he would welcome them, and they would finally have a place where he and Jess could sleep and live and not always be thinking about moving. Always having to formulate an escape. Always leaving, not staying.

He glanced over at Jessie. At least she was getting some sleep. He twisted around to the window and propped himself up on his elbows. The moon was just starting to rise. It was an affirmation that there was no turning back now, boy. Your plan had started.

Actually, thought Michael, the plan had started in the barn that day when he met Jody. When he saw all eighteen horses. Those horses.

Ironically, smiled Michael, it was old McCardle himself who had unknowingly filled Michael in on details that would assure their success.

In the barn day before yesterday, Michael had paused before a hand-drawn map that was posted in the barn.

McCardle had come up behind him. "The hell you starin' at?"

The map was a series of squiggles with one curly double line that was different. Michael had pointed to it. "If this is all your property, looks like you own a river. Can we swim in it?"

"You crazy. Don't own no river. You can't own a river. And you can't swim in the old Putah unless you want to be et up by leeches."

Michael had let it drop, but now he knew where he was, sort of. He was west of Sacramento because the damn South Fork of the Putah River flows toward Sacramento from the west. He knew from the 'Rivers' report he had to do at school. There may be fish, probably are, but he doubted if there were leeches.

He was good at maps, and if they were west of Sacramento, about an hour's worth, then they were near Davis. And he was pretty sure the Putah flowed south of Davis, so they were somewhere south of Davis, California.

It was all good.

CHAPTER 19

Someone was pulling at his feet. He tried to pull them away from whatever was grabbing them, but he was held fast.

It took a moment of groggy, then super-sized panic to realize he'd fallen asleep after all.

What?! He couldn't believe he fell asleep. He raised his head to see Jody at the foot of his bed, working on Michael's feet. Next to Jody stood a yawning Jessie. She was dressed, hair still askew, looking like she was ready to go back to bed, not join in a crazy fool plan.

"Shit," whispered Michael. "Sorry."

Jody, his face, expressionless, only mumbled, "Let's go."

Michael took less than a minute before he was dressed. He had the backpack stuffed with anything he thought they might need, like the extra food he and Jessie had secreted the last two days. He also tried stuffing one of the blankets from Jessie's bed. It spilled over the top of the backpack, past the leather strap. It looked awkward, but it was important that he keep Jessie and himself warm.

"Okay. One at a time. We don't need three of us on the stairs."

Jody parted the door a crack, then wider. Without a sound, he stepped into the hallway and was gone into the darkness.

Next was Jessie. She gave Michael a last look which he answered with a smile and, "We're good."

She made it just outside their bedroom door when a sleep disturbed voice echoed down the hall.

"Who is that?" It was muffled but carried well enough so they all heard.

Jessie froze. She did not move. She did not make a sound.

Michael had to do something, but what?

"I said, who the hell is in the hallway?" It was McCardle, more insistent. In another moment, he would be up and they would be screwed.

Michael thought about making a run for it. That wasn't the plan and they would be more than screwed if he did that. He knew Jody was already outside wondering what they were doing.

He was about to speak up, with some inane comment about not being able to sleep, when he heard Jess's voice.

"It's me," she said in a quiet voice.

"Who?" answered McCardle.

"It's Jessie," she said louder. "I just got some... water. I was thirsty."

Michael let out a breath. Brilliant Jess. Good girl.

But McCardle didn't answer. Michael imagined him trying to decide what to do. Trying to decide if she was telling the truth.

"I'm going back to bed now," said Jessie when there was no response.

They all strained to hear whether McCardle was going to get out of a warm bed, deal with a little girl and see what the hell was really going on or stay where he was.

Finally, came an exasperated response. "Get back to bed and don't get out. Jesus."

The faint creak of bedsprings signaled the whale rolling over but not rising.

Michael leaned out into the hallway afraid Jessie was really headed back to bed, but she had already disappeared down the stairs.

Michael slipped off his shoes, stepped into the hallway and pulled their bedroom door to. He was the heaviest of all three of them and he was sure he knew where the squeaks were in the hallway floorboards. He didn't know why, but he was filled with a sudden confidence that the plan would work and that this day would see him and Jessie finally free.

Sliding most of the way, he made it the length of the hallway and down the stairs. He slipped on his shoes at the back door and ran across the yard to the horse barn.

He'd never been around horses much, but he hadn't figured on the excitement it would cause when they were awoken in the middle of the night.

He heard the disturbance before he made it to the barn. Jody and Jessie were already inside. Jessie was hard up against the tack room wall watching eighteen jumpy horses stamping and neighing and pulling at their ropes.

Jody must've known this would happen because he was already making his way down the line of horses with a bag of treats, whatever horses like to eat and don't get much of. It was a grab bag of miscellaneous items but whatever they were, every horse that Jody patted and fed something to quieted down. It took ten minutes but when Jody was done, every horse had turned their heads to see what was going to happen next.

Michael smiled. Sweet, sweet freedom was going to happen next.

CHAPTER 20

It was almost four a.m. by the time Michael and Jody had untethered all the horses and retied them in two groups of nine. Since Michael had no clue how to do it, Jody had saddled two horses and attached the leads of each group to each of the saddled horses.

"Time to go," said Jody.

"No."

Jessie hung back.

Michael tried an encouraging smile. It was going to be tactically brilliant or looming disaster that he hadn't told his sister the whole escape plan.

"C'mon Jess. It'll be fine."

"M, I'm not."

"What's her problem?" Jody hissed, casting a quick glance at the house. "We gotta go if we're doing this."

Michael sighed and turned to Jody. "Horses. She's afraid."

"Now!?" exclaimed Jody, his eyes widening in disbelief. "Now she's afraid? Where was she when she heard the plan?"

"I didn't tell her that part."

"Just great." Jody saw Jessie had her head down. It was defiance if he ever saw it. He made a decision.

"Screw it," he said, putting his boot in one of the stirrups and swinging up into the saddle. "Good luck you two."

"Remember, Shippen Travers," said Michael. "Somewhere near Bullhead, Arizona. We'll be there."

"Yeah. Sure," answered Jody as he gave a quiet clicking and guided his horse and the six attached to him out of the back of the barn. "Right."

Michael thought Jody might have smiled, but maybe not. In any case, he knew he'd never see the kid again, but they parted as if they would, as most people do.

Michael returned to his sister.

"M, I'm not going with. I'm staying."

Crunch time. Time to sell the goods. Michael knelt in front of Jessie.

"Okay. Two things. No, make that three. First. We stay together, no matter what. We don't separate. We're all that's left of the family, except whatshisname in Arizona. Just us. So we stick."

Jessie brightened and started to speak but Michael stopped her.

"Second, sometimes… well, sometimes we have to do the hard stuff. Stuff we don't like, or we're scared to do. Like now."

Jessie started to shake her head.

"Cause now we have to do the next step and that might be hard."

"No, Michael. No."

Michael continued as if her objections were really affirmations. "Third. I will protect you. I have so far. I will always do that. You will be safe. I promise."

When she didn't answer, Michael sealed the deal. "Jess, I promise."

"I'm scared."

Michael stood and walked over to one of the remaining horses Jody had saddled for them. He took hold of the reins and led him over to Jessie.

"I knew you would be. That's why I had Jody pick out the gentlest horse for you."

"You did?"

Michael nodded but remembered his conversation with Jody.

'How the hell should I know?' Jody had said. 'I don't ride 'em. Just find the oldest one, I guess.'

Michael had. At least he hoped he had. Every plan had its risk.

"Ready? I'll help you up."

"Promise?"

"Yes. Now come on. I'll hold your reins. Gotta get outta here."

Under the moonlight, they headed out the back of the barn, away from the house. They made their way through the cornfield, cutting a disturbing path through the young stalks.

Halfway across the ten-acre field, Michael could see where Jody had veered. That was an essential part of Michael's plan.

Michael and Jessie going north, Jody east.

CHAPTER 21

Once again, Stan regretted not having anyone to handle security or reception at the OID building. Downtown had promised somebody here full time, round the clock, but that promise was made to take effect when the archive units were completed. With the current slowdown, and now having to divert crews to the repair of the glass office, that would be months in the future.

And now, after eight o'clock at night, the buzzer was insistently grinding away.

At least they had the foresight to install a camera above the new security door when the whole alarm system was installed. There was an intercom too, but its inaugural was still weeks away.

So, all Stan had was a silent picture of two men on the video screen. Two men standing under the bare bulb shuffling back and forth, and now once again pushing the door buzzer. One was well-dressed, suit and tie. The other was smallish, sunbaked, with a mustache and dirt-stained overalls that showed a full day's work. He could tell by their movements they were about to give up and leave.

Fine.

Stan leaned closer to the monitor. There was something innocent about them. Moreover, he didn't believe they were hitmen come to finish the job Ilsa Pokovich had started. He'd never seen Mexican hitmen before and didn't believe he was seeing them now either.

He could see the two were talking. Finally, the well-dressed one, reached into his coat pocket, produced a small leather case from which he produced a business card. He took out a pen and wrote a word, one word, on the card. This he held up to the security camera.

Stan leaned closer. There was no way to focus the camera and the card was so close it blurred out, but not before Stan saw the one word written on the card.

'Marston'

He shoved aside the files he had been sorting and hobbled to the door. The metal latch made a clanging sound that echoed throughout the building. Especially at night, it reminded Stan of a jail cell with its steel finality.

Even though the two men had been waiting at the door, they still seemed surprised when someone actually opened the door.

"Hola," Stan said.

The two men took off their hats and held them in front of them.

Stan stood aside and let them enter.

"Miguel Martinez," said the well-dressed man, offering his hand to Stan with a business-like smile when they all had stepped inside. Martinez was dressed in pressed chinos and a freshly starched shirt. His leather jacket had the logo of the Eastern Hills Landscape company on it.

"Detective Wyld." Stan shook his hand. "Come in."

Stan nodded to the other man. He wore working-man's overalls and would nervously smile, then lower his eyes.

"What can I do for you?" asked Stan as both men stood before him. Stan had not yet closed the door, unsure of where this was going.

"I'm the owner of Eastern Hills Landscaping, sir." He handed Stan a brochure from his pocket, then proffered his business card.

Stan took them both and wondered seriously why they were soliciting business at 10:30 at night.

"We handle Mr. Marston's estate grounds and we have for twelve years. He is one of our best clients," added Miguel proudly.

He pointed to the brochure in Stan's hands.

"Brand new advertisement, see? You can see how proud we are of our work."

Stan studied the brochure. It had the Eastern Hills company logo on the front, but when he unfolded it, there was a full spread of the Marston grounds in all its spring glory. It was spectacular. And if he were ever to have enough lawn or shrubbery or anything resembling true landscaping, he'd surely talk to Mr. Martinez and the geniuses at Eastern Hills. But, he didn't. He and Bea moved into a condo last year. He had sold all his gardening equipment at the garage sale when they sold the house.

Stan handed him back the brochure, smiled and shook his head. and indicated the grounds outside OID's door.

"I'm sorry Mr. Martinez, but we don't even have two bushes out there, just a parking lot.

Miguel Martinez looked confused.

Stan continued. "And all contractors have to go through Sacramento Police Department Facilities and Maintenance department. They're located in the headquarters building on 15th Street."

Stan kept his hand on the edge of the door.

Miguel Martinez looked at the driver who looked lost, then back at Stan when he finally understood.

"No, no, no." He waved his hands in front of him as if trying to erase everything that had transpired up to this point.

"Come. I'll show you," said the owner of Eastern Hills Landscaping, as he moved past Stan and headed for the glass office. He moved right through the opening to the conference table.

The driver stared at his boss then turned to Stan with an apologizing smile. He started toward the office and waved Stan to follow him.

What the hell. Stan shut the door with a bang. By the time he got to the office, Martinez had spread out the brochure again and was waiting for Stan to join him.

"Mr. Martinez," Stan said solicitously.

But Martinez held up his hand to stop him. It was obvious Martinez was having trouble figuring out what he wanted to say.

Finally, he nodded to himself and began.

"We take care of Marston estate for twelve years, okay?"

Stan nodded.

"I own my company. I get the contract to do landscape work. A big job. Makes me very happy to have this work. We do the work twice a week. Same thing each week. Same. Same. Never changes. First the lawn, then rake the..." He stopped when he realized he was getting off the track. Again, he waved his hand erasing the air.

"Okay. We don't send a bill. Check comes before we do that, understand?"

Stan wondered how soon he could move them back to the door without seeming too rude, but he nodded and said, "Marston was a good customer. I get it."

"Yes! Yes! Every week. Always. For twelve years, always a check. And..." He paused for dramatic effect.

"And, we never speak to anybody! Never! Twelve years and we never speak to anybody. Check arrives. We do the work. Check arrives. Always."

He looked at Stan as if he had just revealed the secret to life.

"I see..." But after that Stan had nowhere to go.

Martinez waved his hands again. "So, okay, last week, Jorge..." He indicated the driver who was standing near the office entrance. "Jorge arrive as always to do the lawn and rake and so on and..." Here he produced a business card and attempted to read the name.

"And... Detective Stinger..."

"Steiner. Detective Steiner."

Martinez nodded as if that was what he just said. "Yes, and your other officer, Maz…"

"Mazurski," filled in Stan.

"He talk to Jorge for a long time. And keep asking if Jorge ever see anyone around. Anyone around in the last few weeks. He said it was very important. Very important!"

Stan straightened up.

"Okay. Jorge comes to me and tells me this and how important it is. Do we see anybody ever when we are there? Very important says Jorge."

Jorge nodded in agreement.

"Do we ever see anybody there? Answer is yes. I did. When I take these pictures…" He tapped the brochure. "I saw someone. A woman!"

"Sit down Mr. Martinez."

He did while Jorge remained standing.

"I need you to describe this person. As best you can. Can you do that?"

Martinez split his face with a smile. "No."

"No?"

The smile broadened even further. "No description. I have picture!"

Martinez reached inside his jacket and set a small digital camera on the table.

Suddenly Martinez seemed embarrassed by the small size of the camera.

"Sorry. The camera is all I have. But it takes good pictures." He pointed once again to the brochure.

"Of course. Yes. Now, can you show me the picture."

Martinez hit the ON button. A faint electronic signature chimed, and an image appeared on the back screen of the camera.

"I took so many, for this advertisement." He struggled his way through the images.

It was all Stan could do not to grab the camera and start paging through himself.

"Next one or two, maybe," said Martinez fully concentrating on his task.

A half minute went by. No one said anything.

Martinez brought his face close to the screen. Then turned to Stan and handed him the camera.

"Here. Here is the picture of the woman."

Stan brought the camera up close. The screen was only three by two inches. It appeared to be a section of the rose bushes that fronted the house. They were crimson and yellow in alternating bushes. The roses were clearly intended to be the focal point of the picture, but Martinez had framed this shot so that too much of the house was shown. And in that part of the house was a window. In the window was a woman, but the image was too small.

"Mr. Martinez, when did you take this?"

Martinez took the camera back and pointed to the electronic time and date stamp in the lower corner of the frame.

"About a month ago."

He tried to hand the camera back to Stan, but Stan was already searching for a cord to plug into his laptop. Jake and Mallory always had one at their fingertips. Anytime they needed anything to do with the computer or the digital crap they had lying around, well, all they had to do was reach into the nearest drawer and there it was.

For Stan, not so much.

Martinez hesitated. "I, uh, have a connection cord if you need one."

Stan slammed the lower desk drawer closed and took the cord. He found the right connection on the laptop and let Martinez plug in the camera.

The computer registered the camera attachment and Stan opened the picture folder.

They both sat before the laptop as Martinez once again scrolled through the pictures.

"Here," he said quietly. "Here it is."

Stan focused on the image. It was much larger now. It was clear it was a woman. But...

He swiped a small area around the woman and clicked the mouse. The selected area expanded to fill the screen.

"I take good pictures, yes?" asked Martinez.

Stan didn't answer because the image of the woman now filled his screen. There was no mistake.

"Dear God."

He was so entranced with the image on the screen, it wasn't until Martinez nudged him did he realize it was the Fax beeping and grinding away across the room.

Reluctantly, he left Martinez and the computer and went to retrieve the Fax. When was the last time they received a Fax? He couldn't remember.

Two sheets. The cover sheet had the logo of the Plainfield PD, addressed to Detective Steiner. It referenced Anna Chase and her mother and the woman they interacted with. Below the cover was a detailed sketch of that woman.

As if he needed any more evidence of shit they missed, Stan took the sketch and held it up to the computer screen. The hair was different. The woman who had been with Anna Chase had dark hair, possibly a wig, while the picture Martinez had taken had lighter, blondish, hair.

But the faces.

It was Martinez who stated the obvious. "Both same woman."

"Yeah," breathed Stan. "Her name is Samantha Barnes."

But all he was thinking was, poor Jake.

CHAPTER 22

It was already after 9 A.M. when Mallory braked to a hard stop, skidding within inches of Stan Wyld's pickup. Trying not to aggravate her throbbing head any further, she eased herself out of her Honda. There was little room left in Sacramento's On-Going Investigation Division's mini-mart sized parking lot. It was straining to contain all the work vehicles.

As she skinnied between Stan's truck and a gleaming flatbed truck, with shiny wood slats plugged into the sides, she noticed the name on the side was Charger Clean, a clean-up company.

There was a small pang of guilt as she realized the detail cleaning crew was here to make sure all of Ilsa Pokovich was thoroughly excised from every square inch of the glass walls, floor, desks, coffee cups...

"Okay. Don't need to go there," she said out loud.

In front of the flatbed were two more, progressively cleaner, vehicles, from the same company. Guys in white suits and masks were busy pulling what looked like an industrial vacuum cleaner out of the back of one of the vehicles. Anonymous white tradesman vans were neatly parked in the center of the small lot occupying the remainder of the free spaces. Two construction cranes were idling at the edge of the lot, their arms extended skyward. Cables snaked from the top of their arms through the skylight of OID.

And to top it off, gracing Jake's coveted parking spot, was what, she could only guess, was assistant to Captain Carruthers,

Asshole Samuels' Crown Victoria. It was parked at an angle, ignoring any striped lines, saying 'I don't give a shit who tells me where to park, I can goddamn park anywhere.'

The cooling engine was still ticking.

Great.

With two hands, she strained to pull open OID's security door. As soon as she did, a blast of air propelled her inside. The vault size door nearly slammed shut.

She couldn't identify why there was a whirlwind until she ventured further. And looked up.

"Holy crap."

Above her, two of the skylights had been removed and now being lowered into place were two massive panes of half-inch glass. Destined to be the new walls of the glass office.

Maintenance crews had yesterday taken care of the big chunks of glass. Now the minions from Charger Clean were using everything from tiny makeup brushes to battery powered dust suckers to one large industrial tank of a vacuum; all to remove every particle of tempered glass. Particles that had inexplicably gotten into every part of their office, including the bottom of half-filled coffee cups, inside desk drawers, with some found at the very bottom of Mallory's purse.

She stood at the threshold of the glass office. She saw they had moved the conference table to the far side of the office where the least amount of glass had been blown. Four panels had been blown out in the mixture of 9mm and .45 caliber bullets. The crime scene photos documented the damage but with the missing part of the glass walls, Mallory felt exposed.

As she scanned the rest of the floor looking for Stan, she tried to ignore the cloying smell of sanitizing disinfectant that washed over her. No Stan.

And then, above the different screams of the assorted vacuums and the whine of taut cables sliding over pulleys lowering the glass, she could hear Samuels. He was ten feet away and easy to identify as the only one with an apoplectic complexion and waving his arms.

"The hell is going on here?" shouted Samuels. He pushed past two men in hard hats that were exiting the OID and made his way to the man who had a walkie-talkie and 'Sherman' stenciled on his hard hat. Samuels grabbed the man's arm and spun him around.

The man ignored him and kept speaking. "Let me know when it clears. Got that?" He clicked off and listened for the response.

Samuels persisted. "Who's in charge and what the good goddamn is going on here?"

The man with the walkie-talkie gestured to someone else behind Samuels. "Get him outta here."

Samuels shook off the two hands that gripped his arms. "Let go of me." He approached Sherman again and commanded the space in front of him. "I'm Lieutenant Samuels and I demand to know who's in charge and what it is you think you're doing."

Sherman finally lowered his eyes to Samuels. "You're in the way and you're in violation of a shitload of safety rules by standing here without a hard hat and you're in violation of my good mood by being here and being an asshole." Sherman gave Samuels a shove. He raised the walkie-talkie again. "Clear yet?"

"Yes," came the tinny reply.

"Bring 'em down."

A burly assistant super stepped between Samuels and Sherman. He handed Samuels a hard hat. Samuels took it and flicked it away and started advancing again. This time the burly assistant bumped chests with Samuels, who then tried to get around him.

The assistant brought his full beard close to Samuels' ear. Mallory couldn't hear but she could imagine what was being said, as the assistant took Samuels' arm, bent it into an uncomfortable position, and guided him back to the entrance. Mallory stepped aside, gathering only the briefest shouted words, "...for your own protection."

Mallory dashed to the temporary rack set up toward the Archive office. It had hooks containing orange vests and hard hats. She grabbed a stylish yellow and white hard hat. Inside the hat were a pair of safety goggles. She slapped on a bright orange vest and went in search of Stan.

She found him resting on a pile of pallets in the temporary archive office. His phone was pressed to one ear, the other covered to block out the construction din.

Before she could say anything, he paused his conversation, covered the phone. "Good. You're here. We've got a shitload of trouble. You heard from Jake?"

Before she could answer, the archive door slammed open, bouncing back and hitting Samuels from behind as he barged in.

"Stop this! Stop this now!" he shrieked at Stan.

Samuels moved past Mallory right into Stan's face.

"Who in the holy hell authorized new glass for this idiotic fishbowl of yours? The plan is to tear it all the hell outta here and replace it with real offices! Was it you Wyld?! Don't you know the plan? I thought I made it clear, this whole OID shit is going to be replaced. We're shutting you down. Your precious grant, kaput! And no more of this glass crap. We'll take it and make it all into coffee tables. Tear it all out-"

"Can't do that, Samuels."

"Can't do what? I can do whatever I say. Whatever the Captain says. Got it?"

"I mean, you can't cut coffee tables out of tempered glass once glass's been tempered. You see, tempering-"

"Screw that! Who called in all these cranes and who authorized this?"

Stan pointed to an official-looking document tacked to the plywood wall.

"Looks to me like it came from Carruthers himself."

Samuels spun and ripped the sheet as the clip holding it went flying. He scanned it, squinting at the signature at the bottom. In one motion, he balled it up and threw it.

It bounced off Mallory.

Samuels' eyes widened, recognizing her for the first time. "And what the hell are you doing here? You are restricted from working. You're under investigation missy. You need to be gone, like yesterday."

"She's with me," answered Stan calmly. "She's... invaluable. She stays."

Mallory hid a smile and stood a few inches taller.

"On whose authority?" began Samuels. Then, as if he'd been sucker punched, he gave it up. "Screw it." He slammed open the archive's plywood door. "Whole place is a freak circus."

"Thanks for that," she said, nodding toward the retreating Samuels' ass.

Stan held out his hand for Mallory to shake.

"What?" she asked but took his hand anyway. He gave a preemptory shake and released her.

"Congratulations. You've been promoted. You are now partner, a full partner with OID."

"I..."

"Should've done it from the beginning. Jake said it and I agree. You have instincts. Instincts, we, Jake and I, don't have. You are a value. But you already knew that didn't you?"

Mallory blushed. She didn't want to, but she did anyway. The turnaround from enduring Jake's sarcasm to praise, even long distance, was almost too much. It made her at once wary and at once warm. And Stan's acknowledgment of her value was reaffirming.

"Thanks. I mean it. Thanks," she said. "But, why now?"

"Because you need to find those kids and because Jake's got trouble and because I'm leaving."

"What?"

"Here. You need to see this." Stan handed Mallory an envelope. He pushed open the archive office door and limped toward the main exit.

CHAPTER 23

Mallory upended the manila envelope and let the items slip out. She pawed through the items.

"Stan, what have you given me?" asked Mallory.

She unfolded the three-panel brochure from some landscaping company. Clipped to it was a business card of the landscape company's owner, according to the card. It had pictures displaying admittedly the most spectacular landscape designs she had ever seen. Right away, she recognized the inside picture. When she unfolded it, there was the Marston Mansion, the crimson park, set off by the truly breath-taking scenery. It hardly resembled what she remembered but then again, she hadn't been concentrating on the flowers and shrubs.

Underneath the brochure was a picture. She could tell right away it was like the one used in the brochure. Taken from a different angle and showing more of the house, it wasn't used for that reason. That, and there seemed to be two people standing in one of the windows.

She strained to see who they were. One was a woman, but that was all she could ascertain.

Next though, was a paper printout blowup of the window and what were now obviously two women.

"Shit." Mallory didn't need to strain to recognize Ilsa Pokovich. Pokovich was in the Marston mansion! She was standing with her arms crossed, obviously watching the photographer take pictures, not realizing she was going to be in one.

But Mallory was not prepared to see who was next to her.

Samantha Barnes.

"It cannot be."

Stan had printed out the enlargement because at the bottom he'd scrawled a note.

'Taken 3 months ago !!!'

"What?" She did some fast calculating. Not only had Samantha Barnes, the bitch, been in the mansion three months ago, but she'd been there with Ilsa Pokovich.

They knew each other.

Three months. That was before the head of James Marston fell at Jake's feet.

Head swimming with this, she looked at the last item. As if to mess up her day even more, she faced an artist sketch that had been Faxed from the Plainfield PD. Again, the resemblance was certain. Samantha Barnes stared back at her.

It wasn't computing. Who was this lying bitch? She wasn't just involved with James Marston and Ilsa Pokovich, she was also with eleven-year-old Anna Chase on the other side of the country.

She hurriedly shucked off the construction vest and hard hat and chased after Stan as they both exited OID, she double timing to catch up.

"Whoa," she said. "You're leaving, going where? And what about Jake? And whatshername?"

Stan tossed his cane inside his truck and swung his leg with the heel cast inside. Before he closed the door, he answered Mallory.

"I have people searching for Samantha Barnes. Jake's fine, pretty much. We're in trouble. OID. Seems somebody leaked Anna Chase's name to all of the media outlets within 50 miles of New Jersey. Most of the East Coast wants us lynched because we're trying to arrest one of their Middle School girls for the murder of James Marston."

"That's crazy. Does Jake know?"

Stan laughed. "Sure he does by now. That's his trouble. Going nuts out there dealing with the fallout. So much he stayed there overnight."

"What about...?" She meant Samantha Barnes, that bitch.

Stan knew who she meant. He shook his head and slammed his door.

Before he started the truck, he lowered the window. "All right partner. Your job. Find those kids. Call in Susan. Call in whoever you want to help. Your job now. I've gotta go put out this fire downtown."

She couldn't make out what else Stan was saying before he accelerated out of the parking lot because the startup of rigging cables and crane hydraulics and shouted directions drowned out everything.

It was so loud, Mallory didn't know her phone was ringing until she felt it vibrate.

She answered without looking at the caller ID. "Jake?"

Two things she realized right away. It wasn't Jake and whoever it was, was battling a terrible connection. So bad, she only caught a few words which made little sense. She checked the phone's screen. It showed an unknown number coming from an area code with which she wasn't familiar.

She disconnected and tried texting Jake. She waited a half minute. Nada. Time to concentrate on finding... the kids.

The kids. Michael.

"Arrg, you stupid idiot!" she shouted.

The realization that she'd had the way to get to the kids all along knocked her back against her car. She began spinning through her past call list, scrolling as fast as she could, looking for not a number but a date, the date that Michael Cooper had called her. The night he had called desperate for someone to rescue him and his sister from the Fourth Redeemer church. There was a number attached to that call. It was simple she'd call back. She should've thought of this earlier. Way earlier.

Her hand shook as she scrolled. She had to figure out what to say when he answered.

'Uh, hello Michael, this is Detective Dimante. Remember I saved your ass before, well- '

No.

'Michael, you remember me, Detective Dimante. Well, not really a detective-'

No.

'Hey, Michael, tell me you still have that good ol' stuffed-'

No.

She found it, punched to return the call. It rang and answered.

Michael's sarcasm shone through with his prerecorded greeting. "This is me, text me. I don't do voicemail."

"Smartass kid." Mallory gripped the phone hard as she waited for the beep. She'd leave a message anyway.

"Michael this is Mallory Dimante with the Sacramento PD. Please return this call immediately." She tried to keep any real panic from creeping in, just urgency.

She disconnected. However, when it came to texting the same message, she capitalized IMMEDIATELY.

And she waited.

No call ever came.

And the text box remained empty.

Her phone rang again. She slipped into her Honda so she could hear without the construction confusion.

Again, the area code she didn't recognize, but this time the connection was good. The voice was clear. There was only one problem.

She was talking to a dead man.

And he had a story to tell.

CHAPTER 24

Michael tried to ignore the breaking dawn and instead focused on the lights ahead.

When Jessie had asked where they were headed all he did was point straight ahead. The glow of Davis California was their guide.

And even though the lights looked close, Michael knew they had one obstacle to pass. He'd seen it on McArdle's map. And judging by the glint of the rails from his left and from his right he realized they'd arrived.

Railroad tracks.

He wasn't sure, but he guessed that the horses were not favorable to crossing railroad tracks. His first clue was when they stopped and wouldn't move forward.

Jessie had been doing well up to this point but now she seemed filled with uncertainty.

"M they're not moving. They won't move."

"Oh yes, they will. I'm going to have to lead them across. I saw this in a movie. You stay on."

"What are you going to do and why do I have to stay on?"

Michael slipped off his horse and gripped the reins of Jessie's horse. He looked both ways. Four sets of tracks. Two must be North the other two South, he guessed.

Well, nothing coming. He let his horse wander some feet away, content to explore the grasses that lined the tracks. He concentrated on Jessie and her horse.

"Come on Dumbo," he urged.

The horse reacted to his name which startled Michael. He'd been pretty sure horses don't ever recognize their name but now he wasn't so sure.

"His name is not Dumbo," objected Jessie. "He won't do anything if you call him by the wrong name. I saw that on TV."

"He doesn't know who he is anyway. That was TV hooey." Michael tried to affect a soothing tone. "Come on Flower or Bumper or whoever. You can do this."

Michael stepped over the first rail onto the creosoted wooden tie, but the horse didn't move. With Michael pulling, the reins were stretched taut and there was an immovable determination in the horse's eyes.

Finally, still with Michael cajoling, Flower or Bumper reluctantly stepped over the first rail.

"Can I get off?" asked Jessie with an insistence bordering on a statement.

"No," muttered Michael. "I'll do this."

"But..."

"No."

"What about that?" Jessie pointed to the west. Michael knew what it would be before he turned. It was hard to tell how far away the train was, or how fast it was coming but coming it was. The headlight twinkled in the distance.

Either way, he figured he had a few minutes. With calm resolve, he smiled and spoke quietly.

"Jess, slowly get down."

"How? He's too tall."

"Put your foot in the foot thing, the stirrup."

Jessie checked the left side of the horse. "M, it's too far down. My foot won't reach. You help."

"Jess I don't want to move right now. You'll have to do it."

Michael checked down the tracks. He couldn't tell, but it didn't really matter which of the four tracks the train was on. He was standing in the middle of the southbound tracks. The unmoving horse flesh known as Flower or Bumper or whatever was straddling the northbound line.

And, the light was noticeably larger. Maybe it was his imagination, but he thought he could detect a rumbling.

"Jess just lean over to the left. Let your foot slide down until it reaches the metal loop. Soon as you do that put your weight on it swing your other leg over. Then lower yourself."

"M, I can't…"

"Jess now."

In the predawn light, the horse shifted a bit as Jessie moved.

"Okay, okay. I think I feel it," said Jessie, as her foot slid down a bit.

"Good."

Michael could just make out her form as she moved down the side of the horse.

Then she disappeared.

"Jess!" Michael shouted.

"Michael! Help!"

The horse jumped to the side, its hooves trying to find secure purchase on the railroad ties.

"Jess!"

Michael leaped and stretched over the horse, but not in time. To his dumbfounded amazement, he saw Jessie hanging upside down. Her head was inches above the railroad tie, her foot looped through the stirrup.

The horse stared, its eyes getting wider. Michael held it fast. If he moved now, it would bounce Jess's head off the rails.

"Michael, I… I'm stuck," she blubbered.

Michael regripped the reins while he leaned down to Jessie. Her arms were flailing. Trying to prevent herself from banging against the rails, she tried to grab onto anything. She found Michael's shirt collar and begin pulling herself away from the horse.

"Jess! Just wait! Wait!"

Then he froze.

It wasn't the panic on Jess's face that made him pause. It was that his shadow was now sharply etched across her.

Adrenaline gripped him. He turned only to see the train's headlight moving with the sway of the train. It no longer twinkled but shined with a steady and uncaring approach.

Grabbing Jessie by the shoulders, he lifted her up, hoping to take her weight off her foot and free it.

Instead, she began kicking, jabbing the horse in its side.

"Hold still. Quit kicking."

He saw Jessie glance over his shoulder.

"Michael!"

Michael pulled away from the horse who stomped back and forth. The rumble from the train was unmistakable.

"Hold onto my shoulders".

Jessie latched onto Michael with a death grip while Michael reeled around and fumbled with her foot and the stirrup. His fingers worked like clumsy claws. The sweat rolled into his eyes.

"Michael please!"

Michael leaned over. "Climb over me."

"I can't."

Michael was face-to-face with foot and stirrup. It was far too easy to see because he now had plenty of light burning down on them.

And now a sharp warning horn blasted. And kept blasting.

He twisted Jessie's foot ninety degrees and worked it back and forth, twisting until came free. The sudden release made him lose his balance. Both of them crashed to the ties between the rails which now vibrated up and down.

With only a glance at the train to try and figure out which track it was on, he made a decision and carried, really dragged, Jessie north across the rest of the rails.

They collapsed down the shallow embankment.

Michael turned to see the horse frozen like an entranced deer in an approaching headlight.

"Sorry," was all he could say to the horse, as the engine roared by, its horn still blaring.

It was a passenger train, Amtrak or some such. Blurred faces whizzed by, never seeing them in the early morning gloom.

Michael raised up from the ditch and peered under the cars as they swept by, but he could not make out the carcass of the horse.

And just like that, the train was gone. The red light on the last car swayed and jumped, receding harmlessly.

Jessie kept her head buried in Michael's back.

"The horse..." was all she could manage. It was a question in the statement.

In the glow of the pre-sunrise, there stood Flower Bumper, either in shock or blissfully ignorant.

"Is he dead?" whispered Jessie.

Michael stood, amazed. It was if the train had passed right through the dumb horse.

"Is he?"

Recovering Michael stirred. "No, he's fine. We're fine."

He pulled Jessie away. "Jess, we're fine so let's get the hell away from these tracks."

"But your horse?" asked Jessie, "Where is he?" She peered around Michael and searched the other side of the rails.

"He's the only smart one. Took off running when the train came."

Jessie persisted. "Then what are you going to do about my horse?"

Michael scanned the direction they were headed before the train and horse situation arose. He could make out lights in the distance including a marquee of a hotel. And now that the train had passed, and his pulse had subsided to pre-panic levels he could hear the occasional car and the whine of a lone semi on a distant highway.

"C'mon. Let's get some breakfast.

But Jessie wouldn't move. "We don't have any money for food and what are we doing about the horse?"

Michael turned and looked at Flower Bumper who still stood straddling two tracks, looking lost.

Leaving the horse in the middle of the railroad track was not part of his plan. As a matter of fact, his plan had stopped about a mile before this. His grand plan, discussed with Jody, was to abandon the rest of the horses back in the field, which he did. The plan was, let them scatter, confusing all who came looking for them. And the plan had also called for them to slip off their own horses as well. Still, it had been dark, and it had been so convenient to just keep riding.

In the distance, Michael could see the welcoming glow of crimson hotel lights. And the plan, the revised plan, came fully formed.

He took the reins and for some reason, Flower Bumper had no hesitation about high-stepping over the rest of the rails and rejoining them.

Michael put his face right up to the horse's snout. "Now you decide to move? Where was all this energetic bravado a few minutes ago?"

Flower Bumper ignored Michael and pretended he didn't hear him, only giving a sidelong glance when Michael turned away.

"We're taking the horse?" asked Jessie.

"We'll use the horse."

"Sell it, so we can eat?"

"No," answered Michael. "I'm going to give it away."

CHAPTER 25

Michael appraised the establishment as they got closer. It wasn't a Hyatt or Marriott but a good imitation. An off-brand chain but it was three stories and the parking lot was half-full. A collection of SUVs, sedans, and coupes occupying multiple spaces.

"Perfect," said Michael, satisfied.

Jessie hung back. "For what?"

"You'll see."

"We going in?"

"In a bit."

"M, we're just kids, they'll throw us out."

Michael tied the horse to one of the lampposts a few posts down from the entry. He retrieved the backpack that he'd had strapped to the back of the saddle.

He reached in his pocket and found the treat Jody had given him before they left. He offered it to the horse who looked suspiciously at the apple, at Michael and Michael's outstretched hand. He made no move to eat it.

"Maybe he doesn't trust you," Jessie quipped. "Maybe he thinks you're going to leave him on some more railroad tracks in front of another train."

With the lights from the hotel lobby, Michael could see the horse clearly wasn't interested.

"Okay," said Michael. And he took a bite of the apple, then handed the rest to the horse.

The horse stood there.

Michael gave up just as an obscenely large SUV pulled up followed almost immediately by a camper.

"Here we go," said Michael.

"We're going in now?"

"After these good folks."

It took long minutes for the occupants of both vehicles to get out and stretch. Michael was happy to see two kids both about ten or twelve years old get out the SUV. Even better they had a dog.

They must've been driving all day and night, thought Michael because, even though it was just past dawn, the only item the kids were talking about was getting into the hotel pool.

So eager, they were oblivious to Michael and Jessie and the horse.

Michael turned to Jessie. "You have one line to say when we get in there, okay?"

Jessie could see through the windows to the reception desk. "M, they'll throw us out."

"Trust me."

"Is that my line?"

Michael laughed. "No silly. Your line is 'Let's go tell dad'."

"Let's go tell dad."

"See. You got it. It's easy."

"You want me to say that?" questioned Jessie.

Michael nodded.

"To who?"

"You say it to me."

"When?"

"You'll know." Michael felt a nudge on his arm. Evidently, Flower Bumper now wanted the apple.

"Here you go horse. Thanks for your help. Have a good life."

He turned to Jessie and gave thumbs up. "Let's go."

They left the horse and followed the last of the stragglers into the hotel lobby.

Michael took a sniff. They must put something in the air he thought. It wasn't bad though, not overpowering, just like there was a flower shop next door. Smelled like a snooty hotel which was perfect.

With Jessie trailing, he made straight for the reception desk. Of the two clerks on duty - a pimply-faced girl with green highlights and an older man who looked like an overweight B-movie Mafia enforcer, he chose Scarface.

"Hey Mister," Michael said, addressing the man, who turned away from helping one of the customers checking in. He seemed immediately suspicious of Michael.

"Mister, you know you've got a horse in your front yard."

The man studied Michael searching for the punchline. "A what?"

"There's a horse in your front yard. We saw him from our window upstairs." Michael pointed to Jessie. "She didn't believe it was real, so I came down to show her."

"And he's eating some of your flowers," added Michael.

This stirred the man.

"A horse?"

"Yep, in your flowers."

The man exchanged glances with the pimply faced girl. "Where?"

Michael pointed. "Out there where the pretty flowers are."

Jessie came up and tugged at Michael. "Let's go tell dad."

"Good idea," agreed Michael. "He won't believe it."

While the two desk clerks had moved to the window to confirm the horse tale, Michael, spying the sign pointing to the breakfast room, headed that way.

CHAPTER 26

Jake had to shout to be heard over the boarding announcements and the crying baby. "I'm at Newark. About to board. Your text said it was urgent. Is it about my dog? What's wrong?"

On the other end, Mallory, confused, held the phone away from her ear and looked at it before she resumed the conversation.

"Jake, the dog is fine. I wanted to make sure you got my message about Florida."

Jake misunderstood. "The girl? Goddamn circus out here. Tell Danni to clean her house. Someone in Forensics leaked the girl's name as a suspect in Marston's death last night. Media here went crazy. Place was crawling with everybody; New York TV and God knows who else. The locals were doing their best to keep them from breaking down the Chase's front door."

"I know," shouted Mallory, not meaning to.

Jake rambled on, trying to make himself heard.

"Two things about this Anna Chase. Her only connection seems to be some TV commercial she was in, shot out here in Jersey with some L.A. production company. The kid said they made her hold a glass during the commercial. That's where they got her prints, I'm sure. And she said she'd be able to give a good description of the woman producer. The mother saw the woman too. So, I had an artist from Plainfield working with the girl and her mother, doing a sketch-"

"Jake! We have it already!"

"They'll scan and Fax it to you later. You can work on finding the production company."

"Jake...Jake..." shouted Mallory, trying to interrupt.

"And this Anna's never heard of Marston," Jake hurried on. "Not Marston, not any of his films. Has never really been outside of Jersey. Never been in Marston's car. She's a bright kid. Cute. I think she'll give us a good description. How's it going there?"

"Jake! Shut up a minute! Don't get on that plane."

"What? Sorry, hard to hear. Make it fast, we're boarding. What's urgent? You said it was urgent."

"It was. It is." She thought for a moment of telling him about Samantha Barnes, instead plowed on. "There's been a change of plans. Jake, you're not coming home. You're going to Florida."

That had been four hours and one flight earlier.

The irony was never far away from his thinking. It made him smile. He never even had to leave the state but once when he was with Robbery-Homicide. Now, he was racking up airline miles working on cold cases. Maybe it made sense. As time goes, events fade, people move and hide, try sometimes to bury themselves, put as much distance and crap between what they did or was done to them and their new life.

Only, now he wasn't in Sarasota, Florida to rediscover a new life.

He was here to dig up a dead man.

The place had that false cheery air of forced optimism. Jake sat in a comfortable chair in the little alcove where the resident's mailboxes were located. As if sensing the Second Coming, people, ancient of days, began gathering around the mailboxes. Jake had to move his feet back to avoid a couple of the old men angling their walkers to be in the best position when the U.S. Mail arrived.

It was a few moments later when the mail truck pulled up. The mailman, used to the throng, smiled as the residents parted to let him distribute the few letters into the individual boxes. Their eyes alive, watching for their box to be opened, for some communication from a relative or the dwindling number of friends to be deposited. Later, if they were one of the lucky few, to be opened and read and re-read and replied to in hopes of getting another reply. Hoping to get something in the mail to show they were not forgotten. That they could still thrill to a picture of a great-grandchild, a graduation, a birthday.

Small pleasures.

When the mail was gone, those that had not received any that day eyed him as the visitor he was, wondering who the lucky resident was that had someone come to see them.

Knowing it wasn't them only reinforced their loneliness and made the shuffle back to their rooms that much longer.

"Detective?"

Jake rose. "Yes."

"I'm Mrs. Freemont. You're in the wrong lobby. Took me a while to find you."

She was middle-aged in a nurse's uniform. Thick around the middle with a kindly face that gave out a wan smile. He imagined he was the youngest person she'd see that day, save the mailman.

"I wasn't sure. This looked like the main entrance."

"It is. But the person you're meeting is in the extended care facility. This way."

She turned and led him out the door and down a concrete path across the parking lot to a two-story building.

The sign next to the entry door said, 'Pelican's Lodge'.

"This is our facility for Assisted Living and Memory Care."

"Memory Care?"

She turned and gave Jake an understanding smile. "Alzheimers. Early dementia."

Jake nodded.

"Everyone here gets three meals a day and has the advantage of 24-7 nursing care. Most of these are one-bedroom apartments, though we have a few larger units for family stays and Respite care."

She was used to giving sales pitches, Jake realized.

"We have a full schedule of activities – Coffee club, reading group, baking club, Musical recitals, movies, even bus excursions around town."

They proceeded down beige corridors lined with pleasant framed landscapes and triptychs of flowers and ships sailing unknown seas. A respectful solemnity to the place, like the lobby of a funeral home.

Mrs. Freemont turned. "We have you set up in one of the small chapels. I've asked the two policemen to wait outside."

"Policemen?"

"Yes," said Mrs. Freemont looking confused. "I thought you requested two uniforms from Sarasota to join you. Though why I'm not sure. Anyway, I've had them wait outside the chapel. I didn't think it appropriate for them to be in the chapel."

"Yes," said Jake, affecting a knowing countenance. "That was thoughtful." Still unsure why Stan or Mallory wanted local cops to join him.

When they turned the next corner, the two uniforms stood up as they approached. One was a tall skinny sergeant, the other a black woman with a leather bag.

"Here's the chapel. They're inside waiting for you." Mrs. Freemont gave a serious smile. "I wouldn't spend too much time. He tends to get agitated."

"Thank you."

Mrs. Freemont glanced at the two cops, then Jake, and proceeded back the way she had come.

"You're Detective Steiner?" asked the tall cop, offering his hand.

Jake took it and nodded.

"I'm Sergeant Wilson, this is officer Onja from our Forensics division."

Jake shook the young woman's hand. "Forensics. Fingerprints. Of course." Jake finally understood. "Thank you for making yourselves available."

"Anything for California, you know," said Wilson, though he didn't appear to be thrilled to be in a retirement home babysitting a beat-ass detective from the Golden State.

"I'll just have you guys wait outside here. I need to talk with him first, but I'll get you in and out of here as fast as I can."

"Sounds good," said Wilson, speaking for both.

Jake pulled open one of the double doors of the chapel and stepped inside. The settled air was warm and close, suffused with the echoes of thousands of unanswered prayers. Half-dimmed bulbs in electric candles lined the fake stucco walls and gave off a tender light. Weakened sunlight lit the three stained glass windows above a miniature altar and splashed varying hues on the only other two people there.

The man was in a wheelchair, and while his head was drooped a bit and tilted at a dispirited angle, his eyes were sharp and followed Jake down the aisle.

The woman was a big woman, as Jake could see when she rose to greet him. She didn't appear happy to see him.

"Detective? You the one from California?" she demanded.

Jake held out his hand which she took reluctantly.

"Detective Jake Steiner." He fished out a card and gave it to her.

The woman was about to speak when the man interrupted her.

"Steiner! Is that Jewish?" The voice was throaty and phlegmy as if he hadn't spoken in a day.

Jake regarded the man.

The eyes searched Jake for a reaction.

"Half Jewish," replied Jake.

"What's the other half?"

Jake took a seat at the end of the pew opposite.

"The other half is part Irish, but mostly just Asshole."

The old man grunted satisfaction.

Jake held out his hand. The old man flicked his a little and Jake had to take the initiative and do most of the pumping when they shook.

"I'm Detective Steiner, Mr...?"

Jake held his breath, waiting to hear the words he had come to hear.

The man brought his head up. His eyes bore into Jake.

"I'm the real one, detective. I'm Rudolph Rendell."

CHAPTER 27

The voice was rasp and grit. Years of tobacco and carny life had left him wrung out and pummeled like a twisted dishrag. Still, there was fight.

"So, what kind of cockamamie operation are you running out there?" He nodded toward his companion, who, Jake surmised judging by her facial hair, had once done a stint as the Bearded Lady somewhere.

"She tells me you got things all balled up. Don't know your ass from shinola."

The old man's attendant started to open her mouth, but he waved her down.

"And it looks like it takes an old man with half a brain who even though he can't remember what he had for breakfast is gonna have to straighten you the hell out."

The speech left spittle on the man's chin. The old man ignored his companion as she wiped it away.

He stated it as a question and a challenge.

Jake said, "Prove it. You say you're Rudolph Rendell, show me the proof then."

The old man sat back a bit and he grinned. But it was a grin one does to keep from crying, and it only animated the left side of his face. The other side was slack and used up like a deflated tire.

"See," he started. "There's the rub sonny. They took it all. Everything. Goddamn sons a bitches. See, I brought 'em in and they charmed me, and I loved 'em and they pretended, and they took from me after I showed how to do everything I knew."

Jake let the man roll on.

"It was that goddamn relief agency, you see. That European one. Rescuing kids from shot-up parts of Europe, they said. Hungary was where they supposedly came from, but I don't goddamn believe it. They was spawned from some unholy pit, I tell you."

The light from the windows shone on his face, lighting it in a deep crimson. He didn't seem to notice.

"Oh, I was doin' great back then. We were. Had the circus. Carnival. Two actually. Ran the circuit, north in the summer ran south in the winter. And they caught me when I was feeling good. The wife and me. We said, sure we can help out some unfortunates. Sure, we can.

"Well, fuck that day. It was a black, black day when I agreed. Had to talk my wife into it a bit."

He looked at Jake with tears in his eyes. "Worst thing I ever did."

He cleared his throat and continued after a moment.

"So, yeah, I brought 'em over here. Sponsored 'em. Fed 'em and put clothes on their back and schooled 'em and they pretended all the while pretending to be grateful, you know...."

He stopped. He worked his jaw, the words he wanted to say were caught in the past and came with difficulty. "It's all gone. All of it."

The old man's eyes spilled over.

"You see, they just up and took my life. That's what they're good at."

"Who are they?" Jake asked, not really buying the act.

The old man rumbled on past Jake's question.

"So, what're you gonna believe? Me? My say-so? Do I have to have her go down to the bank and drag out my birth certificate for you? They took away my car so no driver's license. What'll it be?"

"We're going to take your fingerprints."

"Oh." The old man sat back, then recovered. "Oh. Well, yeah." He showed his hands, brown and age-spotted. Knuckles outsized. The skin beneath the nails was white from years of using muscle to earn a living.

"But, see Sonny."

The old man turned them palms up. "They took those too."

Jake stared in disbelief at the smooth and shiny finger pads. Tiny cracks spidered across them like ice on an uneven lake.

"How?"

The old man looked him straight. "You have to melt it. Melt the skin away so it forgets who you are. It forgets to grow back as you. It just skins over and forgets."

"But-"

"There was a time I could've taken them and if we'd been alone, I woulda tried, by God, but they held what I treasured most."

"What do you mean?"

The old man glanced at the large woman by his side, who looked away.

He turned back to Jake. "My first wife, Frances."

"They threatened you with your wife if ..." Jake indicated the man's hands.

"No. No." The old man gave Jake a pityingly look. He reached out with one hand and gripped one of Jake's hands. "I feel sorry for you, son. You don't know who you're dealing with here do you?"

Jake sat silenced.

"They wouldn't just threaten me. They wouldn't force me to do this by threatening to kill my wife. That would be too easy. Too...merciful."

"Merciful?"

"These are caged animals!" the old man growled. "Vicious. Uncaring. Unfeeling. I wasn't prepared. But you need to be. You need to think like they do. They have a sick pride in what they do."

Jake sat back remembering Stan's words. 'Stop believing every asshole has your sensibilities.'

"I don't understand," Jake asked. "Why didn't they just kill you?"

The old man gave a deep sigh and shook his head. "They brought me and Frances into a dirty garage. It was cold. Very cold. They tied my hands behind my back. Lashed me to a steel post. All along I believed they still had some shred...of... I guess I still had hope. That was my mistake. I hoped it would all turn out okay. That they would finally leave us in peace. That they were just...trying to buy our silence with fear.

"But I was wrong. I knew that as soon as they ripped off all of Frances' clothes."

The old man looked around as if he was seeing where he was for the first time.

"I prayed then. Hadn't prayed since I was a kid. But I prayed. I promised Him anything, everything if it would just end."

He turned back to Jake.

"It didn't. They forced Frances down on the freezing concrete floor. First to her knees. Then they put her on her back. They tied her hands to an oil drum. They wrapped chains around her ankles and jammed the chains around an engine block. She looked so helpless and she was shivering. She could not stop. She was shaking so bad, her head kept bouncing on the floor. I...couldn't look. But I did because I truly believed this was going to be the last time I saw my wife."

The old man's eyes narrowed. "I expected to see a gun, to feel the impact. I hoped it would all be over. I think I even pleaded for my life. I know I begged for hers. But there is no mercy with these people, these scums. There was no gun. That would've been mercy.

"From the back of the garage, I heard the scraping of metal along the floor. They were dragging something. I couldn't see until they pulled it in front of me. It was a rusted, upside down side panel of some old Ford. They grabbed a handful of dirty, oily rags and tossed them in, spread them out, making a nest."

The man gripped both sides of the wheelchair.

"Then I knew. I knew what they planned to do. I could see it as if it had already happened. I could read their sickness. I looked at my wife. But she didn't yet understand. I knew that when she realized she would fight with everything she had."

Jake remained still.

"You see," the old man continued. "My wife was eight months pregnant."

Jake felt the hair rise on his neck. "What...did you do?"

The old man lowered his head and shook it, scattering images that would never be unseen.

"I kicked. I yelled. My feet were still free. I kicked out at this hellish cradle and sent it spinning. I wanted to distract, to stall, anything so my wife wouldn't understand. My only hope was so her last moments were..." He shrugged.

"I never saw the gun." He touched his right knee. "They shot out my knee."

The old man looked pleadingly at Jake. "And I was glad. Because it was the beginning of the end I thought. It was going to be over soon. I could hardly breathe for the pain but that was okay because I knew it was about to be over for both of us. But a second bullet didn't come. Bastards! Instead, they brought out a knife.

"I saw my wife's eyes go from the knife to the car bumper. And then she knew."

"One of them knelt down and scored a big 'X' on her stomach at the highest point. She was thrashing on the ground, I...I...screamed...I promised them anything. Anything! If they would just stop. Stop and leave us. Just leave us be."

The old man's companion wiped her face and took both of his hands.

"And they did. After having their fun, they put the knife away. They left me tied. They left my wife shivering on the concrete floor. They took every material thing we owned, including JOYLAND. Everything. But they didn't stop there. They took more." He raised his hands. "You see they took our lives, our self, our souls and left the shells."

He raised his head. "You see, when you really look at it, who are you? What are you? Not the things you own. Not the material things you've gathered and built. It is yourself, your identity. The ability to wake up in the morning knowing who you are, where you've come from, who you love, what you like, what you want.

"They left us our bodies to breathe and eat and function, but they took everything else, including our hope our plans, our life together. Our unborn son."

Rendell paused, in grief, Jake thought, but it was just to catch his breath. He'd been hollowed of all that had meant something to him long ago. What was left was razored raw and it fueled his story.

He shifted in his wheelchair and began again. "In the years that followed, we would get mocking postcards asking how our son was, asking whether we were trying to get pregnant again. Always threatening to drop in sometime and say hello.

"They discarded us like garbage. We were a toy to be teased and threatened. Nothing more."

Jake started to object.

"You think I could've done something, don't you? I see it in your eyes. You blame me for my silence."

"You could've gone…"

"The police?! I did! You smarmy bastard. I did." Rendell's head went back and he gasped for breath. The Bearded Lady touched his shoulder. He waved her away.

"I did go to the cops here," he continued. "I… neither of us could take it anymore. It was like we were back in that garage every day. Every shittin' day. Finally, we just wanted to end it. We knew the postcards came from California, so we told the two detectives here the whole story. They didn't believe it, but they said they'd check it out and get back to us."

"Did they?"

"Of course." The crooked smile settled into a sneer. "Of course they did. And I know they did because my wife and son were killed in a car crash a week later. Yeah, I know the cops got to them because I got the condolence postcard a few hours before my wife and son even got in the car."

Jake swallowed hard.

"Here." The old man dug out an envelope. It was an 8x10 manila envelope, dog-eared at the corners with the slim contents held in by the metal clasp at the back.

"This is it, detective. Everything I know. Pokovich was one of the names they used. But I taught them about disguises, about pretending, playing a role. That's what being carny is all about, you see. Reading other people, being what they expect to be, so you can fleece 'em. Or kill 'em.

"So, here. Their history and pictures."

"Pictures?"

Rendell coughed. "Sorry. Not what you're hoping for. Pictures from when they first arrived decades ago. See, they made damn sure I never got anything on film after that."

He looked away, up to one of the little stained-glass chapel windows. The depiction was a stylized Jesus offering a helping hand to a lost beggar. He seemed to be lost in thought for a moment, maybe realizing he was releasing remembered events he no longer had to remember and for which he was no longer responsible. A moral load that he could finally pass off to someone else.

When he turned back, he took in the whole chapel, finally settling on Jake. He seemed deflated as if the race he'd been running was over and over was all that mattered.

"You have no idea, son."

Rendell's bony hand reached out to cover Jake's. It was a simple and gentle gesture but was cut with a sad, harsh whisper.

"Good luck and may God be with you."

CHAPTER 28

McCardle watched as the rusted Dodge K car paused at the mailbox, backed up, turned and headed down the long gravel driveway, leaving a dusty trail.

"Now what?" he asked to no one in earshot for everyone on the farm was busy assisting the police investigators combing through what little was left of the personal belongings of the three young horse thieves. Bastards.

That Jody kid was easily spotted. How many kids show up at a McDonald's with three horses. Now the police had him back upstairs, taking turns being good cop, bad cop. McCardle was confident they'd have the other two in hand shortly.

The old Dodge swung past the hedges that surrounded the house. Damn near rear-ended the two CHiP vehicles neatly parked side-by-side.

McCardle saw the driver, a small little man, pull himself up against the steering wheel. His face was pressed up against the windshield as if he'd never seen highway patrol vehicles before. The car shifted into reverse, began to back away, and braked to a stop after only a car length. The little man sat idling.

McCardle had had enough with back and forth. Was the guy lost or what? He sidled up to the driver's window and knocked on it.

The little man inside remained staring straight ahead not acknowledging McCardle.

McCardle knocked again. "You staying or are you going," shouted McCardle.

It took a moment but Pitic cut the ignition, opened the door and got out.

McCardle could see he was sweating and shaking a bit as if he had a bit of palsy. Still, the little man attempted a pleasant façade even though he didn't say a word. Just smiled and fidgeted.

"Who the hell are you?" challenged McCardle.

Pitic handed McCardle a business card.

McCardle took one look at it and guffawed.

"The hell is this? Bill Smith private investigator? Who the goddamn is Bill Smith? It sure isn't you."

Pitic glanced around to make sure nobody was nearby and then whispered.

McCardle leaned in. "What did you say?"

Pitic licked his lips and cleared his throat. When he spoke up, it was in a high piercing Eastern European cackle.

"Said I'm here to pick up the kids."

"What kids?"

"Those two kids that are here."

McCardle gave him a hard look and turned toward the house. "Follow me. Let me introduce you to our state cops. They can help you deal with those three kids."

"Three?"

"Yeah three. The one I had here already and the two new ones that came the other day."

"There's three?"

Something wasn't right. McCardle turned and faced his little man. "Just what's your business with these three kids? Are you with CPS? If so, you'll probably have to get in line behind the cops. You do know they stole all my horses."

Through all this Pitic just kept shaking his head no, no, no. "I'm private, just looking for those two kids. I need to take them."

McCardle looked him up and down. The shaking was worse, and the sweat was just running off him.

"You okay mister Bill Smith?"

"I'm just here to pick up those two kids."

"Yeah, it's what you keep saying but you'll have to talk to the cops so come this way."

But Pitic didn't move. "I don't want to bother them."

McCardle approached Pitic. "I don't know what your deal is Mister Smith. You say you're private. You say you're here to pick up these kids. You don't want to talk to the cops. What's going on? Anyway, I told you those kids aren't here."

It was as if Pitic was a minute behind in the conversation. "Horses? What horses?"

McCardle pointed to the barn. "You see that barn. That barn had 18 horses in it this morning or last night. Now, they're all gone and so are the three kids. Well, one kid was caught thanks to the cops. He's upstairs being grilled. You need to talk to them if you want to get the other two kids."

Pitic had heard all he needed to hear. He backed away, opened the car door and with a shaky hand pulled it shut. He started the ignition but before he backed out of the driveway, he rolled down his window. "Which way did they go?"

McCardle wasn't going to answer but relented. Maybe this asshole can find the rest of my horses. Screw the kids.

"Look, I found a trail through my cornfield. Stalks all trampled. Seems they headed off northeast."

Pitic started backing out as soon as he heard the direction they went.

"You find them, you bring them back here," shouted McCardle. "I want my horses back. And, they're going to have to answer for being horse thieves too."

Pitic couldn't have pushed the accelerator any harder. Gravel flew, and he just missed the mailbox by about 6 inches.

McCardle took another look at the business card. He tore it in two and dropped it in the dirt.

CHAPTER 29

"Well, look who has come to visit, boy. It's Detective Jake Steiner all the way from Florida and New Jersey come calling. What can he want?"

The dog padded past Mallory and went to Jake, tail moving.

Mallory made a show of checking an imaginary watch. "You just get in?"

Jake held up his hand. "Okay, I know I'm late. Shoot me."

"I can do that. Bend over."

Jake stood on the threshold and greeted his dog with a pat to his side.

Mallory smiled at the scene. "Dog missed you."

"Maybe."

"He paces."

"Back and forth?"

"Pretty much. He missed you," said Mallory again in a quiet voice.

"Stan?" Though Jake knew who she meant.

"Your dog."

"I don't know. He seems Mr. Nonchalant whenever I leave him."

"He paces when you're not around."

They both glanced at a whooshed-out mutt, head on paws.

"He doesn't appear to be the jewel of excitement."

"Jake, he's just waiting to be fed."

"He can stand to lose some weight." Then. "Aww man. What have you done to my dog?"

Jake knelt in front of Jake who now had a red kerchief tied around his neck. The dog looked at Jake with a baleful look that said 'I'm sorry. Couldn't help it.'

"And he smells," stated Jake as he took a good whiff of Jake's fur.

Again, the baleful look.

"I gave him a bath, Jake. He needed a bath."

"Maybe. But now he smells like wet dog and some sort of lavender pomade."

"It's called 'Spring Morning.'

Jake looked at her accusingly. "Is it a dog shampoo? The vet didn't mention hosing him down with 'Spring Morning.' She said to use a flea shampoo to keep the bugs away. This'll probably be a clarion call for every flea in Sacramento. Come everyone and chomp on my lavender soaked dog."

"You don't deserve a dog, you know."

This stopped Jake. And for a moment Mallory felt guilty and regretted it because he did look as if he had his doubts.

"I mean. This is your first dog, right?"

Mallory glanced down at the dog who had nuzzled up against Jake's leg.

"I mean, he obviously likes you for some unknown reason, so you're doing something right with him. Just remember, he needs a bath every week, at least. They're not like cats, you know, they don't groom themselves."

She looked at him and gave him an encouraging smile.

"Look. You haven't killed him yet and he seems well-fed. Just remember hygiene. Once a week."

"We'll shower together, won't we boy?"

Mallory moved to fill the slightly awkward pause.

"He's a good dog, Jake. I've had dogs. I know. And he seems dedicated to you. I don't know what you've done to endear him to you, but whatever it is, it works."

Jake shrugged "Well, we work together, don't we Jake?"
Jake wagged at the attention.
"Um. You want to come in?"
Jake looked past her into the condo.
The invitation hung for a moment while Jake hesitated.
"Some other time," he said, finally. "I need to get home. Water my plants."
Mallory laughed at the mental picture.
"Okay. Here then." She held out a leash. It was red and green and made of woven nylon. "It's a new one. Kinda goes with the kerchief."
Jake looked at the leash.
"Thanks. I already have one," he blundered, then recovered. "But I guess it's good to have two. So, yeah, thanks."
He turned and followed the dog who had already loped his way to the car and now sat obediently next to the passenger door awaiting Jake's valet service. When the door opened, he hopped in and sat primly on the seat, seeming, if not eager for, at least accepting of his vehicle harness.
Mallory leaned up against the door. She observed how carefully Jake adjusted the straps and made sure every part of the dog was inside before he shut the passenger door. She saw him ruff Jake's fur before he shut the door. It was a personal thing. A communal thing.
And then she was sorry she hadn't insisted he come in for coffee or just to sit down. Loneliness comes in many forms and usually never shouts or makes itself known. Just hovers. And hurts.
Before they drove off, the dog turned and looked back at her. The red kerchief was still on his neck. It kinda matched the color of Jake's red Corvette.
They made a handsome couple.

"She means well, I think."

Jake gave a sidelong glance to his dog. "Maybe she only had poodles before. Little toy ones. They would've loved to be drenched in that Spring Morning stuff."

He scratched Jake behind the ear.

"Don't worry. It'll wear off before you know it. Just don't go rolling in a dead rabbit to get yourself some manly smell, okay. I don't need to deal with that."

Jake adjusted himself on the seat.

"Always the stoic, aren't you?"

Jake studied the dog's shoulder. He knew where to look to see the scar but, if you didn't, you'd never know he'd been tossed out of the back of a station wagon, along with his three brothers.

Jake remembered that night. He and Stan had just finished slogging through a mountain of witness reports. He was tired, headed home. The rusted brown Chevy wagon had been coming toward him.

Kids. A kid driving. More of them swarming the back seat.

At first, when the cardboard box was tipped, he thought they were toys, stuffed animals. Thought some wiseasses in the Chevy's backseat had been screwing around and tossing crap, beer cans or bottles, out the window in front of oncoming cars.

But they weren't bottles of Bud or cans of Rolling Rock or toys or stuffed animals and they hit hard in front of Jake.

Four of the pups and then for good measure the box they had been carted in, all hit and bounced and rolled. The Chevy with a girl waving a scarf out the passenger window went accelerating past Jake as he stood on his brakes. Laughter and thumping beat of bass speakers screamed past and faded quickly.

When Jake jumped out of the Corvette, he was unprepared for what he saw. He'd worked scores of traffic accidents, stabbings, gunshot wounds, had stuck his finger in busted arteries and had cradled dying kids, but he'd not experienced having to pick up the bent and broken remains of a malnourished litter.

As gentle as he could, using the box from which they dropped, one by one he placed them carefully against the cardboard sides.

He knew that two were dead, but it would have been wrong to leave any there. One's eyes were closed and its breathing shallow. The last one had a bone sticking out of its shoulder and appeared to be crying.

'They're Weimaraners,' said the girl who took the box at the animal hospital. Jake was reluctant to give it up. Still, he insisted on walking the box into the hospital himself.

It had taken using all his off-hours patrolling that stretch of highway. Waiting. It was three months later when he had arrested the driver of a rusted-out Chevy for DUI. It was a good arrest and Jake followed it through to arraignment and sentencing. It was the second DUI for the kid and he was only 20.

That same night he swung by the animal hospital, just out of curiosity.

One dog had made it, said the girl who had taken the box that night. One dog. He was still there. Tough to adopt out a dog that's been injured, she'd said. Most people don't want damage to their animals.

Jake had allowed himself to be led back to the cages. Just to see, he'd told himself. Just to see what a survivor looked like.

The girl opened the cage of a medium brown-haired dog with the name Admiral handwritten on the white name board above the cage.

"He's still not 100% I think," she'd said, but the dog named 'Admiral' had lifted his head and even before he left the cage was wagging his tail in an energetic thump-thump.

The only evidence of his trauma was the shaved hair and scar that was still evident.

"We still keep it shaved because we've had to do a few surgeries. Normally, we wouldn't have done them…"

Jake looked at her. "You wouldn't? This is an animal hospital isn't it?" Then, he knew better.

The girl looked unsure about how much she should explain that this was an animal hospital, but it was also a business and the staff needed to be paid and the facility maintained and multiple surgeries like the ones done on this dog usually were never in the cards.

"But, he seemed to have just a great attitude, you know? And we all thought after what he went through and being the only one left, well…"

Jake had knelt and touched the scar. Admiral had bowed his head as if embarrassed about his disfigurement. It was an unspoken bond, Jake believing that the dog may have actually remembered him. Maybe remembered being rescued. Maybe not.

Now, even under the passing streetlights, Jake could see that the scar was still there, though the hair had grown over. And he knew the limp was almost gone. But, now a new, ragged crimson scar on his left side was surrounded by a circle of shaved fur thanks to Ilsa Pokovich.

Damn resilient, thought Jake. A soul that has seen the worst of man and still not lost his trust.

"Proud of you, you know," Jake said.

Still, it had taken Jake two months of coaxing at the shelter to even get Admiral back into a vehicle. There had been a number of trial runs until finally, the day came, and the dog trusted him enough so he was able to take Jake out of the shelter and home.

It was trust now that allowed Jake to sit proudly in the passenger seat knowing he wasn't going to be tossed from the moving vehicle and trust that his protector wouldn't let him be shot again.

"And, I'm really, really sorry about the lavender."

The dog glanced at him then resumed his scanning of the road ahead. And Jake the dog wasn't particularly surprised when Jake the man made a U-turn and headed back the way he'd come.

CHAPTER 30

Jake stood before Mallory.

"I forgot to return the kerchief. I don't believe he needs it."

The dog nudged his leg. Jake knelt and undid the kerchief. Mallory watched him, bemused.

She took it when Jake handed it to her. "I thought he looked good," she said, trying not to sound offended. Which she really wasn't.

"Maybe," Jake mused. "Maybe if he needed to score with some saucy bitch."

Mallory paused before she said, "It used to be my kerchief."

Jake stepped back and regarded her with a slight smile. "You didn't need any help to score?"

Mallory shook her head slowly side to side. "No."

The dog looked up, first to Jake, then to Mallory, then back to Jake.

Mallory stepped back, hands at her side. She couldn't stop herself. As if she was being directed by someone else. As if someone else was talking.

"He approached me. We locked eyes. He reached up and unbuttoned the first button of my shirt. I didn't object. He continued and released each button. He reached in and cupped each of my breasts as if he owned them. His hands would've slipped inside my panties, had I been wearing any. His hands moved around traced the curve of my ass. He pulled me to him. He kissed me with a surprisingly gentle kiss. I didn't respond. Not satisfied, he cradled my head in his hands and tried again. I still didn't respond. Unsure of what was happening he stopped until I took his hand and led him to my bedroom."

"That happened?"

She moved only to take his hand. "Not yet."

She led him to her bedroom and before she closed the door she whispered to the dog.

"Nope. Sorry."

When the door closed, Jake put his head on his paws, swallowed twice and listened. Satisfied that all was going well, he closed his eyes.

Instead of her leading him she was surprised when, holding hands, they both move towards the bed together. He turned her toward him. His grip was sure and firm when he lifted her to him, the kiss was warm and insistent and lasted agreeably longer than she expected.

Jake started on the top button on her plaid work shirt, and continued undressing her expertly with a smile, a knowing smile, but still slightly unsure, like a teenage boy who asks permission with his eyes when he's experimenting for the first time. He loosened her jeans. They fell on their own to gather at her feet. She stepped out of them and stood before him.

"Why didn't you tell me how beautiful you are?"

"Jake-" She ran her hand along her scar.

He took her hand away. "That's not you."

"How do you know?"

He didn't let her say anymore. He leaned in and kissed her neck. She shivered, feeling the light scratching from two days of not shaving. As his hands smoothed down her naked back, she held her breath until he gripped her from behind, then she pushed him back.

He hesitated until she smiled and began undressing him. He helped because there was a quiet urgency building between them.

Mallory fell back on the bed and then propped herself up on her elbows, admiring who stood before her.

He was the man she had imagined. The man she'd seen once before with someone else. The man who she thought she knew. She knew then what was about to happen wasn't going to be perfect or spectacular, just special. They had danced. They had touched. They had spent working time together. They had fought, they had laughed together.

Now, there was nowhere else to go but here.

From the first time she'd seen Jake, she'd felt the pull, like no other time before. Like water cascading where it had to go, this was always going to happen. Even if she didn't know it, voice it to herself, admit it, deep down there was always going to be their two circles intersecting. There would be no experimenting this night, no tantric positions, no discussing what each one liked. There was just the irresistible need to be close and satisfy the other.

He knelt on the bed and pushed her hair from her face. He lowered himself to her and kissed her again. She was the one who started exploring first, running her fingers over his chest, down further until she knew how ready he was. He moved over her and let her guide him.

They both reacted as one as he entered her. Both amazed, because they fit together perfectly as if two halves had found each other. And they moved together as one. And they came together. And to Mallory's surprise, it was perfect.

CHAPTER 31

Jake watched, propped on one elbow as Mallory slipped out of bed and opened the window. Backlit by moonlight, she appeared to Jake as someone he knew and didn't. Standing there, she seemed... purposeful. Purposeful. Not tremendously romantic, thought Jake. But there she was. Nothing hidden. Everything she was, was there. It was unnerving, yet...

He sat up. "I think I've never seen you before."

"Jake."

"I mean who are you?"

"Who am I?" she answered without turning.

"You're not Mallory, the Mallory I see every day. The Mallory who lied her way into working with Stan and me. The Mallory who plies us with pastries. The Mallory who has tremendous insight yet can easily bungle an interview. So, who did I just kiss?"

"And screw," she added.

Jake beamed. "Twice, I'd like to add, humbly trying to keep the pride out of my voice."

"Can you ever really know someone? Even if you make love to them..."

"Twice."

"...Even if you sleep with them for 30 years. Even if you eat every meal with them. Even if you plan your lives together. You can't know."

"I don't know." He shifted, piled two pillows together and sat up. "Now that I think about it, you seemed to know a good bit about me. You knew I owned my building. You knew my parents had willed it to me when they died. It was as if you had studied the blueprints of the building. When we had the two kids, you turned right toward the guest room. How did you know it was there? How did you know where to go?"

Mallory sighed, turned and rested her bare butt on the windowsill.

"You were born in Newark, Delaware. You had a brother, Clyde, but you called him Jeeli, he died in a car accident when he was sixteen. You have a sister, Sarah. She's in Atlantic City. I don't know what she does. You are the oldest sibling. You father was a firefighter. Your mother was a housewife, I think. You played football in high school and went to the University of Minnesota on a scholarship. You graduated cum laude. Your parents moved to California while you were in college. They put down roots, first in Los Angles, then here in Sacramento. Your mother had pancreatic cancer and your Dad died shortly after she did. He was shot on the street in a robbery gone bad.

"Shortly after that, you joined the department here. Worked your way up. You partnered with Stan. You never married. You seem to play around a lot. You're sarcastic to everyone, including me. You work hard. You care."

She stood. "And you have a big heart."

"How... do you know so much?" Jake asked. "How?"

Mallory gave a short laugh. "There is a story about the Sultan of Brunei or someone like that. He was fastidious about cleanliness. He demanded that every inch of his palace be cleaned every day. So clean, that there wasn't to be a speck of dust anywhere. His servants came to him and said they did their best but admitted that there was no way they could know if the palace was as clean as the Sultan had demanded. You know what the Sultan did?"

Jake shook his head, mesmerized.

"Every night he had his favorite wife spread a light coating of sand into every corner of the palace. In the morning, the servants cleaned up every bit of the sand, thereby assuring the Sultan that the palace was as clean as he demanded.

"I scattered sand all over your life Jake. I cleaned it up the best I could."

"Why?"

Mallory went to bed and kneeled next to Jake.

"Because you kissed me. Months ago."

"I did? I don't…"

"Remember? You kissed me on my head. The day we found my brother's grave. You leaned over and kissed the top of my head. Jake, that kiss meant more to me… than anything we've done here. Then anything we might ever do. I had to know who you were. Who was the man, that when I needed it most, showed me tenderness, showed how tender he could be."

"You make me sound like a cliché. Like the cop with heart of gold."

"No. You're a man, not a cliché. And, I love… what I know about you."

Mallory slipped under the covers and snuggled against him. "So far, anyway."

When Jake awoke the sun of a new day blasted in, lighting up everything. He watched as Mallory emerged from the shower, toweled off and proceeded to get dressed. He had a strange feeling. It took him a moment to identify what it was.

It wasn't guilt, it was luck, he decided. He felt lucky. The guilt that he felt was only because he reminded himself about their age difference.

He cleared his throat. "Stan's looking better, don't you think? Pretty sure he'll be a hundred percent soon."

Mallory stopped with the towel and stared at Jake. "What are you doing?"

"What?"

"You're talking about work and Stan."

Embarrassed, Jake started to get out of bed, but Mallory pushed him back. She climbed onto the bed next to him and sat cross-legged.

The view was incredibly alluring, and Jake settled back and admired what was before him.

"Don't look like that," admonished Mallory.

"Like what?"

"Like uncomfortable."

"It's just-" started Jake.

Mallory put her hand on his chest. "You wanted to get past the awkward."

"Awkward?"

"Jake, we work together. You think you're going to feel weird, self-conscious, probably embarrassed that I dragged you in here. You want to talk about anything else but us and... you know..."

"Last night?"

"Right. Last night. But it's daylight now. No moonlight, no... urgency. And we can see each other and remember and regret... if necessary. And that's why it's awkward."

Jake smiled but said nothing.

"Of course, maybe it's not awkward for you," Mallory ran on. "Maybe your self-confidence is through the roof and you are happy and satisfied with your performance and you've completely written off the other person's... performance or their perception of their performance."

Jake held up his hand to stop her.

"What?" she asked. "What is it?"

"I made coffee."

"What? When?"

"Last night when you were in the bathroom. I set a timer."

"You made coffee."

"Smell it?"

Mallory sniffed, then nodded.

"Yeah," Jake shrugged. "I thought it might be awkward for you and you would want to talk about anything but what went on last night and I thought we could discuss the difference between Arabica beans and Columbian beans while we sipped coffee. So, you wouldn't be uncomfortable, and we could avoid saying what last night meant."

"Which was?"

"Weird."

Mallory covered her face and jerked away. "Shit! All my fault. Me talking about cupping my breasts, leading you in here. And you did it, like a pity fuck and you didn't want to but you were playing nice and you felt sorry for your delusional partner because not only did I drag you into something, complicating any kind of professional relationship we have... had, that there's plenty of regret to go around..."

Mallory stopped because Jake was laughing.

"What?" she asked, demanding an answer.

"Weird was the wrong word. It was just... I realized I've never spent the night with..."

"What? A demanding bitch? An idiot?"

"With a friend. I've never spent the night with a friend. And..."

"And what?"

"And it was oddly comforting." Jake turned on his back. "I liked it. I like you. I liked us last night."

He raised his head. "You did too."

Mallory struggled to keep her smile neutral, but the overwhelming feeling was to touch him again, to make sure he was really here, that what had happened, had happened.

Instead, as a protective reflex, she ran her hand along her scar.

Again, like last night, he took her hand away. "Don't. I told you, that's not you."

"How do you know? We made love in the dark. I could've been anybody. You couldn't see everything."

"I see you every day. That's not you."

Jake pulled her on top.

"And it's not dark now. And I very much like what I see."

Later, after he left, though she tried not to, she let long unused tears fall into what Jake told her were a combination of Arabica and Columbian bean coffee. She cried for the silliness and she cried with gratefulness.

CHAPTER 32

As they were leaving the breakfast room Jessie said, "Where to now? Find another church?"

She was smiling because she had just eaten well, and they were free, and she trusted that Michael had a plan.

"Church. Funny, ha-ha. No," he said. "Now we go for lunch."

"With what?" she asked. "I saw you got nothing from the cash machine and nothing plus nothing is nothing. Like you always said."

"We're okay."

"Sure," she mocked. "How 'bout I get some cardboard and some crayons and make a sign and stand by the side of the road if that's your plan. Like the beggars we see."

"No, we're going to get our car serviced."

"What you mean to get our car serviced? What are you talking about?"

"Look, I saw it one time when good old dad had the car in for service. They have a nice waiting room. They've got apples, juice, coffee, all kinds of stuff to eat while your car is being worked on."

"So, what. We don't have a car."

"Doesn't matter. We can wait with the rest of the proud owners. Chow down while waiting for our imaginary car."

"This is your plan?" she asked. "We escaped a nice house and a farm."

"It wasn't a nice place," interrupted Michael. "You were just tired of moving around. That's why you thought it was nice."

Michael saw the look on her face. It was the same look when he told her she'd have to ride a horse.

"Look, it'll all work out," he continued, summoning up his trusting voice. "You just have to trust me. We'll be in Arizona before you know it."

Michael kept up the smile until Jessie turned and went into the women's bathroom.

Some plan. Sure, the ATM didn't give him any money. Maybe because he couldn't remember the password. Maybe it was a bad card. Maybe there was no money. Didn't matter.

He'd figure out how to get some dough somehow. For some strange reason, now that they'd eaten well, now that they'd escaped from the McArdle's, he had a good feeling about their future. And it involved transportation and it involved arriving in Arizona and it involved being on the ranch. And it involved being away from all the shit that had just been happening.

It was a funny feeling, being unsure but confident. Kind of conflicting, but then again, their life so far had been pretty conflicting.

He'd seen a Toyota dealership about three blocks away and that's where they would head just as soon as Jessie came out of the bathroom. They'll just saunter down there, to the service entrance and sit down like they're waiting for their car. If somebody asked them why they're there, they'll just say 'Hey my dad is out there looking at new cars while we get ours serviced'. And yes, we will have another apple thank you'.

It will work, thought Michael.

And he was pretty sure it would, right up until the moment he saw the two cops.

Two local cops, local Davis county sheriffs, passed Michael and Jessie just leaving the breakfast room. He and Jessie had their pockets and the backpack stuffed with bananas and oranges, boxes of strawberry yogurt and a few blueberry muffins. Michael had even toasted four slices of bread, peeled open six little plastic tublets of peanut butter and six of the grape jelly and, remembering to spread butter on one side, had even made two PB&J sandwiches.

And they would've made it out and to freedom if Jessie hadn't taken so long in the bathroom.

When she finally emerged, he had turned Jessie around when he saw the smarmy assistant manager point directly at them.

"Jess!" Michael hissed. "Get back in the bathroom."

"Why?"

"Just go. Stay in there until I call you."

"Why?"

Instead of answering, Michael gripped her shoulders, turned her around and held the bathroom door open for her. He gave her a nudge that didn't give her a chance to object.

He took a casual pose, leaning up against the hallway across from the bathrooms. Through quick glances, he saw the cops had rejoined the assistant manager and were now staring in his direction.

The cops nodded to the assistant manager and headed down the hallway, dark shades, creaking leather, and local attitude.

To Michael, they seemed poised for action, not knowing whether he was a crazy homeless urchin with a weapon, or if Michael was going to go rabbit, bolt for parts unknown, leading them a chase.

Michael did neither. He stayed where he was, slouched up against the hallway wall as they approached. With his sister in the can, where was he going to go?

Both cops looked back to the manager seeking assurance they had the right kid. The manager gave a curt gesture and that was all they needed.

They kept their distance but flanked him on both sides. He could see his image reflected in their dark glasses.

The younger of the two took charge. Before he spoke, he moved his wad of Juicy Fruit to the other side of his mouth.

"Hey, son," he began. "Are you staying in this hotel?"

The assistant manager stole up behind the officers to hear what was being said.

"Son," the younger one said, pushing his cap back in a fake casual manner. "What room are in? If in fact, you are staying here."

Michael didn't move. And he didn't answer.

"Son, asking you nicely. What about it?" All fake polite, just as Michael had come to expect.

He stayed propped up against the wall and he didn't answer to 'Son asking you nicely' type shit.

He thought about making up some random room number and had made up his mind to spew forth something like thirty-four or 'the one on the left on the top floor' but looking past the cop he saw the corpulent assistant manager shake his head either as a warning or in general disgust at the level of homeless kids these days. It was hard to tell, maybe both.

Two things happened in the short space of Michael's hesitation.

Jessie emerged from the bathroom and the cop, the beefy one, losing any patience he might have come in with, made a grab for Michael.

Michael, fortified with two helpings of make-your-own waffles and a large apple and several blueberry muffins warmed and slathered with two plastic tublets of real butter, was slow off the mark.

Just as the cop got his arm, Jessie let out an alarming scream. Michael swung the backpack up from the floor, roundhouse, connecting squarely on the left side of the cop's cheek and jaw.

Things escalated from there.

The guttural growl from the cop combined with Jessie's screaming made for bad harmony.

The cop's hand scissored into Michael's neck followed by legs slamming into the back of Michael's knee.

He did remember his head hitting the side the tile floor, pinned down with the cop's boot on his neck.

The funny thing, next to the drool from his squashed face bathing his cheek, was a phrase he'd heard in school. He couldn't remember the context. Hitler maybe. But, as he thought it, he yelled it, as best he could.

"Fucking jackbooted thug!"

The only effect it had was that the boot on his neck ratcheted deeper until Michael struggled to breathe. He began flailing, clawing at the cop's leg, trying to tear into the flesh on his calf. Anything to make him remove his boot. Michael panicked, searching for any way to escape. All he saw in his fading haze was Jessie with the other cop, pinning her against the door of the bathroom.

It was the crowd of guests that emerged from the breakfast room that made the cop release him.

CHAPTER 33

Michael opened his eyes and found himself staring at the acoustic tile ceiling.

The sounds were unfamiliar - general busyness, a whoosh of a door opening, occasionally some garble on an intercom.

But the smells he knew.

It was the impersonal perfume of a hospital.

Shit! He was in a hospital.

"Jess!" Michael croaked. He tried to turn his head but there was a collar or some type of apparatus securing his neck and head. His throat was on fire and he tried to swallow but had no spit. Then he remembered. Goddamn cops.

His speech came out as a weak rasp. A garble that even he didn't understand, but it was enough to bring Jessie to his side.

She pulled a chair over to the bedside so she could look down on him since he couldn't turn his head.

To Michael, she looked awful. Scared, tired, mostly lost. It was all his fault.

"Hospital," was all he managed.

Jessie nodded.

Michael fought against the pain in his throat. "Gotta go."

Jessie's eyes widened.

"Leave. Us. You and me. Go."

Jessie shook her head. She glanced at the door. "M, they want to arrest us or something. For running away and the horses."

Michael nodded. "So, gotta go."

Jessie stared at him, frozen, uncertain She glanced over to the door again.

Michael reviewed his grand escape plan. What worked and what didn't. Scatter the horses. Jody going one way he and Jessie the other. Hit the ATM. Withdraw dough. Transportation to Arizona. Not quite how it was working out. Still, they had a chance. No one seemed to be attending to them. And hey, they were just kids. Kids aren't going to do anything rash, right? They may be able to just walk out.

If his clothes were handy.

He went to sit up, went to swing his legs out over the side and that was when the handcuffs on his left wrist jerked him to a stop. He saw his left wrist was shackled to the bed rail.

"The hell is this?" garbled Michael, yanking once, twice, on the cuffs. Every time he did that the one loop slid along the bed rail, metal on metal, making a decidedly you-aren't-going-anywhere sound.

"Having trouble, kid? Giving the staff trouble, are you?" The older overweight cop leaning against the doorway sniggered.

"Try and bust out, asshole. What you did to my leg I ought to have you up for resisting arrest and disorderly conduct and attacking a member of the Davis Police Department."

He leaned in so Michael could see the name on the badge, Jace Bonnetti, and get a full slug of just-been-chewed pepperoni pizza breath.

"You are mine." The cop then nodded his head toward Jessie. "Toto too."

It was all Michael could do to not spit at this slob of a cop.

Instead, he laughed. His speech wasn't completely back to normal, still, he made his derision clear.

"Hey dickwad, is this the best you can come up with? Is this the best you could do with your life? Tell you what, go home and tell your wife that you've been abusing kids. See how that goes over, you shitface."

"Talk all you want kid. It'll do no good. I've heard a lot worse."

He pulled out a key from his ring and unlocked the handcuffs.

Michael pulled himself up in bed. "Jess, hand me my clothes. We are so out of here."

"You're right, son. We have a nice place for you to wait until CPS gets here."

"You're taking us in?"

The cop laughed, turned and shared a laugh with the other cop now in the doorway.

"Taking you in? You have been watching too many cop shows. Damn straight, we are. Aren't we Artie? You know they used to hang horse thieves out here."

"We stole nothing." But, even to Michael, it sounded hollow as he couldn't muster much conviction.

"C'mon. Hospital released you. They did all they could for your throat, but they said there was no cure for you being an asshole. Let's go."

"I don't think so," said Michael.

"You don't think what?" The cop stood full height, ready to deal with anything.

"You're not taking us anywhere."

"Don't give us trouble kid. We'd hate to see you bawling your eyes out all the way down the hallway while we dragged your sorry ass outta here,"

But Michael was busy digging into his jeans pockets.

"Just get dressed. We'll be right outside."

"Wait," commanded Michael. His tone made them stop.

When they came back, he had a look of confidence. As if he knew something they didn't. And they hated that look.

"What?" demanded the younger one,

Michael found what he was looking for. It had been jammed in that little jean pocket on the right side, the pocket he never knew what it was for.

He carefully extracted a business card. At least it had been. Now the corners were bent over, frayed all the way around, barely holding together.

The cops watched as Michael took his time unfolding it. He re-bent the corners back to the original shape and flattened it as best he could. Finally, he presented it to the younger cop.

"Here. Careful."

The cop took it and read it. He handed it to the other one, then took it back. It showed the logo and title of the Sacramento Police Department.

"Call it," is all Michael; says. "Call it. You'll see."

"Who the hell is this Detective Wyld? Why are you giving this to me?"

"Just call."

"So, you have some detective's card. So, what?"

"His personal cell is written on the back."

The cop turned it over. There was a faded, nearly unreadable phone number in faded blue ink.

"Call him."

"All right, kid. Exactly what is this?"

Michael smiled and winked at Jessie.

"That, you pig-faced assholes, is my get-out-of-jail-free card."

CHAPTER 34

Jake was tempted to ask, 'Now what?' when the phone rang again, just after he'd ended a call. But it wasn't the call he'd been waiting for. It wasn't Stan letting him know he'd found the kids. It was Mallory.

"Hi," he said. "Hey, listen. Perfect that it's you. Thought we could reconvene where we left off."

"Jake," she interrupted. "This is business."

Silence.

"Oh," Mallory laughed, embarrassed. "Yeah, hi," she said softer, acknowledging the past few days. "I'll start again. Hi. How are you?" She sounded like a high-schooler to her own ears, but Jake seemed not to notice.

"Where are you?" he asked.

"Why?" This was going to go off track if she let it and as much as she wanted it to, she'd called for another reason.

"I'm home, but listen-"

"Good."

"Jake, we need to do something."

"You're telling me."

"Jake! I mean it."

"So do I." She could imagine him smiling and looking to the dog for approval of his fabulous wit.

"You need to meet me," she said, mustering a level of seriousness.

"That's where I was going."

"We need to go back to Marston's screening room. Where we found them, you know?

"Not really what I had in mind."

"Sorry, but there's something we need to do."

She could hear him sigh, abandoning the pursuit. "I give. Why back there?"

"Because we missed something huge."

He tried not to sound annoyed. "Rodriguez and Danni's team have been all through there. They scraped and vacuumed and sifted and got down on their hands and knees and picked at and sucked up everything. They analyzed the blood on the silver tray as Peter Berlin's. Danni made the determination that it was the same or similar daiishka that took care of both men. Mal, everything was taken care of, down to the smallest detail."

"Yeah, that's what I'm saying. Everything to the smallest detail. But they missed... we missed, all of us missed one important element."

"Okay, what?"

"Jake, how did they get in?"

"Same way we did."

"You saw how Susan and I got in," Mallory persisted. "Those nails were rusted. They'd been there, that way for a long time. You think whoever did this to Marston and Peter Berlin, pulled off the plywood, marched them in somehow, and when they were done boarded the place back up?"

"Could be."

"With rusty nails? In the same holes as before?"

Jake leaped ahead. "Mal, you're saying there is another entrance, right?"

"Has to be."

"Well, no one saw anything like that. Neither Rodriguez or Danni. There were no trap doors in the floor. Nothing. There was only the front entrance."

"I know what they didn't find. But..."

"What?"

"I have a feeling."

Jake knew better than to argue. Both he and Stan agreed there was something their assistant had they didn't. Feelings. Hunches. Whatever it was, it had worked in the past.

Jake began to pick up on Mallory's drift. It may not be important, but two things started to nag. If there was another entrance, then someone went to some effort to conceal it. And it is unusual to have only one entrance to an office. Jake remembered the size of the block of which the Marston screening room office was a part. It was at least twice as deep as the Marston office. Which meant the entrance didn't exit onto a back street.

The second thing that bothered him, now that she raised it, was the whole screening room tableau, staged as it was, rankled as if unfinished. As if he and Mallory had only uncovered part of the mystery of what had happened.

"All right, when?"

When Mallory didn't answer right away, Jake laughed. "Okay," he said. 'How 'bout half hour."

"And bring Jake."

"He's no bloodhound."

"I just miss him. Then again, you never know."

CHAPTER 35

A Sacramento rain was sluicing down the whole block when they pulled up to the Marston office in Jake's Corvette. It made the shuttered storefronts feel even drearier. Even though the area needed a thorough hose down, the only result was wet litter, soggy newspapers draped half into the gutter, smeared graffiti and the insistent ripeness of urine reanimated.

The old weathered plywood with the rusted nails had been removed and replaced by Danni's Forensic crew when they had completed their work. In place were three new pieces of plywood, overlaid with chain link screwed to the plywood, then draped with yellow crime scene tape, crisscrossing the entrance and woven through the holes of the chain link. The intent was to keep out the curious and the wandering street ambassadors from once again using it as their personal encampment.

It looked break-in-able, except for the sizeable Sacramento PD padlock that secured the two sections of chain link.

"Shit," exclaimed Mallory. "I didn't even think we'd have trouble getting in." She went over and hefted the padlock. It was round and heavy and wasn't going to be convinced to open with any item she had.

She turned to Jake. "Sorry, dragged you down here for nothing. C'mon." She took the dog's leash and let him wander over to one of the cement benches that haphazardly lined the sidewalks. "Sorry, boy. Wild goose chase. Probably a dumb idea."

Jake dog appraised the bench and did his business.

In the daylight, the street was deserted, especially in the rain. The other storefronts in the block had been forsaken long ago and had their own makeshift barriers, most with spray-painted 'No Trespassing' warnings.

Jake studied the whole entrance. "Well, if there was ever a need for another entrance, now would be the time to know about it."

"Yeah. Sorry, let's go before we get soaked." Mallory started to lead the dog back to the car. "Jake. Coming?"

He was smiling. And holding a key. "I'm not a detective with Sacramento PD for nothing." He turned, inserted the key, jiggled it a bit and released the hasp. He slipped the lock in his coat and pulled the two sections of chain link aside.

Mallory and the dog joined him.

"New plywood and new nails," said Mallory, examining the wood.

"And shitty carpenters. Seems they missed with the nails on this side." He grasped the edge of the board. It pulled away from the rotten doorframe easily. The dog was the first one through. He sat waiting until both Mallory and Jake squeezed in.

The lobby was pretty much as they had last seen it, torn up couch, busted chairs, stained and lopsided coffee table. Some of the itinerant homeless residents had even tried their hand at redecorating, mostly, it seemed, with spray paint and urine.

The muted sound of rain outside and the malodorous air inside Acme Distributing exuded an atmosphere of hopelessness to the whole venture.

Jake, even though he knew better, tried the light switch anyway. It flopped uselessly.

Mallory clicked on both the flashlights she'd brought. Jake switched on a battery-powered lantern with industrial strength bulbs that lit the place with a nuclear glow. Their shadows were sharp against the warped paneled walls.

"May as well start here," said Jake. "Maybe there's some access to an adjacent business." He began exploring one side of the lobby, Mallory the other. They knocked along the wall, probing for openings, hollows, hidden hinges. The dog watched the tap, tap, tap for a minute then wandered off.

Jake yanked a ripped piece of paneling off the studs. Dust and a cache of dead spiders and their desiccated meals came with. Behind it was a brick wall. With the butt of his flashlight, he knocked against the bricks.

"Anything?" asked Mallory.

"I'm up against a brick wall. Literally."

"I have concrete block here."

Jake made a short foray into the projection room. Not surprisingly, it was as big as a closet and there wasn't room for any sort of egress.

"I don't know, maybe this is a buster," sighed Mallory, uncertainty about her 'feeling' beginning to build.

"Probably," agreed Jake. "Moving on then." Jake picked up the lantern and they made their way through the padded double doors into the screening room proper. Both stopped. The dark was tight against them and the lantern did little to help.

Both noticed it, but neither said anything about the smell. The leftovers of something gone very bad lingered and now suffused the walls, the carpet, the folding seats.

Jake dog held back and pressed against Jake's legs. He nudged him forward. "Let's go you hound. Nothing here now," said Jake with encouragement.

"You hope," answered Mallory.

"Hey, listen, I never asked you how you knew this whole place was here in the first place. One of your famous feelings?

"I was hungover. So, it was luck, a good memory, and a hot shower."

"I knew there was a secret to this business."

"No, look," continued Mallory. "I already told you this, but you were probably too busy mansplaining something to me to hear what I said."

Jake showed mock indignation. "I would never."

"Right." Mallory smiled. "Okay, remember, we had Peter Berlin's notes and locations which put him right about on the next block and I remembered that inventory I did of Marston's places. It just... fit."

"And you just up and drove here."

"Yeah, with a chauffeur. Isn't that how you'd up and do it?"

"And now here we are, like Nancy Drew and one of the Hardy Boys, as Carruthers would say, banging on walls looking for a secret passage."

Jake set the lantern down on an armrest of one of the back seats of the screening room. "Well, if it's here, if soothsayer Dimante is right, this is where it will be."

"I don't know. I'm not always right. I was wrong once last year."

Mallory raised her flashlights up to the ceiling and traced the whole perimeter. Acoustic tile that had once been white was now evenly cigarette stained to a warm, phlegmy brown. The whole ceiling appeared undisturbed. It was obvious no one had exited through the roof.

Jake crisscrossed the small room, going along one row then the next, back and forth until he arrived at the front where the rest of James Marston, Jr. had been found. The whole front row was still covered with fingerprint powder. Even so, both Mallory and Jake stopped to stare at the furrows in the carpet where Marston had probably struggled.

"Jake?"

"What?"

"Where's the dog?"

CHAPTER 36

"Here boy," called Jake. "Where are you?"

Nothing.

"Jake! Come here."

Both strained, listening for anything, but there was no Jake dog padding his way back to them. No barking. No whining.

Mallory and Jake exchanged glances.

"Did he go back to the lobby?" asked Jake.

Mallory shook her head. "I would've seen him. Besides, he would've come."

"You take that side," said Jake.

Mallory nodded as they both approached the white screen from different sides of the room.

She tried again. "Jake? Where are you?"

There was no response.

Both arrived at their respective edges of the screen at the same time. There was a small gap behind and they both slipped through.

The lantern lit up the area, so much that they could see a short passage extending away from the screen on either side.

Jake started down his side but didn't get far. Framed marquee movie posters, some five feet tall clogged the passage. Like a connoisseur trying to decide on which Andy Warhol print to purchase, Jake flipped through the whole pile. There was nothing but a solid sheetrock wall behind.

"Jake. He's here," yelled Mallory.

Jake pushed the whole collection back against the wall and made his way to the other side.

The dog, which had been lying on the floor, got up and began wagging as Jake got to them.

"He was just lying here. I think he may not be fully recovered," said Mallory as she stroked the dog's back.

Jake raised the lantern to get a better view of the small passage on this side of the screen. More movie posters were jammed into the space, but the area in front of an electrical panel was clear.

Jake looked at the dog, who was still wagging his tail. "You okay boy?" asked Jake.

The dog looked at Jake, then Mallory, then at the electrical panel. To Jake, it looked like the dog wanted to bark. Instead, the tail picked up speed.

The electrical box was a standard grey box. The master cutoff lever was on the side of the box. Jake opened the cover. It appeared to be a normal electrical circuit box. Two rows for circuit breakers, about twelve on each side, lined the box. None were labeled. The only writing was on the inside of the metal door.

Some joker had scrawled 'DANGER 50,000 OHMS' on the inside of the box's cover.

"Be careful," said Mallory after seeing the warning. "And what's an ohm?"

"It's a joke," said Jake, as he began to switch each of the breaker switches on and off. Just like the light switch in the lobby, they flopped uselessly, side to side.

"What did you expect?" asked Mallory. "Place has been abandoned for years."

"They're duds. These don't do anything. They don't control anything. They're useless." Jake closed the breaker box door, snapping it closed.

"Try the big handle," suggested Mallory.

"Mal, I'm trying to tell you, this is a dummy box. Or it was working at one time, but some idiot just mounted it up here as a prop. A joke." He pointed to the '50,000 Ohms' scribble.

"Fine. Can't hurt then. I'll do it."

She reached up and with both hands pulled down the big handle.

"I wasn't-" started Jake.

Jake dog barked as the paneled wall moved.

Mallory gripped the edge of the panel and pulled. The wall slid back easily revealing a dark, man-sized opening. "I guess I am right once and…"

"Quiet!" Jake hissed.

"What?"

At the same time, the dog moved past both of them and disappeared into the gloom.

"Jake!" Jake stepped in front of Mallory and called for his dog again. "Jake come back here you! Now!"

The only sound was the light clicking of dog claws moving away.

"Quick!" He held his hand out to Mallory. "Let me have a flashlight."

He switched off the lantern and aimed the flashlight beam into the darkness.

"Jake," he called again, but the darkness and the silence was the only despairing answer.

Jake unholstered his gun. "Stay behind me and keep your beam aimed down. And quiet."

"Jake, you know me. I'm always excited to follow you into the depths of the unknown danger if you answer one question."

"Make it quick."

"Do we need backup? You know, those highly skilled officers rigorously trained to deal with a possible shitstorm of life-threatening issues that might be down this passageway."

"What for? I'm working with deadeye Dimante. Your reputation is legend. I have no fear."

"Jake. C'mon."

Jake sighed. "Hey, I'm not even sure anyone's at the end of this. You weren't even sure this was here. This was your hunch, remember."

"Yeah, but if I'm right, whoever is down there chopped off people's heads. You remember that?" She pulled out her phone. "I'll call for backup."

"Okay. Compromise. I'll follow my intrepid dog. If I'm not back in a minute, or you hear a boatload of trouble then call. Look, if you call and a whole SWAT team arrives on Mallory Dimante's hunch and there is only an empty warehouse, you will have squandered all the good glow you garnered from not shooting Stan."

She hated when he was right. "One minute," was all she could muster.

Jake pulled on a set of gloves from his pocket and headed off into the darkness, the flashlight doing little to illuminate what hallway there was.

Mallory cradled her flashlight between her shoulder and her cheek as she stabbed the power button two or three times until the phone woke. Just in case.

"Shit! No bars. Figures." She debated going back to the lobby to get some coverage or follow Jake. She swished the phone in the air and checked again. Nothing. She may as well have been 100 feet underground.

She looked back toward the screening room and past that to the double doors that led to the lobby.

She checked her watch. It had been all of twenty seconds. She pulled on her own gloves.

"Forget this." And started down the passageway.

CHAPTER 37

It appeared the passage turned because Mallory could only see the distant glow from Jake's flashlight reflecting off a wall. He'd turned a corner and was well ahead.

She made her way along the wall. When her fingers brushed the side, she realized the wall was made of metal. Cold and almost rusty. It left a metallic juice trickling in the back of her throat.

She came to a turn in the passage. Suddenly it was all dark. No reflected glow. No flashlight at all.

"Jake!" hissed Mallory.

Again. "Jake!" louder this time.

"Quiet," came the answer from further down the passage.

Mallory continued blindly until she bumped into Jake's back. She could hear Jake dog's breathing as well. All three of them were crunched together before what she could now see was a door. Because she could see faint light leaking around the frame. A blue light.

"Stay… behind me," whispered Jake.

She couldn't see it, but she knew he had raised his Glock.

"Going in fast or slow?"

"Easy and slow," answered Jake. "Hold his leash." Jake handed the leash back to her. "Keep him tight with you."

Jake took a deep breath, reached out and tried pushing the door open. It wouldn't budge.

He peered close to the crack between the door and the jamb, where the latch would be. There was a lock. He couldn't tell what kind it was, whether he'd be able to jimmy it or not. Decided not.

"Screw it," he murmured.

He pivoted back to Mallory. "Forget slow and easy. It's fast and hard. Move back a ways."

"Shit. You going to shoot the lock?"

"Well, yeah, unless you can somehow wish it open."

"I'm moving." She pulled on the leash, guiding the dog back down the passage.

"Mallory, whoa. Kidding. I'm not shooting the lock off. Where did you learn that? Your film-noir cinema class at college? The sound in here would deafen us for a week and, besides, I'd probably miss anyway."

"So, what's the plan?"

Jake pulled out a small rolled-up leather pouch, the size of a few pencils, bound with a rubber band. "I told you before. A detective is always prepared. I'll pick the damn thing."

"This is your idea of fast and hard?"

"Probably just hard. I haven't done this in a while."

"We have all day."

Jake ignored her and began work on the lock. "When it goes, assuming it does, I go, you stay."

"Jake, we'll be right behind you."

"Not. Not until I know what's there." He paused. "How's that backup?"

Mallory shook her head even though he couldn't see it. "No go. No cell coverage. You think we should bail and wait?"

"Probably, but I don't hear a sound on the other side. Odds are no one is around if it's that quiet."

"Unless, of course," mused Mallory. "They know we're coming and are all waiting on the other side."

"Stop trying to cheer me up."

Mallory trained the flashlight on the lock for Jake while he fiddled with what looked like a few small odd-looking metal prongs. She could see Jake's hands contorting up and down and around and hear a few pissed-off sighs from Jake as he worked.

She held her breath, listening for the lock to give or for someone on the other side to begin blasting the shit out of the door. She tightened up on the leash, gripping it with both hands.

When it happened, it was softly satisfying, a yes-you-did-it click, like they'd hit some surreptitious jackpot. The door slowly swung open.

Both strained to hear anything else while searching what they could see. With Jake on his knees, Mallory had a better view.

The only light in the room came from the center of the room where a cadre of computer monitors glowed blue with a swirling screen saver. The familiar smell of an office wafted over her - plastic, idling computer warmth, abandoned coffee.

Jake rose up, gun ready. He swept the room from his position. When no one popped up returning fire, he relaxed.

Mallory joined him. The dog, ready to run and explore, was restrained by Jake who took the leash.

"Let's find some lights."

He used the flashlight to scan the wall until he found the switch. Turning it on, it lit up a room the size of a smallish office, with warm fluorescent lighting and two doors on the far wall. In the center of the room was a large L shaped table on the other side of the computer terminals. Moving around to see it better, they saw one arm of the L was occupied with what was, according to the label on the side, an automatic scanner. It was two feet high and as wide. Cables snaked out the back and led to the computers.

A feed tray, that looked as if it could hold hundreds of papers, yawned open. A collector basket was hooked on the other end. Both the tray and the basket were empty.

"I don't get this," said Mallory. "This has an academia feeling. Like some research facility office, or document archival place. I mean, why else have some oversize scanner?"

"It feels..." began Jake.

"Benign.," completed Mallory. "Yeah, I know. Like the only people who work here, have pimples, glasses, and bad breath."

With a sinking feeling, she thought that maybe the connecting passage, the locked door, all had nothing to do with Marston and the gruesome scene in the screening room. Maybe it was a bizarre coincidence that the two were connected in this old warehouse. It was possible no one had ever come from where she stood into the Marston screening room and slaughtered Marston and Peter Berlin.

If that was the case, they had just broken and entered the computer room of some run-of-the-mill document center.

"Jake. Maybe I was wrong. Maybe this is all innocent. Maybe we shouldn't be here…"

Mallory stopped when she saw Jake. He was standing in front of an open closet door. He was holding up a woman's black wig.

"Look familiar?" he asked.

Mallory moved closer. "Not my style." Still, it did look as if she'd seen it before, but she couldn't place where.

And that's when they heard a distant door slam.

CHAPTER 38

Both Jake and Mallory ducked down behind the line of computer terminals. Mallory pulled the dog close to her. He seemed to understand when Mallory made a 'shh' noise to him. The low growl segued to an urgent whimpering whine. The tug on the leash was insistent.

Jake left them and crabbed to the other side of the room where he had a clearer view of both doors on the far wall.

Mallory couldn't see either door from where she and Jake dog were. She could only listen as whoever it was was busy with what sounded like boxes they were sliding along the passageway and coming toward them.

Mallory heard no conversation, so she believed it was probably a single employee coming to work, pushing or shoving more permission forms down the hallway. Not looking forward to a day full of computer drudgery.

This was going to be an extremely embarrassing moment, Mallory was sure. She tried to rehearse a plausible excuse for what would be an undoubtedly scare-the-ever-loving-shit moment out of some computer nerd.

'Oh, great', she thought. She looked across to Jake who had trained his gun on the general area of the two doors.

"Jake!" she hissed. "Don't shoot! It's a mistake."

Jake didn't turn.

"Jake!"

When he gave her a quick glance, she signaled for him to lower his weapon.

What? he mimed, shrugging his shoulders.

When she used both hands to motion down, the leash slipped out of her hands.

Mallory tried to grab for it. Missed.

The dog took off for the left of the two doors, his uncut nails clicking on the linoleum floor. He stopped in front of the door and cocked his head.

The sliding box stopped in the hallway.

Jake and Mallory remained motionless, not breathing.

There was no sound from the hallway.

The dog stood silently, readying himself for who was behind the door.

Jake raised up soundlessly and step by step made his way to one side of the door frame.

The dog gave him a quick acknowledgment, then went back to silent sentry duty.

It took Jake a moment to realize why the person in the hallway had stopped. It wasn't because they might've heard the dog, it was because the lights were on. Whoever was in the hallway stopped because they were sure that when they had left, the lights had been off.

Jake looked up at the glaring rows of fluorescents. Now, they were most definitely on.

He could almost sense what the person was thinking. 'Did I leave the lights on? Am I going nuts? I always shut off the lights. Is somebody in there? Did I hear some scratching?'

That was when he heard the subtle but unmistakable double click of a weapon being readied.

Jake lowered himself down until he could reach the leash. His fingers wound around the leather. He stood and, with a gesture to the dog, beckoned him away from the door.

After making sure that was what he supposed to do, Jake dog reluctantly moved to Jake's side, his attention still riveted on the door.

Jake flattened himself against the other door. Whatever was coming through the door was going to be ready for a confrontation or major embarrassment if they found no one was there. Jake was ready to take advantage of the small window of uncertainty.

Slow or fast he wondered. Slow or fast.

It was fast.

The door slammed open, arms and gun were first through. Jake brought his own weapon down like a sledgehammer. It smashed the gun down. It exploded, just missing the dog and burying in the linoleum floor.

Mallory, like a sprinter released by the starter's gun, launched herself from behind the humming bank of computers, only to find Jake in an awkward tangle, atop of someone she couldn't see, surrounded by hundreds of files and their contents from a split open box.

On the floor at her feet was a .38. Mallory kicked it behind her and lunged, grabbing the legs underneath Jake. Once grabbed, they struck out, hitting her twice in her jaw. Mallory tightened her grip and twisted, rolling herself to the side for more leverage.

The cry of pain echoed the popping Mallory heard from joint, knee or ankle, she wasn't sure which and didn't much care.

Jake rolled off and Mallory found herself staring at a seething Samantha Barnes.

"Hold her," Jake shouted. He took off down the hallway.

"Hold her?"

With her one good leg, Samantha kicked up and out as she attempted to pull out and away from Mallory's grasp.

"You are not going anywhere." Mallory doubled her fist and smashed it into the gut of Samantha Barnes twice. Samantha curled up, doubling in half, wheezing like an aged asthmatic, unable to even begin to draw a breath.

Mallory raised her fist again and planned to smash it into Samantha's nose, just for old times' sake, then thought better of it.

Jake returned almost immediately. "No one else here."

"Where did she come from?" asked Mallory.

"Street entrance, other side of the building. Street's clear."

"For now."

Jake nodded. "Time for that backup you've always wanted."

Mallory pulled out her phone. There was a signal. Before she called, she looked down at a recovering Samantha Barnes. She didn't look quite as good as she had when she was at the hospital pretending to identify Ilsa Pokovich. And she definitely didn't resemble the bitch that had her ass pressed up against the glass office wall, doing Jake.

She resembled a sodden rag. Hair stringy and askew, saliva dripping from her nose and mouth, blouse ripped and what makeup she'd applied this morning was now coursing in several tributaries down her face.

"Comfortable?"

A weak 'Fuck you' was all Samantha Barnes could manage.

CHAPTER 39

Jake stood over Samantha Barnes and for a moment it looked to Mallory as if Jake was going to deliver a few well-placed kicks to the ribs of Miss Barnes. Instead, he reached down and grabbed both of her wrists and secured them with handcuffs.

"Backup?" he managed to ask.

"On their way," said Mallory.

"Fine," nodded Jake. "Let's go exploring." He pulled Samantha up to her feet, then pushed her ahead of him through the other door that didn't lead to the street.

"Jake, wait. Wait for backup."

"She would've called out, alerted someone, even if the gun hadn't already done that. I'm betting there's no one else here."

"Jake, she shot her weapon."

"Yeah," he said, as he gave Samantha another shove. "That was no warning shot though, she was aiming at me."

The hallway to the left was a low-ceilinged affair with strange looking walls.

"It's metal," exclaimed Mallory. "Jake, this is another metal wall." She went to the other side of the narrow passage. Same cold aluminum or tin or steel. She couldn't tell. She sniffed close to it. The odor stuck in the back of her throat and made her salivate. Like biting on aluminum foil, with a bouquet of rust.

As they made their way down the constricted passageway, she flashed back on one of her psychology classes where the rats were trained to follow a twisting pathway in a complicated maze. Part of the experiment allowed the students to change the course by flipping the dividers to an alternate configuration. The rats would be confused. At first. But within minutes they adapted and raced through.

All the students made the appropriate notes in their notebook.

Mallory now scanned the low-slung ceiling and wondered if they were being watched, just like she and her fellow classmates had watched and cheered as the rats discovered the correct path. In the gloom, she reached up to what she imagined was a small security camera but when her fingers touched it, she realized it was a sprinkler head for a fire suppression system.

The hallway turned left, then back again right.

Jake stopped. "You go ahead," he said to Mallory. "Let me know where this ends up."

"Yeah, she's expendable, Jake honey," murmured a revived Samantha.

Mallory stared at Jake who, as far as she could tell in the dimness, kept a neutral expression.

Jake raised his flashlight. Ahead in the dimness was a door. A metal door.

"Change places," said Jake as he pushed Samantha Barnes past Mallory, right up to the door.

"Want me to go first, sweetheart?" cooed Samantha.

Jake didn't answer. Instead, he pushed against the door. When it didn't give, he searched for a handle or knob, anything to open it.

There was none. But there was a keypad.

Samantha leaned back into Jake. "Uh oh. Looks like we can't get in, Jake honey. Maybe if you knock a bit, my friends inside will let you in." Jake pushed her back against the wall.

Mallory moved past them and put her ear to the door.

"Course," continued Samantha. "They may shoot you and your slut. Never know. But I'll try to put in a good word."

Jake turned her around so they were facing each other.

"Combination." His voice was steel.

Samantha smiled. "Or what? You'll shoot me? Torture me? Stick your dick in me again?"

Mallory straightened up. "There's no one in there," she declared. "I'm sure."

Samantha raised her chin toward the door and keypad and addressed Jake. "You figure it out, big boy. It shouldn't take you too long."

To Mallory, there was something in Samantha Barnes' voice that was more than a flip comment. It was a mocking challenge.

Mallory closed her eyes as she felt that peculiar knowing flood through her. "Oh, shit," she whispered. She reached past Samantha and with dread and with a hope she was wrong, she entered the code.

6969.

The lock clicked, and the metal door opened six inches.

"Wow, honey. The slut got it. What do you think about that?"

Mallory didn't want to, but she stared right at Jake. He met her gaze but the look on his face made Mallory melt for him. For now, they both had confirmation of how Isla Pokovich had been able to get through the OID security door and shoot Stan. She was given the code by Samantha Barnes. From the night Jake had taken Samantha to the office. He'd never revealed the code, but he hadn't needed to, she'd been hanging all over him when he opened the security door.

"Jake?"

Jake looked away. "Let's go." He gripped Samantha's arms and shoved her through the door. She didn't resist. In fact, she jumped forward and pulled Jake with her.

At the same time, she screamed, "Now! Shoot!" She tried to drop to the floor, but Jake held her up as a shield, it appeared to Mallory.

Mallory grabbed the leash and flattened herself against the metal wall.

Then there was nothing but Samantha Barnes laughing. "I guess," she said. "I guess they're hiding."

Mallory stepped further into the room. Jake joined her. Neither were prepared for what was there, or the room itself. What wasn't there, were other people.

Except for the bladed ceiling fan creating a whooshing gentle breeze, it was dead quiet.

Mallory looked up. The room was expansive. Twenty, thirty feet high, and easily twice as long. It reminded her of an old classic library with a center atrium and wooden baluster railings holding in the second and third floors. Shelves lined the walls, filled with... not books, but what seemed to be file cabinet drawers. Built-in file cabinets were stacked eight high. A rolling ladder stood in the corner. Each drawer was labeled but Mallory couldn't make them out.

"It's like a-"

"Library," said Jake, finishing Mallory's thought.

"Library, I know, right," agreed Mallory. "Reminds me of where we used to study in college, back in the stacks. All that."

"Except, it doesn't seem there are any books," answered Jake. He turned to Samantha Barnes who had managed to find a chair and was perched on the edge. "What is this place?" he asked, his voice betraying frustration.

He leaned in. "Just what the hell do you do here?"

Samantha Barnes looked mystified. "Don't know Jake honey. I have no idea why you brought me here. Why I've never been here in my life." She brightened. "I know, let's just go back to your place and let me do to you what I do best."

Jake grabbed Samantha's arm and pulled her to her feet. He pulled her backward over to the lowest bank of file cabinets.

"Jake!" shouted Mallory. "Jake!"

He pushed Samantha's face into the front of the file cabinet. She didn't make a sound when her forehead contacted the file cabinet.

"Jake!"

Jake froze but didn't turn. "What?"

Mallory moved to his side.

"What is it?" he pressed.
"Backup's here."

CHAPTER 40

It was just after noon when the moving stabs of powerful flashlights cautiously approached down the narrow hallway. They came in full body armor, helmets and face shields, firearms aimed at the floor.

They were prepared for whatever crazy shit the OID crew had mired themselves in. That, and then having to snake down a narrow hallway, single file, it was a surprise when they emerged into the 'library', as Mallory was now calling it, and to see nothing strange going on. No imminent terrorist threats. No hostages. No precarious situation. Just Jake standing over a disheveled, though still stunning, handcuffed Samantha Barnes. And Mallory, with Jake dog at her feet, sorting through a file cabinet.

Jake held up his identification. Mallory, since she was not supposed to be on any sort of departmental activity, didn't turn around, but continued clawing her way through file after file.

The backup team had swept past Mallory and approached Jake.

"You good?" the team leader asked as he swept the room - Mallory's back, the dog and finally a now whimpering Samantha Barnes.

"Sergeant Richard Stat," he said to Jake.

Jake nodded.

Samantha, who tried to get up off the chair but was jerked back by the handcuffs connecting her right arm to the wooden desk chair, began plaintively whimpering, all the while maintaining eye contact with the lead of the backup group.

"So, who's this?" Stat asked, noticing more than just the handcuffs on Samantha.

"Not sure," replied Jake. "Calls herself Samantha Barnes."

"Aww honey," purred Samantha. "You know everything there is to know about me, Jake baby. As many nights as we've spent together. C'mon." She tilted her head, so she was coyly fixing Officer Stat with her best suggestive gaze.

She turned to Jake and shook her head. "Officer, I have to confess."

"Confess?" asked the Sergeant.

"Yes, I confess he's shit in bed," she said with some remorse. "Had to fake the miserable experience, if you know what I mean." She inclined her head toward Mallory. "And don't take my word for it. Just ask her."

Officer Stat's gaze went from Samantha to Mallory then back to Jake who held up his hands in the universal sign men share, meaning 'I don't know what the bitch is going on about'.

It was answered with an understanding, albeit long-suffering, acknowledging nod.

"Listen, Sergeant, before you sweep the entire place, have one of your guys go out and disconnect, unplug, destroy, I don't care, those two security cameras. One's over the entry. The other over the loading dock."

"Destroy?"

"We don't know where the feed ends up and I would prefer if our presence is not known, if possible."

"Copy."

Officer Stat signaled two of his men, who had also heard the instructions and he began to follow them out while giving the rest of the team instructions to sweep the rest of the rabbit warren.

Before he left the room, he turned back.

"So, what kind of perverted place is this?"

The dog stirred as Mallory had stood. In her hand was an open file folder. Neither Jake nor Stat could see the contents.

"Well?"

Mallory smiled and with both hands had indicated the mountain of file cabinets all around them.

"Working on it."

Mallory was able to tune out the bedlam all around her and concentrate on deciphering what they'd stumbled into. Her stomach was growling from lack of input and that was when she realized she'd been at it for over three hours.

With the help of a bag of chocolate candies she found in the fridge in what passed for a break room, and with the assistance of Sharon Ollestad, her old boss in the IT division, and her new IT flunky, red-headed Jeffrey, she'd figured out what they were surrounded by.

It was so archaically amazing she doubted she could explain to those who were demanding to know.

It had taken analyzing the contents of that first file cabinet for her to figure it out, as she confirmed it all with Sharon and Jeffrey.

"Okay, so first I just attacked the closest file cabinet I came to. Before I slid it open, I tried to decipher the meaning of the label on the outside of the drawer. All the drawers are labeled."

She set the peeled off label down in front of her.

"Okay, I understand what 'Cleveland' means but I didn't get 'LMC98'. In the top drawer were exactly twenty file folders, each jammed with individual papers. Most of the folders had different color sticky notes flagging them."

She set one of the folders down next to the label.

"All have yellow, blue and green, some are tagged with red notes. On the red ones, you can see the word 'Done' is written in neat handwriting, along with a date. Surprisingly, the date for this Cleveland file was only a week ago."

Mallory took a breath. "I pulled out the front folder and opened it and rifled through the bundle of papers inside, hoping something would fall out and reveal itself to me. "

Sharon picked up the folder and spread out contents.

"They are forms. All have the same heading, 'Little Miss Cleveland Auditions – 1998'."

"The hell is this?" Jeffrey muttered to himself. He picked it up. Then picked up another. And another.

The top form was a model release for the Little Miss Cleveland Talent Search. According to the verbiage at the top, the top three little girls would 'win' a chance to be in a secret Hollywood production. The rest was standard boilerplate crap about permission to use the likeness and advertising and other legalese. At the bottom was the participant's name, Jenny Krieger. Her birthday followed April 19, 1991. In parentheses was a warning in italics – ('Only participants born before January 1, 1992, are eligible.)

There were lines for parent's names, address and parent's signature, allowing seven-year-old Jenny to prance around on a stage in a little frilly frock, Mallory guessed, maybe even try and perform some unkempt kind of talent, to win a chance to audition for some unnamed television production it seemed.

And, just for participating, each contestant was evidently paid a small sum.

"So, they paid these kids to just tryout?" asked Sharon.

"Appears so."

Sharon looked around. Scores of file cabinets. Must be thousands of similar model releases. She glanced back at the door through which they'd busted through.

"This whole thing doesn't make any sense. Have you found any evidence that they're connected with any kind of Hollywood production company? Anything like that?"

"Nada. And there's still the issue of the computers, which we haven't been able to crack into yet and the scanner."

Mallory replaced Jenny Krieger's permission form, closed the folder and shoved it back into place.

Mallory would later grudgingly give Jeffrey credit for figuring out the scam. At least he was the one who hacked his way into the computer.

After that, the whole thing made beautiful, crooked sense.

CHAPTER 41

Gathered around the L shaped table in the computer room were Stan, Jake, and Rodriguez from Robbery-Homicide. Pacing behind them was Samuels, the chief undertoad for Captain Carruthers. Opposite were Mallory, Sharon Ollestad, and Jeffrey. Absent was Carruthers.

"Where is the old boy?" asked Stan.

"Don't know," answered Samuels. "Let's get on with this, okay? And what is she doing here, for chrissakes?"

Mallory had, for a moment, tried to stay invisible, but finally just said, "Do not push it. This is all because of me. I don't care what kind of administrative leave I'm on, I found this." She sat up a bit taller.

"She found this," Stan said, seconding Mallory. Turning to Sharon, "Let's get started. What is this place."

Sharon smiled. "Pure and simple. It is a nursery."

It was the last thing the men expected to hear.

"I thought this was a scam?" growled Samuels. "What do you mean, a nursery?"

Sharon took off her glasses and slowly stood. "The files you saw in the other room were all permission forms like the one here."

Mallory passed the form to Stan who read it over then handed it on to Jake.

"Thousands of them," continued Sharon. "Maybe hundreds of thousands, we haven't counted. They're all the same format and all contain the same information. Some go back twenty years."

"Kids, babies, right?" asked Samuels, struggling to follow the train. "So that's where the nursery is?"

Sharon shook her head. "Nope. No babies, at least we haven't found any. These are all kids, maybe five to ten years old. And they all signed up for something similar; either a mini beauty pageant or mostly, the chance to star in some Hollywood production or TV commercial. But there is no production company and there is no production. The scam stops here."

"I'm not seeing the scam," said Stan. "All I see is a kiddie talent agency. And if they're paying these kids to audition for a non-existent TV thing, then they're headed for the poorhouse. That's no way to run a business."

"Correct," agreed Sharon. "But that isn't their business. Their business is identity theft."

"How?" challenged Samuels.

Jeffrey couldn't contain himself any longer. Tired of the older generation slogging themselves through this beautiful scheme.

"Take a look at the form in front of you," said Jeffrey. He stabbed with his nail-chewed finger. "There. At the bottom. See it? Right… there."

They saw it. The child's social security number. And the small type below it that said it was required 'for tax purposes' that the child be paid, and it be reflected with the child's own social security number.

Samuels flicked the form back onto the table. "So what? These are kids. And all this is just on paper. If this whole thing were on computer, some big database and they were doing something like that, well... that would be something."

Stan jumped in. "So, they were paying to get the child's information, I get that. But, can't you get that information on the internet now?"

Jeffrey burst forth. "No! Not until just recently when young kids started to really begin to buy shit online. Then they were exposed. Parents just recently started to sign their kids up to have their identifications protected. But that just started. This... these papers, these forms go back years. Way before anybody thought to protect their kids from getting their personal, most personal information stolen out from under them.

Jeffrey was breathing hard, excited. "Okay, let me make it simple. We have all these ways to send messages, and search engines that generate a lot of data. A lot of useless information too. And as has been proven, it's all hackable, right?"

He looked around the table for agreement. Seeing blank faces, he moved on.

"You can buy adults' personal information in thirty seconds on the dark web because someone stole it. Hell, they can find out who you talked to, read your texts, know that you're headed to the store for broccoli for shit's sake. Nothing is sacred, which is why when the thieves go to sell your and my personal information because we're adults, it goes for pennies because it is so easy to get. It is so hackable."

He stood up and picked up the permission form and held it up high above his head.

"Try hacking this."

Jeffrey was out of wind, but he had one more point to make.

"You know what the safest form of communication is these days? The US Mail. Paper."

He sat down, flushed.

Mallory stepped in. "These people have been nurturing this information, that no one else had, for years. They had a traveling scam it seems. A family business. They sucker women and little girls and boys who want to be famous, want to be on TV. They hold auditions way away from the West Coast. A golden opportunity for a parent in Altoona, Pennsylvania or Burlington, Vermont to make some dough off their kids. They paid them a pittance and in exchange have access to information that will generate thousands over time, with fraudulent purchases, credit card accounts that go bust.

"And the best part to show they were legitimate they actually paid these kids, so no one suspected a scam. And the better part was, they waited. Years. Let the trail go cold. Then one day they blew a hole in the credit life of some kid. Brilliant."

Jeffrey strained to explain, "And this shit is worth a fortune because no one else has it. This is virgin stuff."

Jake flashed on Anna Chase and her stage mother. It fit. They gave up their information in a heartbeat for the chance at piles of dough when little Anna was discovered as the next child star.

"Why the scanner and all the computers then?" questioned Samuels.

"Time was running out," said Sharon. "They're pulling up stakes as it were. As Jeffrey said, times are changing. Parents are wising up. So, evidently, they have been digitizing the information so they could wholesale it online. Batch copying all their paper and selling the information as fast as they can, after they make purchases with it. At least according to the transactions, we found on their accounting system."

"How much of a fortune?" asked Rodriguez, his face set. "Robbery wants to know."

"Upwards of 60 million," chimed Jeffrey without missing a beat.

Rodriguez whistled. He looked at Jake and Stan. "Who are these people?"

Before Stan could muster an answer, his phone vibrated.

CHAPTER 42

The old shit piece of transportation provided to the OID was a Dodge of suspicious lineage. Stan believed the department had acquired it at an auction of seized drug runner vehicles. Or, possibly, judging by the faint fishy odor that washed up from the air vents on these baking Sacramento afternoons, it could very possibly be a victim of a Louisiana flood.

The seats had seen way too many doughnut-fueled asses and had long ago lost the will to live.

Stan always rode with the windows down and fan on full no matter the weather. Tonight was no exception. He'd rather freeze or roast than inhale.

With the wind whipping into the cab, Stan wondered did they really have a stuffed bear that held a secret to this entire mess? He could feel the anticipation. He'd been around too long, was too jaded to believe in things neatly falling into place. Still, he shifted in his seat and started banging on the steering wheel like a rookie speeding to his first homicide.

He hadn't taken the call the first time. But, the second call, from the same number, meant it was business.

And it was. Officer Spinnetti from the Davis PD had in protective custody, two children. And they had his business card. Stan hadn't even remembered giving his card to the Cooper boy.

He immediately felt sorry for the Davis Police Department when he entered the building. It looked like they'd strung two or three Dairy Queens together. Gaudy, misshapen, and smelling of neglect with a hint of departmental ennui.

The smell was the same as the atmosphere. As soon as someone from outside their Police Department or any Police Department entered the building a disturbance in the force rippled through the reception area.

After traversing double doors and a metal detector that seemed only for show as it didn't register anything that Stan was carrying, Stan approached what looked like a watch commander's desk.

"Officer Spinnetti, please. Detective Wyld from Sacramento. I'm expected."

Stan handed the officer his card and flipped open his wallet to show his I.D.

It was examined and passed with a nod.

Stan couldn't sit still and ended up at the memorial board of fallen officers, pictures, and bios. He noted that one of them was a Spinnetti, either father or older brother. Probably, if he looked further, he'd find more of the same family.

Spinnetti, when he appeared didn't seem to resemble either of the pictures on the wall. He was tall with thinning dark hair plastered down with a disheveled comb-over and a tired look on his face. In his hand, he held the arrest papers of Michael and Jessie Cooper.

After greeting each other, Spinnetti started in on the litany of charges. Horse theft, resisting arrest, stealing from the hotel, attacking an officer, making false statements. It was all very interesting, but Stan didn't give a shit about what they were jailed for. All he wanted to know was whether they were all right and what possessions Michael and Jessie had.

Still, when he thought about it, Stan had to give them credit for using a bunch of horses to affect their escape.

As if Spinnetti didn't care or didn't listen. He rambled on. "We got them in the hospital. Kid was kind of beat up after resisting arrest. My partner got him good and shackled though. What a fighter." He didn't say it with any kind of admiration.

"But the kids are okay?" asked Stan.

"What?" asked Spinnetti, probably not believing anyone would care about two little runaways.

"Huh? Oh, yeah. Boy's okay," answered Spinnetti.

"And his sister?"

"Yeah, yeah the little girl too. She's fine. She's with him."

"Great," said Stan, relieved. "Now what about their possessions? What about the backpack?"

"Backpack?"

"Yeah."

Spinnetti turned to the officer at the desk. "See if you can find what stuff the kid came in with. A backpack or something else, or knapsack or I don't know."

Stan watched the desk officer get up and disappear into a back room. He was aware that Spinnetti was jabbering, probably rehashing all the charges against Michael Cooper and Jessie. But frankly, he didn't care. Now that he knew the kids were okay, all he wanted to see was the backpack. To see what it contained. To see if they were really chasing some goddamn stuffed bear.

Spinnetti pushed a piece of paper in front of Stan. "Well, if you're taking the kid and his sister, then here's your assumption of liability form."

He proffered a pen. Stan, without even looking at the paper, scrawled his name.

Spinnetti took the paper back, looked at Stan's scrawled signature, then looked up at Stan. "So, this kid is special right? He must be if you dragged your ass all the way from Sacramento just to pick up some runaway kid and his sister. He must be something special."

Stan regarded Spinnetti. There was no way he was going to go through the whole story of Michael Cooper and what he's been through. Instead, he said, "Yeah, the kid has been through a lot. And he's important to a case."

Spinnetti accepted the vagueness, though he still pushed. "You know," he said. "This is a criminal investigation. The guy who owned the horses is really upset. Pressing charges."

"He got the horses back didn't he?" asked Stan, trying to rustle up some modicum of sympathy for the Davis cop. "I'm sorry they gave you guys a hard time. Unfortunately, the investigation that these kids are involved in is going to be way more important than stealing a couple of horses that have since been returned. Look, I'll be responsible. If they really need to come back and be rearrested or testify or do anything, I'll get them here."

"Okay partner," said Spinnetti. "It's all on you."

The desk sergeant returned, unfortunately empty-handed. He rubbed his chin as he stared at the booking papers. "Well," he said. "Seems there was a backpack or something when the kid was brought in. Or, maybe when the kid was arrested. Don't know. Anyway, we ain't got it."

Stan rolled his eyes. "It's evidence. What does your trail of custody say?"

The desk sergeant took the paper turned it over, scanned the back where there was nothing written then turned it back to the front and shrugged. "Don't know. Your guess is as good as mine. Since the kid's in the hospital, most likely whatever he had with them is still there in the hospital."

Stan forced himself to stay calm. He even managed a smile.

"And which hospital would that be?"

CHAPTER 43

When they entered 15th Street HQ, and after were whisked through security, showed their I.D.s, had Jake's firearm secured in a little wire cage drawer behind a bigger wire cage, and after they had arrived at the lower level row of interview rooms, Mallory noticed that not only Rodriguez but also two of his assistants were lined up with their asses resting on desks outside the interview rooms.

They did not look happy.

Evidently, their lack of success prying anything useful out of Samantha Barnes was affecting their moods, made sourer by having to call Jake as a last resort.

Mallory wasn't sure why she had agreed to come with Jake to the HQ holding area anyway. It wasn't as if Jake could kill Samantha Barnes, though truthfully, she wasn't going to hold him back if that was where he was headed. Anyway, they'd had to check all firearms at security.

She supposed he could jump her and strangle her, but it somehow didn't seem Jake's style.

No, she wasn't sure why she had agreed. Maybe it had something to do with trampling the shit all over your former supposed competition. In a passive, look-who's-behind-bars-and-I'm-not, kind of way.

Maybe it was curiosity. Maybe she wanted to see Samantha Barnes with the perkiness beaten out of her. Drained of all that was so endearing to so many. Maybe it was something like that. Not really female vindictiveness. Just justice.

Yeah. Right.

She was waiting for them in the newly remodeled attorney-client conference room. It had been remodeled in the last few months. When they walked in, Mallory got a good whiff of the new smell of the floor tile and the paint on the walls.

It was a decent sized room with a large one-way mirror at one end, another identical double locked door with a small window opposite the one they had come through. The whole room was painted light green. They used to paint them pink back when they believed that it calmed people down, when all it really did was make them think of barfing up Pepto Bismol.

The steel table, the only item left from before the remodel, was in the middle of the room, anchored to the floor with large bolts through the legs. Its top was dulled with the uncertain sweat of years of felons who had slogged through the room. Two metal rectangular loops protruded up through the center of the table.

The chain was bright brassy metal and it snaked from the metal loop on the table to the cuffs that held the hands of Samantha Barnes. Soft hands, Mallory saw. Nails had been stripped of their polish and trimmed. Standard practice when you're being held for a charge where you're in a shitload of trouble. Where the fear was that you could try and scratch your way through the mesh snake wire that covered your cell's one window. Course that meant you'd have to go through three panes of tempered glass. About the same thickness glass as on the submersible subs exploring the Titanic.

Of course, it could also be so when a catfight erupted from a spurned advance deep in the recesses of the cellblock, the fighting inmates couldn't really harm each other without sharpened nails.

Either way, guess they were taking no chances.

She wore an orange jumpsuit with the redundant word 'Prisoner' stenciled across the front. It was too big for her and

Mallory saw she had pulled down the center of it to give as much a suggestion of cleavage as she could.

Mallory watched Jake. Watched his jaw muscles work. And she realized something. She realized why he had come. And it wasn't just because he'd received Rodriguez's request. She didn't understand all the intricacies of men, but her heart ached for him. Because, in Jake's expression, she saw the juvenile face of one of her own high school classmates, Ronny Miller, so long ago. A nice nerd who had asked Mallory to the prom her junior year. She'd turned him down with a laugh. Derision that said what gave you the idea that I liked you. What gave you the idea that I would go to a dance with you.

And she'd said exactly that to him. Said it off-handedly. Tossed it off. Thought nothing of it until she saw Ronny Miller's face, which registered as much of a shock as if she'd slapped him.

Ronny Miller had turned away, taken a few steps, then turned back to her.

"But, but..." he'd stammered.

"What?" she'd asked him. "What?"

But his face crumpled, and his mouth became a tight line and it was only then that she understood how much hurt she had inflicted.

She understood something else. Ronny Miller wasn't mad at her. In fact, in his own way, he maybe thought he was in love. No, he was mad at himself for being wrong. He was mad at being fooled. Being a fool in his own eyes. He had made the same mistaken assumption men make when searching for a relationship. They erroneously believed that all women were as kind, as self-seeking as they were.

The anger in Jake Steiner's face now was of a little boy being put through the shitter of another of life's lessons. Even with all his female experience, she was surprised at his naivete.

And she could have told him that. She could have told him the Jake – Samantha relationship was always headed down the wrong street that only had a big dumpster for his heart at the end of it. Then again, maybe she was making more out of the whole thing. Maybe he came to view Samantha Barnes the same way one comes to see one's prey finally caged.

Relationships only exist aboard the fragile boat of trust in a beguiling sea of temptation. When one trusts, really trusts, the little boat sails on. When trust isn't there, falls apart, leaves, then someone has, with uncaring treachery, taken a hatchet to the bottom of the boat and scuttled everything.

She was imagining Jake had come to try and figure out how badly he had been fooled. On the other hand, that was probably thinking as she would. Really, she hoped he came to kick emotional sand in Samantha Barnes' face.

"Well, well," sniffed Samantha. "I see you brought the slut with you." She turned her face into a full pout. "Jake, honey. I thought we were going to be alone."

Jake started speaking as if he was totally bored. His eyes never left Samantha Barnes.

"Your mother was Ilsa Pokovich. Your family has run a scam involving the theft of over twenty thousand identities. One of your uncles who went by the name of Ruby Everheart is dead. That leaves one member of your family, Nikolai Pokovich."

Samantha tried not to show she was surprised at the mention of Uncle Nikko's name, but a flutter of eyelids, even with a quick recovery, gave her away.

"Where is he?" finished Jake. "Tell us. And… we're done."

Samantha answered by taking her index finger and sticking it in her mouth then with obvious masturbatory intentions, began to run it over the front of her tunic.

It was mesmerizing watching Samantha's nipples harden.

Jake got up and without a glance backward pulled open the door and left. The door closed with a tiny rush of air.

Mallory was left alone with Samantha.

The two women stared at each. Finally, a small smile crept onto Samantha's face.

"I'm not who you think. This is a case of mistaken identity. Mistaken."

"Identity," Mallory finished for her. "You mean stolen identity, don't you?"

Samantha looked at her questioning. "Who are you?"

"What?"

"I asked, do you know who you are?"

Mallory said nothing.

"Well, I do," whispered Samantha Barnes as she leaned toward Mallory. "I know exactly who you are."

She settled back in her chair, as much as the chain to her wrists would allow.

"You think you're a cop. You think you are what you do. Most people do. They define themselves by their work, their job. Oh, I'm a janitor, or a truck driver or a mail carrier. Crap like that. But you don't understand who you are."

She leaned forward again and in the lowest whisper, so low Mallory found herself involuntarily leaning toward her, said, "I saw you."

"What?" Mallory jerked her head back so she could focus on the woman's eyes.

"Yeah, I saw you in the shadows. I knew you were there. Jake had forgotten all about you. But I knew. I knew you were watching. Watching him use his hands, his tongue. Watching him go down. Watching him shove himself in me. Watching him do to me what you wanted done to you. I came twice just because I knew you were seeing what I was getting and you couldn't have."

She settled back again with a smirk.

"Mistaken identity. You were mistaken. You thought you could be me. Have what I have. Do what I do. You can't. You never could. I know what you are and what you'll always be. You're scarred trash."

The smirk stayed.

Mallory resisted the urge to touch her scar; to run her fingers down it and feel it like the ugly appendage she always thought it was.

She stood instead.

Yeah, she was scarred, so what. It only mattered when you let it matter.

At last, she smiled at Samantha Barnes, who when she saw the confidence of Mallory's smile, lost hers.

"I wouldn't plan on ever getting out," Mallory said it simply and plainly. "I wouldn't plan on anything resembling a normal life. Ever. Because you now have a new identity. One whose name in any language is 'fucked'. You see, they found evidence, fingerprints I believe, on the inside of the car. And the house."

Samantha breathlessly blurted, "I used…"

"Gloves? Were you going to say you used gloves? Were you going to say that you used gloves and there could be no fingerprints?"

Samantha licked her lips, glanced sideways at the one-way mirror.

Mallory clicked her tongue. "I guess they weren't very good gloves. I guess that leaving fingerprints all over the place wasn't part of your 'plan', was it?"

She turned and grabbed the door handle and opened it but before she went through she turned back to Samantha.

"On the positive side, it looks like you'll be able to enjoy a full lifetime of female companionship back in the women's wing, I hear.

Samantha Barnes hadn't moved.

"Oh, and every day, when you're down on your knees worshiping at the hairy crotch of someone whose name is very likely Big Bertha Smiley, tell her I said 'Thanks.'"

The color drained from Samantha Barnes face.

Women, too, sometimes forget that not every other woman plays by the same rules.

Mallory found him standing outside on the steps to the jail. His face was turned to the sun and his eyes closed.

Mallory watched him. He was smiling. That was something else about men. They recovered a lot faster than women when tossed into life's shitpile.

Mallory went to his side and grabbed his arm.

"Okay?"

He looked down at her and smiled. Smiled at her, this time. "Sure. Why not?"

Mallory put a serious look on her face, "You can lean on me Jake, you know."

Jake continued to stare at her, then said, "Do you always have to end a sentence with 'you know'?"

"Often." Mallory smiled, relieved.

"Besides, do I look wounded or look like I may fall over?

Before she could answer, his phone went, breaking what mood there was.

He checked the number. It was a familiar number, but it didn't come up as someone he knew. And even better, it definitely wasn't a reporter's number. But because he wasn't going anywhere, including to bed or heading off to his local establishment for a drink, he answered it.

"Yo."

"Um. Is this Detective Steiner?"

"If it sounds like me, it is."

"I just thought I'd get a message machine. Sorry to call but I just wanted to call and thank you. Thank you so, so much."

"Who is this?"

"Oh. Yes, this is Katherine Chase."

Pause, waiting for recognition.

"You were just at our house."

Jake got it. "Anna. Anna Chase. Yes. Of course. Your daughter. What do you need Mrs. Chase? Why are you calling?"

"To thank you!"

"Thank me, why?"

"Well, we're here, and it's all thanks to you."

Jake looked at Mallory who had a quizzical look.

"You're where?"

"Here. In California. And thanks to you."

"You're in California? Why?"

"Because you made it possible."

"I did?"

"I mean to tell you, we'd just about given up on Anna getting any kind of film or TV work, until you came along. Jeez. You were a godsend, and I mean it. My husband was about to divorce... Well, never mind. Anyway, we're here. We have a contract and everything and I just can't thank you enough. I mean it."

"Mrs. Chase, you sound very happy, but I don't believe I had anything to do with you or your daughter having success."

"But you did. If it hadn't been for you, oh my gosh. If you hadn't come out and if my Anna hadn't posted that video with her and all news people, we'd still be in Plainfield doing what we always did, pretty much nothing. But, now. Wow. Do you know, I have an agent! Well, I mean Anna does. And we have signed a contract with an agent and we're going, well, Anna is going to be on a show and they said maybe she'll be able to sing with her favorite singer and a screen test, not just an audition and we're just so excited. And I just had to call and say thanks."

"I don't think I did anything, though I'm very happy for you."

"You did. You brought all those reporters and TV people to our house. After you left, we did interview after interview. Anna was on most of the New York TV stations. Her story got picked up by the TODAY show and a few late-night shows and now, here we are."

"Mrs. Chase, I only left you a few days ago."

"I know! Isn't it amazing?"

"It is at that."

"Just think, she'll be singing on one of those idol shows and just a few days ago, she was nobody and we were doing everything we could and now look at us."

"Wonderful."

Her voice dropped. "And, just between you and me, I don't think that producer lady is the person you're looking for."

Jake turned and looked back at the jail. "Oh? Why?"

"Because she was right. She told my Anna that she'd be a star someday. And now she's on her way just like she said. So, I don't think she was a bad person at all."

"That so?"

"She gave Anna good advice, she predicted her future."

"Her future, yes. I'm very happy for you and Anna."

He looked at Mallory. "Futures are sometimes very hard to predict. I have to go."

CHAPTER 44

Stan saw the two Davis County cops lounging outside the hospital door. He handed the fat one a card as he brushed past them.

"Hey! You the CPS guy or what?" the fat one asked before he studied the card.

"Oh. Ok. Sacramento."

Stan pushed open the hospital door. The room was dark. The sick greenish glow of the fluorescent above the hospital bed was the only light. Stan saw Michael and Jessie. Jessie was trying to help Michael get his T-shirt on over his neck brace.

She saw Stan first and she nudged Michael to get his attention.

With one arm stuck straight up through the T-shirt and his head barely poking through, Michael was able to turn his whole body and see the detective.

Michael's upraised hand gave a thumbs up and there was a muffled "Thanks for coming".

"If you would help me with this," said Michael. "We can get to the bus station quickly."

"Or a church," said Jessie. "Where we usually hide out."

"Very funny," said Michael.

They were able to pull down the T-shirt. Michael's head emerged fully. He twisted his head, right and left, stretching out his neck.

"We're supposed to be in Arizona, but we've been a bit travel-challenged."

Stan looked at both kids. They seemed older, wiser, and just plain tired. He remembered the first time he'd seen them, that night in Olive Park which now seemed forever ago. Michael, shaken, defiant, and proud. And protective of Jessie.

"So, how are you guys doing?"

Jessie gave a weak smile and a quiet, "Okay."

"Never better," seconded Michael. "Except for a few cops I'd kick the shit out of if I were bigger. I'm just fine. Jess is just fine. We're anxious to get a move on. Can you give me a hand?"

Instead of what he wanted to look for, Stan had to help Michael get dressed. He found Michael's pants and had him sit on the bed while he held the waist open. Michael rolled back on the bed and came forward landing both legs into the pant legs.

Michael struggled to stand and shuck the pants into their proper position.

Stan could wait no longer. "Where's the backpack?"

"Backpack?"

"Or knapsack or something you're carrying your stuff in. You have it?"

Michael tried to turn his body to look around the room finally turned back to Stan.

"I don't know, maybe. It was with us when the cops accosted us, beat the crap out of me, dragged me into this hospital, wanted to arrest me. All that shit. If I had time and knew a good attorney, I'd sue 'em for child abuse. Especially the fat one."

"You don't know where it is?"

"The backpack? Not a clue. Ask the stormtroopers. They may have it. Look, it only had crap stuff in it. Stuff we'd gotten from goodwill, plus a few things we grabbed from Aunt Jane's house when we left. Nothing that's worth anything. We can get new stuff when we get to Arizona. It's okay, we don't need it."

"Not okay" replied Stan. "I need to see it."

Michael straightened up, finished zipping his pants. "Really, we don't need it. It's just crap. Besides, we just want to get outta here, get going."

Stan took Michael by the shoulders and addressed him straight on. "Michael, this is important. I think you have something that I really need to see."

"Like what?"

"Michael, do you have a teddy bear?"

Michael started to laugh but it hurt too much. "Ow. Damn. Are you here to pick us up or to get some freakin' stuffed animal?" Michael waded into sarcasm. "I'm so glad I called. If that's all you're interested in. We don't need your help. We can hitchhike to the bus station."

"Michael…"

"Or hitchhike all the way to Arizona if that's what it takes, but we just gotta get outta here."

Stan didn't move. "Michael it's not at the police station. The backpack. The police say they don't have it, that it was with you when you are arrested."

"What is it with you cops? Look, I appreciate you coming to bail us out of hospital jail, but now it looks like you were just here to rummage through our stuff, which I don't know where it is. If you can find it, you can fucking have it. We are leaving. C'mon Jess."

But Jessie didn't move. She stood with her head down.

"Jess, what is it?"

It was at that moment Jessie brought the backpack out from behind her back.

Neither Stan nor Michael said anything until finally Stan approached Jessie and held out his hand. "Can I have it?" he asked.

Jessie handed him the backpack. Stan immediately turned it upside down and dumped the contents out onto the hospital bed. A variety of hotel breakfast room staples fell in disarray. Sweet rolls wrapped in a few napkins, also a few yogurt containers, a couple of plastic spoons, two apples, what looked like a change of clothes for Jessie and Michael, and a jacket for Michael and a few random socks.

And, lastly a stuffed bear.

It fell with some weight and lay there on its back looking up at the three of them. It had a crumpled hat that seemed to be sewn on, a red vest, one side of which was loose and folded back. It had small funny eyes and the fur, what was left of it, was matted in different directions the result of haphazardly being thrown to the bottom of the backpack and ignored.

Michael awkwardly leaned over the bed then turned to Stan. "Okay here's your bear let's go, go, go."

Stan kept staring at the bear. He couldn't believe that this little thing was responsible for all that had happened. There didn't seem to be anything on the outside that was abnormal or would give him a clue to its importance. He grasped it by one of the ears and hefted it. It wasn't just stuffed with fluffy ticking, there was something of weight inside. He suddenly had trouble swallowing.

Stan knew he should put it in an evidence bag which he didn't have. Instead, he began to lower it back into the backpack and that's when he saw the subtle bump on the back underneath the bear's vest. He held the bear up and with his pen, pushed up the vest so he could see underneath. A portion of the bear's fur was neatly cut to make a flap. He pushed at the flap with his pen, but it wouldn't budge. He knew he couldn't go any further, as in reach in with his fingers and rip open the flap, which is exactly what he wanted to do.

Regretfully, he lowered the bear into the backpack and tied it closed.

"Okay let's go," he said.

Michael looked at the collection on the bed. "What about our stuff? We collected all this. We may need it. It's a long bus ride to Arizona."

Stan reached into the pile of clothes, grabbed a jacket for Michael a sweater for Jessie. He handed each to each kid, picked up the backpack, filled it with what was left on the bed and started out of the hospital door.

"Listen," said Stan. "I'll get you all new stuff. New clothes, shoes, socks, underwear, whatever you need."

Michael smiled at Jessie who smiled back. They trailed Stan out of the hospital room.

"Now we're talking," said Michael. "And how about some bus fare while you're at it? And, listen, I want a receipt for the bear."

However, Stan was already way ahead of them steaming down the hospital hallway.

CHAPTER 45

Stan set the backpack gingerly on the back seat of his car. Jessie slid in on the other side next to it. Michael, using both hands, one on the dash and one on the door to steady himself, lowered down on the passenger seat. He tried not to wince or cry out, but his neck hurt like hell.

Even so, he gave directions. "Bus station, please."

Stan looked at Michael, admiring his bravado. "No bus station kid. You're coming with me."

Michael tried to address Stan directly, but he could only turn so far. "Not back to that McArdle asshole." It wasn't a question.

"No," said Stan. "Someplace quiet, safe, until we sort out some issues."

"Back to Detective Steiner's?"

"Not possible. I have someplace better in mind."

Michael didn't know what that meant, but at least Detective Wyld had rescued him from the hospital, saved him from being arrested. So it was probably a good bet he and Jessie were not to be dumped back into the lap of CPS.

Stan navigated out onto I 80. Traffic was light. The sun had just set. As he drove, he could feel the nuclear heat from the backpack in the backseat. He wasn't afraid of the bear exploding. Hell, the kids had dragged that backpack and the bear in it all over creation. Still, the knowledge that the bear held a secret just made it radiate with a curious intensity. The detective in him just wanted to jam on the brakes, stop the damn car, rip open the backpack, tear off the bear's vest, cut away the flap in the back and find out what the hell is going on.

He could imagine Jake doing just that. Mallory too.

He checked Jessie in the rearview mirror. She was fast asleep. He was about to ask Michael about where he'd been, what they'd been doing when he noticed that Michael was studying the side mirror intently.

"What are you looking for?" asked Stan.

Michael stayed riveted on the mirror. "I'm looking for ghosts," he said. "Ghosts from our past."

He turned to Stan. "I think we're being followed."

Stan checked his own mirror.

"Michael, we are on a freeway. There are cars, some in front of us, some are behind us. Yes, we're being followed. Followed by all the people that work in Davis probably trying to get home to Sacramento. That's who is following us."

He stole a glance at Michael and wondered if all the kid has been through had given him a case of paranoia.

"Think I'm crazy all you want. I'm not," said Michael. "Listen to me, I think we're being followed." He angled so he could get a full view in the mirror. "It's a tan piece of shit Chevy. Looks like a beat-up Nova, probably '86 or '87." He turned to Stan. "You have a gun?"

Stan checked his mirror again. Without picking up contagious suspicion, Stan did notice a light tan, possibly a Nova, that was behind them and changing lanes when he changed lanes. He purposely moved from the right lane to the centerline and then back again to see what would happen.

He executed the maneuver. The car behind them just stayed in the right lane.

Shit, I probably did it too quickly, he thought. He tried again. The car moved behind him. Coincidence.

"Enough," muttered Stan.

Michael stayed glued to the rearview mirror.

"Michael tell me about the bear where did it come from? Where did you get it?"

Michael settled back in the seat. Still, Stan could tell his focus was still on the side mirror.

"The bear isn't ours. Well, it's sort of Jessie's. It's a long story."

"We've got time until we meet Mallory."

"We're going with Detective Diamante?"

"No. Just a rendezvous of sorts. So, we've got time. Tell me about the bear."

Michael sighed. "Okay. When Ruby, crazy Ruby fox-face was taking care of us, she had toys and stuff. In that smelly trailer of hers, there was this bear. She always kept it in the same spot on the mantle. Once in a while she would pick it up and set it in front of us like we were all part of some crazy family. I don't know, it was creepy."

"But, how did you get it?" asked Stan.

Michael sighed. "And after all the shit with her that happened, the cops went through her place and sorted all the stuff that they thought was ours. They bagged it up and gave it to Aunt Jane. So, when we were heading out I just grabbed the backpack and stuffed it full of stuff that I thought we'd need. I thought I'd grab the bear for Jess."

Michael stopped, remembering. "I thought…"

"You thought what?"

"I don't know. I just thought it would comfort her. It was as if it was a symbol, you know. The three of us, me, Jess and the bear. We'd all made it out of that crazy place in one piece. Maybe it was for me too. Sort of like a Three Musketeers thing, I don't know. Like we were all fellow survivors."

"Now," said Michael, taking his eyes off the mirror. "You tell me what you want it for. What is so important that even after you saw me lying in the hospital, beaten to shit from a clear case of police brutality, almost the first thing you asked was, 'Michael, where is the bear?'"

Stan shook his head. "It's important. I don't know why. That's the truth. People have been killed for it Michael, and a lot of people, a lot of bad people are looking for it."

Michael shivered. "Then we are being followed," he said. "It's not my imagination. And I know who it is. Fuck, I know who it is."

"Who?"

Michael found himself breathing fast. "He's a little brown snarly shit. Worked with crazy Ruby. He's been after us. He found us twice, but we got away. Drop-kicked him in his jaw last time we met."

"Who is it?"

"His name is Pitic or something like it. I heard crazy Ruby call him that. And I don't think he's going to stop until he gets what he wants."

Stan once again checked his mirror. There was still a car behind him. The headlights looked familiar. Maybe. Maybe not. Without thinking about it he pressed his right arm to his side. A slight bulge of the gun gave him reassurance as it always did.

They'd agreed to meet at a Park 'n Ride off Capitol Avenue just off the freeway. When Stan pulled in, he saw Mallory standing by her old red Honda. He pulled alongside and turned off the engine.

Mallory opened Stan's passenger door and reached in to hug Michael but stopped when she saw his neck brace.

"What the hell happened to you?"

"Police brutality," enunciated Michael.

Mallory looked to Stan who shrugged. "I think he gave them some trouble."

Mallory addressed Michael. "Well, Bea will take good care of you. Both of you. Where's your sister?"

Stan nodded toward the backseat. "Asleep," he said.

"Whose Bea?" asked Michael.

"Detective Wyld's wife," replied Mallory. "She's got a lot of practice these days of taking care of injured people."

Mallory straightened up and looked at Stan. "Where is it?"

"It's in the backpack in the back seat," said Stan.

He grabbed the backpack by the top loop and handed it to Mallory. She unzipped the big flap and reached in. She shuffled through the few clothes and disparate food items until she found it then carefully removed the bear and returned the backpack to the seat.

"Wow," she said. She turned to Stan. "It looks so normal. You sure?"

"Heft it."

Mallory got a good grip, lifted it up and down. While she had little experience with kids' toys, it did seem to have more weight than a stuffed bear should have.

"Quick as you can," said Stan. "You and Jake get this to Danni, I want to know. I'll be there as soon as I make a detour to Marston's place. Carruthers, again. Something I must see, he said. Oh, he is insisting on interviewing these two." Stan indicated Michael and Jessie. "He was adamant when he heard I had them with me."

"Drama queen," Mallory muttered.

"I think he's trying."

"Very," agreed Mallory.

"Agreed," said Stan. "The bear is paramount. So, off you go."

Mallory cradled the bear as if it was a baby. She motioned to Stan to follow her. She led him over to her car, away from Michael and Jessie.

"Jake gave me a message for you."

"And?"

"He said to remember the Bearded Lady. What does that mean?"

"He said that? Just like that?"

"Verbatim. He made sure I repeated it back to him."

Stan got a far-off look. "It was an old case. One of our first. Doesn't matter the specifics. The Bearded Lady was a man."

"So, red isn't always red, the floor isn't always solid, and the beard isn't real."

Stan shook his head. "No. The beard was real. That was the problem."

Michael strained to hear what they were saying but the freeway noise blocked everything out. He was so intent on eavesdropping that he didn't see the car that caught up to them and pulled into the Park 'n Ride, just as Stan got back into the car and Mallory drove away.

It was a car with familiar headlights and it stopped one row away and sat idling with its lights off.

When Stan finally pulled out of the commuter lot, out into traffic, so did the other car.

Like a bee waiting for an opportunity to sting, it was always a few cars behind.

CHAPTER 46

"Where are we now?" asked Michael. He strained to lean forward and see through the darkness. They swept past two pillars and headed up a curving drive that seemed lined with shrubs. The headlights flashed across trees, expertly trimmed so no branch touched the ground, and even in the headlights Michael could see the place was filled with beautiful grass, green but showing brilliant emerald as they climbed the drive.

"Just a quick stop," said Stan as he pulled up to the only other item in the circular drive. Stan recognized it as Carruthers' staff car. It was parked at an odd angle, one wheel up on the sculpted concrete border.

"Won't be long. Probably." He turned off the lights and shut off the engine. The quiet rushed in.

Michael's eyes adjusted to the dark. He peered out of his window. They were in front of a large mansion. He noticed the grand sweep of the place, the windows, the long stretch and turn of the structure.

"I don't think they know you're coming," said Michael. "Either that or no one is home."

"I know that car. He's here. Probably near the back of the house." Stan hoped he sounded reassuring.

"Some house. You'll need a map."

Stan turned. "The name Marston ring any bells? James Marston?"

"Why?"

"This is his place. Was his place. You ever hear of him?"

Michael ran his memory like a tape through a machine. Nothing. He shook his head. "Nope."

Stan turned back and surveyed the dark façade of the place. Even though there was a sliver of a moon, the place did look deserted, almost now a little neglected from the last time he'd inspected the place. Not so much neglect, more like some disconnect, as if something didn't belong. He idly wondered when the last time the Mexican gardeners had been here. Or the housecleaning crew. Had they even shown up after they found out Marston was dead?

Of course, he realized. According to Squinty Saunders, the attorney, some charity, some Hollywood actor's charity had inherited it. If they'd already taken possession, that would explain his feeling. That was it.

He swung back to Michael. "And you've never been here?"

"Here? No. No way," answered a surprised Michael. "I don't even know where we are."

"Okay, you kids stay in the car. I won't be long."

"Nah, I think we'll tag along."

"Michael!" said Stan, harsher than he meant to. "Stay here. With your sister. I'll be right back."

"There are no lights on. It looks weird. We should stick together."

"Just stay and look after your sister."

"She's asleep," said Michael without diverting his attention from the building. He noticed at the far end of this Marston mansion was a section that seemed to be two, maybe three, stories easy. The moonlight, sliding in and out of the clouds, reflected off what he now saw were soaring glass walls. And down at the bottom, he thought he detected a small orangish glow and movement from inside. It was the only sign that anybody was even there.

He went to call Stan's attention to the light, but he was only in time to see Stan push open a large oak door and step into darkness.

He watched as the door closed by itself behind Stan.

Michael settled back next to his sister. Because his head still hurt like a mother, he kept it straight as he could while he dug in his coat pocket until he found the hole in the lining. He raised the coat to bring the bottom of the coat closer. Through the hole, his fingers touched what he'd been searching for, the cell phone he'd lifted from the fat cop, whose name he only remembered as Butz. True that.

Michael smiled as he fingered the phone, just checking that it was still there. He always had a hole in one or both of his coat pockets. Even on the rare occasion when his mother would spring for a new coat for him, the first order of business was to carefully cut a slit in the pocket lining. And not at the low spot where all his coat stuff would exit out but right near the top, toward the outside.

He was genius at secreting what was needed to be hidden at the bottom of the lining, then pretending he had nothing in his pockets. Cause you never knew when you were going to need stuff.

He'd never been searched before, but the other cop, the one that twisted up his neck, had made him turn out his coat pockets. And he had. Even flapping them so that smug asshole could see there were no illicit drugs, no knife, no massive cans of pepper spray, no six-shooter, nothing that could do harm, in his coat.

He always told the truth. Nothing in my pockets. See dickwad.

Jessie stirred. "Where are we?" she mumbled.

Michael was about to answer her when he saw she'd gone right back to sleep.

He leaned back in the seat. From his vantage point, he could still see the end of the house and all the glass walls and the orange light. Still there.

Down at the end of the driveway, by the two entrance pillars, the little brown man pulled the two sides of the iron gate together and securely locked it.

There was no leaving now.

CHAPTER 47

"Where's Stan?" asked Jake as soon as Mallory walked in.

Before she could answer, he continued. "And where are the kids?"

Mallory ignored him and Sharon Ollestad and her young IT assistant Jeffrey who were assembled in the OID office. She cradled the bear, moved to the conference table in the center of the room, and set it down.

No one moved toward it

Only Jake the dog came up and greeted Mallory. She absently ruffed his neck.

"Stan? Kids?" persisted Jake.

Mallory smiled at Jake. She couldn't help it.

"Kids are with Stan," she said. "He's on his way. Carruthers, when he heard Stan had the kids, demanded he stop at Marston's. Said he had something Stan just had to see there, plus, ever since he took over the investigation, he's been insisting on re-questioning of the Cooper kids. Must figure he can kill two birds with one stone. Stan thinks Carruthers is trying to set an example."

"Of what?" asked Sharon.

"I don't know. Maybe his version of proper investigative procedure. Who knows. Anyway, Stan said he won't be long."

Mallory took the chair directly in front of the bear and looked around at the OID office. It was the first time she'd really seen the whole office repaired and back to normal.

Gone were the big chunks of glass of course. The long conference table was now restored to its place in the center of the room.

Four panels had been blown out in the mixture of 9mm and .45 caliber bullets. The crime scene photos documented the damage, and with the four glass panels missing, there had been a true feeling of exposure by everyone moving through the office.

Now, toady Samuels objections notwithstanding, everything was back together. Glass restored. It felt like it always had to Mallory. Perfectly contained.

Cleaning crews had been and gone and done their work well, having removed and sanitized the area where parts of Ilsa Pokovich had landed. They'd been meticulous in placing everything back on a desk nearest to where the item fell, but Mallory knew Jake had spent hours re-arranging the desks and their personal items to get it back to what was normal for OID.

"Okay," said Mallory, indicating the bear. "Here it is."

Before they moved toward it, both Sharon and Jeffrey snapped on latex gloves.

Once again, Mallory felt foolish for not taking precautions with gloves when she handled the backpack and removed the bear, but damn, she thought, the backpack and probably the bear too had been banged all over creation, dragged through the mud, rained on, and who knows what else.

She relinquished her seat.

Sharon pushed Mallory's chair back and, standing against the table, reached down and rotated the bear all the way around.

Before them sat a scraggly, furze-covered teddy bear, about twelve inches tall. Red vest, green hat, both sewn on, and both rumpled from being neglected in the bottom of a backpack.

No one said what they were thinking. Something this innocent, a child's companion, loveable and cushy, cost a life, maybe more.

Sharon looked at Jake. "Sure we don't need the bomb squad on this?"

It was Mallory who answered. "Sharon, this thing has been dragged all over, tossed around, dropped. If it had any kind of explosive, it would've incinerated those two kids a long time ago."

"Plus," added Jake. "Whoever wants this and is willing to die to get it wasn't doing it just to stop it from exploding. There's something inside."

Sharon gave a twitch of her head as she regarded the stuffed bear. "Still, one person has died trying to get it, another wounded trying to keep it. Go figure."

"Okay," said Jeffrey as he slid his chair over next to Sharon. "Let's get to it."

Jeffrey, the new wunderkind from SacPD's IT's department had the look of a cliched Ichabod Crane, gawky, pointy nose, large Adam's apple, and glasses held on with a rubber band. All that was missing was a half-finished can of energy drink by his side. Still, Mallory realized with his impatient nerd intensity this unkempt kid was probably the best person to extract what needed to be extracted. And he seemed confident in what he was doing which made Mallory feel better.

Sharon hefted the bear, judging its weight. She faced it straight on and smiled. "Hah!"

She pointed the face of the bear toward Jeffrey. "See it?"

Jeffrey adjusted his glasses. His gloved finger reached out and traced the two eyes of the bear.

"Damn. Yeah."

"What?" asked Mallory.

Both Jeffrey and Sharon turned to Mallory. "A camera," said Jeffrey. "One of the bear's eyes is a camera."

"Well, at least we know it won't explode."

"Unless…" mused Jeffrey. "They decided to booby-trap it so prying eyes such as ours would regret trying to open it up."

"Jeffrey," admonished Sharon.

"Just sayin'."

Sharon turned the bear over and got a good look at its ass. "Nothing here."

She turned it around so she was facing the back. The red vest was wrinkled and showed results of having been folded up many times.

Sharon grasped the vest and pulled it up high onto the bear's back.

The tan furze was in better shape having been under the vest, but Sharon noticed a flap, the same flap Stan had seen. With two fingers she pulled the flap aside. The crackling release of Velcro filled the quiet room.

Mallory realized she had been holding her breath. She let it out in a whoosh.

Everyone else shifted in their seats.

Sharon tilted the bear so the lights above illuminated the inside.

Jeffrey leaned in, then reached in and released a snap. With both hands, he lifted out a small, cigarette-sized black case. Attached to it were two leads leading to a battery pack nestled deeper into one of the bear's legs. Those he kept connected. Two other leads that ran to the camera in one of the bear's fake eyes, he pulled out of the black case.

"Okay. There you go." Jeffrey took the black box and checked it over as if he had invented it. He showed no hesitation about shoving anything into any of the receptacles. And if there had been any, Mallory realized, he would have had no indecision about playing with the controls on the face.

Mallory and Sharon and Jake moved in closer.

"So, it's a recorder of some kind?" asked Jake.

"Isn't everything?" responded Jeffrey with sarcasm barely held in check. Then, remembering his place in the pecking order, he amended his answer, trying to generate wondrous agreement.

"Exactly! A recording device. Standard military or black-ops issue, I think.," he said, waxing on, inventing bullshit as he went.

"Connected to the camera in the eye and powered by, what I'm sure is a lithium battery pack."

"How do we access it?" asked Jake.

Jeffrey turned the case around. On the back side was a small, inch-long cover. Using a paperclip, Jeffrey inserted it into a tiny hole next to the little cover.

Out popped a miniature memory card.

Jeffrey held up the tiny card and smiled at Jake. "We access it easily."

CHAPTER 48

Mallory watched Jeffrey with some level of awe. She had initially treated the bear like an explosive device. Afraid if she moved it too much this prize they had been after would delete itself. Somehow. She harkened back to her early days with computers and a single keystroke mistake that had wiped out a sixteen-page research paper she'd slaved over for two weeks.

It was a fear that never left her no matter how many thousands of hours she sat at a keyboard. She looked at Jeffrey and realized he had no such fears. He had never blown up 16 beautifully typed pages of 'Tilting at Windmills – Man of La Mancha, the Philosophical Interpretations'.

Jeffrey exuded the attitude of cyber superiority. Nothing could hurt him, and he was absolutely sure he could do nothing to destroy anything important.

The world was all so simple to the inexperienced.

Jeffrey began calmly going about what he planned to do in his over-explanatory way.

He addressed the group. "All right, now with the memory card I ejected, I plan to insert it into my own invention, my own black box, that acts as a firewall, protecting the laptop in case there is something harmful on our card. Then I will recover whatever is on it, probably pictures and or videos. All I have to do is…"

"What is that thing?" asked Jake pointing to the black box between the computer and the recorder. "Some sort of connecting thing?"

Jeffrey turned and was about to give Jake a detailed explanation of the digital extractor that he'd built himself when he caught Sharon boring into him.

"Jeffrey, who cares how just do it! We want everything off the card." She continued to hover over him.

Jeffrey shifted in his chair and observed his boss. "I will. I was just describing what I have to do so we all knew what I was doing..."

Mallory grabbed his shoulder.

"Jeffrey!"

"What?"

"Shut up and get on with it."

The nerd light went on. "Oh, okay. Will do."

Both Mallory and Jake joined Sharon in hovering over Jeffrey.

"Okay. I'm on it. Leaning over me doesn't make me go any faster, you know."

Jeffrey shuffled his shoulders then let his fingers fly over the keyboard.

"Yeah," he muttered. "Some sort of connecting thing."

All eyes turned to the laptop as they expected visuals to begin to march across the screen.

Nothing.

He repeated his manipulations. Once again everyone watched the laptop.

Nothing.

"Jeffrey!" There was a warning tone in Sharon's voice. "Tell me you didn't cock something up, here. Tell me again how you know what you're doing."

Jeffrey said nothing but once again repeated his keystrokes.

The result was the same.

Sharon slumped a bit. "God, I knew we should have sent this off to the FBI."

"Well, dear Sharon," stated Jeffrey. "They would have found the same thing on this card that you see. Or don't see."

He didn't bother turning around to address her.

"They would have found nothing, just like I did.

"Jesus, man," Jake said, pointing to Jeffrey's black box. "You sure that thing's working? You sure everything is going through?"

Jeffrey didn't bother to glance Jake's way and he certainly didn't bother to check his connections.

"What you don't see is what you don't got," quipped Jeffrey, happy with his humor.

"Then what's that mean?" asked Jake, pointing to small red light on the side of Jeffrey's invention.

Jeffrey turned it around so he could see. He stared at the red light with something akin to admiration. Without missing a beat and speaking as if he expected the current sequence of events to unfold just as they had, he said with forced casualness, "It's... loading something. Big... very big because it's still loading. About a terabyte-"

"Look!" interrupted Mallory.

On a black background, a scroll of white numbers streamed upward. Jeffrey rocked forward abruptly, the smile gone from his face.

"Uh oh."

He tapped the face of the laptop unnecessarily twice.

"Je-sus!"

"What is it?" asked Sharon shouldering in close.

"Damn. It's showing there's little memory left for anything else. Thing's huge."

They all watched mesmerized.

As suddenly as the numbers began, they stopped. The last one on the list was highlighted.

Jake leaned in. "They're dates."

Jeffrey was about to object when he saw Jake was right. "Yes," he murmured. Jeffrey tapped the screen and slid his finger over to a round icon at the bottom of the screen.

He leaned back so all behind him could see the laptop's screen.

"Was hoping there were pictures or videos," exclaimed Mallory. "Not just a list of dates. Damn."

Jeffrey slowly turned his chair so he was looking at Mallory. His voice cracked with a nervous agitation. "These are videos. Thousands of them."

He pointed to the extension that followed every date. "They're videos. A shitload." He took a breath. "Okay, where do you want to start?"

Jake looked at Mallory. "Start with the last one," he said. Mallory nodded.

In answer, Jeffrey tapped the icon.

The screen jerked alive, handheld swishes showed a dark screen with flashes of light, then a few seconds of figures, imprecise visions of people backlit, then it centered on a blurred white light. There was audio too and Jeffrey held the control on the side of the laptop to raise the volume.

"Let me see. I can't see," complained Sharon.

"Can you copy it at the same time?" asked Jake.

Jeffrey stopped the playback, adjusted the laptop and turned up its volume further.

Everyone turned their attention to Mallory's laptop. Mallory scooted in closer and felt the dog nuzzle up against her leg.

"Hey, boy," she said absently.

"Here we go," announced Jeffrey.

Once again, but clearer now, the swishes of dark and light gave way to the blurry light which now came in to focus. The audio was up and the moving image that came on the screen was in black and white and was a large group of young people in a darkened house, hunched over, lurching forward and sideways, bumping into doorways and each other. They appeared to be mumbling and drooling. The audio also had an undercurrent of a raspy irritating buzzing.

Mallory's eyes widened as she realized what it was.

"Holy shit. I know this. I know this!"

"What...?" was all Ollestad got out before Mallory blurted, "Marston! It's Marston! His film. Blood and Honey! I've seen it. I just saw it. Shit, this is Blood and Honey. But what's it doing on... this?"

Jeffrey pointed to the lower edge of the screen.

"It's not. Technically. The camera is recording the film off a screen. See the slight movement? This recorder is at the back of a theater watching... whatever it is."

"Blood and Honey," supplied Mallory. "And we know the theater. Been there."

"Yeah, well..."

They all watched for another half minute.

Mallory whispered, more to herself than any of the group, "This is where the beekeeper gets it. He goes up to the top of the house, and..."

She stopped because the view on the laptop shifted, tilting down so only half of the film was visible. It took a few seconds for the recorder's camera to make the adjustment but when it did, it revealed a row of seats and a figure in silhouette, sitting in the front row.

The action of the film was masked completely as the recorder in the bear was tilted down enough to eliminate what was on the screen and was now just showing the figure.

There was enough light now to discern that it was a man and he sat unmoving watching the film.

"That's Marston," Mallory said. She said it quietly because no one moved on the screen and no one watching the laptop moved. Mallory found herself holding her breath.

The picture jiggled slightly and widened out to reveal two figures now behind and on either side of Marston.

They saw what looked like a looped cord rise up behind Marston's head until it hung like a death's halo over him.

In a coordinated movement, the loop came down encircling Marston's neck. The figures leaned out of the frame, tightening the wire. Marston's hands went to his neck, his legs, bound with zip ties, flew up into frame and even above the exhortations of the beekeeper on the screen they heard the strangled cries of James Marston, Junior as the sharp wire cut into him.

The outline of a woman moved from the aisle to calmly stand in front of a thrashing James Marston. When she turned to face him, there was no doubt.

Ilsa Pokovich stood full in the flickering light of Blood and Honey and laughed. She did not seem to be the cancer-stricken Ilsa Pokovich they'd met. This one had a vengeful energy, reflected in her beaming face as she watched a frantic man struggle for his life.

She came closer to Marston and stood towering above him.

For a second his hands left his neck and his arms came up in desperate supplication, begging, just as her head tilted back and she began to laugh.

The video ended before his head came off but not before a pair of hands came around to the front of the video and began to clap.

They all moved away from the laptop, feeling as if they'd all been in a crash, all seen someone jump, all watched a man die. Only not the way you expect death to be. This was a lash, a vicious, remorseless exhibition of pure revenge. It was breathtaking in its horrific beauty.

Mallory was the first to speak, trying to lighten the mood.

"Film producer, famous for slash films, is himself filmed being killed while watching one of his own films. Multiple layers of ironic."

"Again," breathed Jake. "Show it again."

CHAPTER 49

Stan stood for a moment as the front door swung shut, letting his eyes and ears adjust.

After the dull thud of the front door, there was nothing.

He listened, straining to hear any sound. There was not a whisper. He would've believed he had everything, the place, the immediacy, all wrong if Carruthers hadn't called him after he picked up the kids. In fact. Carruthers had made it sound as if Stan wouldn't be able to sleep nights unless he viewed what Carruthers had to show him.

Well, that was Carruthers' car parked haphazardly in the drive, that and the mansion front door was open, so Carruthers was here somewhere.

Stan wanted to call out but held back. The entry hall was blackness. Even the tote boards above his head that had tallied the profits Marston was making on all his movies were dark and silent.

Stan could barely make out the three other spokes of the house that radiated off the main foyer. All dark. From the last time he had had Rodriguez and his crew chew through the house, inspecting all the rooms, he recalled the three-spoke layout of the place. To the left was dining and pantry and way back, the kitchen. Ahead were bedrooms with EnSuite baths and extras like exercise and media rooms.

To the right was the glow coming from the conservatory.

Like a blind man learning to see, he began to move out of the hub of the house straight ahead down the hallway to the conservatory. Thankfully what little moonlight there was through the skylights, helped. As he started down the hall, he could begin to make out the dim glow of a solitary light or lamp. It was the singular sign of life in the whole joint.

He went up a few steps, past the unlit fireplace. The plush carpet absorbed his footsteps and so made his way silently until he came to the frosted double glass doors that led to the conservatory.

He pushed through the doors and let the warmth and humidity envelop him. And the heady smells, the glorious earthy smells of thousands of exotic and near exotic plants, the water pond filled with lilies and hyacinths, the towering palms and ferns and lichen and loamy soil.

So captivated by the moonlight streaming through the skylights, he almost failed to notice the man halfway slumped on the nearest bench with his back to Stan. He looked to be asleep.

He wasn't.

CHAPTER 50

It could've been an hour or just a few minutes, Michael had no idea when he jolted awake.

He sat up in the backseat of Detective Wyld's car. Jessie was still asleep next to him.

He was awake, but why.

The mansion was still there, still dark. Still no sign of a returning Detective Wyld.

But something had wakened him.

After a few minutes of listening to the silence, he detected a difference in the air. Like when he had his eyes closed he could sense someone approach by the disturbance in the air. Or maybe it was lack of disturbance. A void, a stealthy quiet zone.

And that's what he felt right now.

He settled back and pretended to be asleep, his head turned to the side, his eyes slitted open enough to scan around the car, on his side and Jess's.

Nothing. But that creepy feeling.

"Shit", he muttered as he faked stretching and instead slipped down to the floor.

He checked the window above Jessie.

He turned around and checked out his own window.

What the hell was going on? Still...

He hunkered down and pressed his face between the two front seats.

He swallowed hard when he saw it.

There was a shadow. It was moving along the front of the car.

He was too low to see anything, but the overwhelming feeling of something bad about to happen smothered him.

You don't sneak up on someone if you're planning on welcoming them to the party.

He found Jess's left foot and squeezed it.

Again.

"Jess wake up," he whispered.

He found her calf and pinched it.

"Ow. That hurt," she mumbled.

"Jess, listen."

"What?" Her eyes were open but headed back to her pleasant dreamland.

"Wake UP," hissed Michael. He tried to keep the urgency out of his voice. "Jess! C'mon."

"Okay, okay I'm awake." She started to raise up, but Michael stopped her.

"What?" she asked. "Where are we? And where's the detective?"

"Never mind. We need to be ready-"

Two things happened in rapid order. The door handle on Jessie's door flipped up, the door blasted open and Jessie who had been half propped against it fell backward out of the car.

To Michael's horror, hunched over his sister was the little brown man, Pitic.

Pitic grabbed Jessie by her hair and began to drag her away from the car, over the gravel driveway toward the house.

"No fucking way," yelled Michael. He grabbed the backpack as he launched himself out of the car, propelled full throttle toward the little brown ugly squat of a man.

He meant to hit him full speed square in the back.

He never saw the boot come arcing around to greet him.

CHAPTER 51

The last thing she heard was Michael yelling, "Run!"

Jessie ran, stopping only once to try and see what was behind her. She tumbled into a bush and hunkered down. She was shivering and couldn't understand what had happened. Couldn't understand where Michael was. Couldn't understand where she was.

She remembered climbing in the detective's car, falling asleep. Something about Michael grabbing her, shaking her foot, telling her to wake up. Then being flat on her back on the ground. Seeing that man over her.

Then Michael yelling.

And she ran.

And now here she was, wherever that was. In a bush. Next to what appeared to be a big house. She reached out and touched the stone on the side of the house. It was covered with ivy.

"Michael," she whispered as loud as she dared. She raised up and peered back the way she'd come. "Michael," again.

There was no answer, just the light touch of a breeze that brought the sweetish smell of apples rotting on the ground.

She thought she could see the detective's car. Next to another car. But, there was no movement around either.

She looked the other way, along the side of the house. The place appeared to be even bigger than she'd first thought, now that her eyes were adjusting. There were windows along the ground floor and she could make out at least another story above.

It was too big to be just a house. Like a museum or something. Except there seemed to be no other buildings around.

Michael had yelled 'Run'. She knew he meant 'Run away'.

She was about to head back to the car when she saw the outline of the horrid little man who had pulled her out of the car. He appeared to be searching around the car, maybe looking for her. But he knew which way she ran.

It was only going to be a minute or two before he headed to her. Jessie began to back up, then spun and made her way along the ivied wall to the back corner. What she saw when she emerged onto the back patio made her stop and stare.

Partially obscured by trees, but unmistakable in its familiarity, was a neon sign. It was so out of place, she looked around to see if she wasn't back in Sunshine Acres.

She moved along the patio until her view was clear. It was there. In the middle of a closely mown field. It stood tall. It was bright. It made her smile.

'FORTUNES BY RUBY' in all its multi-hued glory.

"Ruby," she said out loud. "Ruby?"

Drawn toward it, if only for protection, she moved off the flagstones and into the field.

As she approached, she could see the trailer. It was the same! She wanted to call out to Michael. To tell him what she found. That Ruby was still here. Right here!

Green-red light from the sign bathed the side of the trailer where the door was. Above her, bats picked off the unfortunate moths and night insects also drawn to the light.

She stood before the short set of steps that led up to the trailer door waiting, fearing to see Ruby Everheart's face at the small window in the door, just like she'd seen it the first time.

No one appeared at the window.

The electrical buzz from the sign was unrelenting. She looked around for Michael. For anybody. Then she saw the distant shadow of the little man. He was moving away from the cars in quick movements, coming toward her, skirting from bush to bush as if he was stalking something.

"Michael," she whispered. "Come find me."

She clambered up the steps, turned the knob and pulled open the door. She half-fell, half-stumbled into the blackness. She grabbed the knob and slammed the door closed behind her. She squished herself up tight, head buried, arms around her knees, becoming as small as she could.

CHAPTER 52

After a moment. Jessie raised her head. She tried to quiet her breathing because she needed to listen.

She was not alone. Something was heavy and here.

Yes, this was trailer she remembered. This was the sweet-sick smell she remembered, the smell that Michael said was incense. Now, though, there was another... odor.

She held her breath and strained to see into the clotted darkness. The only light, a violet hue shadowed through a crack in the velvet curtains that enclosed the room.

But there was something. She could sense it... and almost see it. A shape, bulky and black, huddled at the far end of the trailer.

In the gloom, next to the dull shimmer from a crystal ball there was a form. A figure at the end of a long table. A hooded figure.

Without meaning to, she whispered, "Ruby?"

The figure remained unmoving and did not speak.

"Ruby are you asleep?"

Jessie moved away from the door.

"It's me. Jessie."

Closer, she could see the hood was tilted down as if sleep had overtaken Ruby Everheart.

Outside she heard a shuffling and footsteps on the stairs that led to the trailer door.

Michael!

Unless it wasn't.

She dropped down to the trailer floor and crabbed under the folds of the black velveteen table covering. She kept watching through a part in the fabric.

The door opened. Light from the sign lit the trailer entry.

On slow, silent feet, Pitic entered the trailer. He pulled the door closed behind him.

Jessie tried not to shift position or even breathe. She knew he was listening for her.

It was minutes, so long that Jessie wondered whether she'd seen Pitic enter at all. In fact, maybe he'd gone, and she was all wrong.

She thought that right up until he spoke.

"Ruby," he said in a soft voice. "I gotta leave. I'll be back." He gave a short, choking laugh as if telling and enjoying his own inside joke.

The door opened, and Jessie could see him back down the steps. Just before he closed the door, he was at her eye level and he seemed to look right at her when he murmured, "Ta-ta."

She waited a few seconds then she slid out from under the other side of the table.

She didn't hear the door lock.

As she raised up, she bumped the table. The crystal ball wobbled. Afraid it was going to roll away, Jessie put her hand out to steady it.

That's when she felt the other hand.

It was cold and slick. It was atop the crystal ball but when Jessie touched it, it slipped off, plopping down to the table.

Jessie jerked her hand away. Her heart began thumping. Did she move the hand or...?

"Ruby?"

No response.

"You're dead, aren't you?"

Jessie wanted to move away but couldn't. She kept watching the hooded figure, waiting for it to move. She didn't understand. Michael had said Ruby was dead. And she knew Ruby was dead.

She knew it. But then why this? Why the sign? Why the trailer? Why the crystal ball, the incense?

Unless maybe she was just sick. Maybe Michael and everyone told her that to make her forget.

But she remembered how caring Ruby had been to her when Jessie wasn't feeling well. Even though Michael called it like 'grooming', she believed Ruby did it because she was kind. She didn't think it was an act. Not completely.

She began to get some courage as she remembered Ruby's barking laugh. And how funny it was watching big hands trying to cook something on the stove.

"Ruby, it's okay. If you're sick, I can get someone…"

Jessie leaned down until she was level with Ruby. She extended a finger until it met the edge of the hood. She hooked her finger under the folds and lifted it up.

The smell of putrefying, contorted flesh seized her. She lurched, wrenching back the hood all the way. Dead, weeping eyes, glistened.

Jessie went to scream when the head fell forward.

And then she did scream. Her shrieks mixed with the pounding on the door.

"Michael!"

She pushed the table out of the way and tried to get to the door. But her feet were grabbed by someone, something.

Ruby!

"Michael!"

She pumped her legs, freeing herself from the heavy velveteen covering that enveloped her, and crawled to the door.

"Michael!"

"Jess! Open the door!"

With one hand she reached up and turned the knob. The door was yanked open.

There was Michael.

But behind she saw Pitic reaching for him.

"M!"

CHAPTER 53

The door slammed shut. Jessie tried to turn the handle. Jammed. Not by a lock, but by somebody's body.

"M! Open the door!"

There was no sound from outside.

"M!"

Jessie used both fists and pounded on the door. She chanced a look behind her. The figure was still there. The hood still in place. It hadn't moved. But the slanted light through the curtains was wavy and danced on the shrunken hand until a finger, one finger, seemed to move.

"M! Please!"

She sank to her knees and pressed her eye to the crack between the door and jamb.

"M!" she whispered through the opening. "M, I'm scared. Are you there?"

She moved so her ear was pressed against the gap. But what she heard, the noise she heard, was coming from behind her.

She couldn't turn, couldn't get up. She huddled in place and made herself very small. She lowered her head down. "Michael," she whispered. "I need you. Please, please open-"

The door burst open.

"M!"

Instead of her brother, the little man, Pitic was there. Pitic grabbed her by her hair and dragged her halfway down the steps then he stopped. His grip relaxed.

Jessie turned to look up. She saw Pitic, eyes wide, staring into the darkened trailer.

Mesmerized, Pitic stepped over Jessie and started back up the steps. As he reached the top step, on the darkened threshold, a bloodied Michael launched himself up the steps and, swinging what was left of his backpack, he connected with the little brown man's head. Pitic sprawled headfirst into the pitch-black trailer.

Michael slammed the door. With a kick, he splintered the wood railing, grabbed two of the wood supports and jammed them between the door handle and the 2x4s on the landing.

"C'mon!" Michael grabbed Jessie with one hand and the backpack with the other.

The wretched high-pitched shrieking faded the farther Michael and Jessie moved away from the trailer. Just before they rounded the corner of the mansion, Michael looked back. The multi-hued glow of the 'Fortunes by Ruby' neon had attracted all manner of digestible insects banging against the lights.

It seemed right that the voracious bats were enjoying a silent, lethal harvest.

CHAPTER 54

"This way," urged Michael. "Hurry up, will you."

"Wait," said Jessie as they reached Detective Wyld's car. The back door was still open where Pitic had grabbed Jessie.

"Wait. You're bleeding."

"So. I'll live." He wiped the blood off his cheek and brushed his hand over his head. Somewhere there was a growing and tender lump as well. That, plus his aching neck, made him light-headed.

"Where's the detective?"

Michael grabbed the metal handle and pried open the heavy oaken door.

"Follow me. We'll find him."

"M, she was in there."

Michael held the door open. "Who? Who are you talking about?"

"You know. Her. The 'Fortune' sign. It's her trailer and she was in there."

"You saw her?" Michael blanched. "They didn't bury her? You mean her body is in there? Right where she used to be?"

Jessie nodded. "And, we touched."

Michael shivered. "You touched her?"

"I dunno."

"What?"

"Her hand… moved."

"Moved? What do you mean? She's dead. Has to be."

Jessie started to cry. "I want to go home M. I'm tired. I just want to go... home."

Michael leaned down. "Me too, kiddo. That's what I want too. We'll get away from all this shit. I promise we will get to Arizona. We'll have sunshine and warmth and cows and horses."

"I don't want horses."

"You don't have to ride. You can watch me, you know. You can slop the hogs or whatever you do to them. You know, feed the chickens and all. Collect the eggs. You can do that. Hey, it'll be nice."

"I just want to go now, okay."

Michael straightened. "Damn good idea. Let's find our copper and get the hell out of here, okay?"

Jessie didn't answer but turned and looked back to the front door.

"C'mon Jess," said Michael as gently as he could. "We'll find him and be outta here."

When Jessie didn't answer and didn't turn back to her brother, Michael touched her shoulder.

"You okay and all?"

Jessie shrugged.

"The trailer?" he asked.

"I guess," said Jessie, nodding. "It was... I thought she..."

"Yeah, well, c'mon. She is dead, really dead, I'm sure of it. And now her little asshole assistant is back with her. Just a happy couple I say. This way and let's get the hell outta here."

Jessie followed Michael into the gloom of the cavernous main room. He paused to get his bearings, get a feel for direction because now, looking every which way, through the dimness he could see they were in a big hub and spokes of hallways led off in multiple directions. And shit, he was tired too. Tired of being the responsible one now that he let himself dwell on it. He tried not to think about their life before. Before all the shit that had happened. Back when even his father and mother seemed reasonably, if not happy, then at least accommodating to each other and to him and

Jessie. He wanted to go home too. He wanted to go back and start over. It would all be different, he was sure.

You made your own way in the world he always believed and were responsible for the hell that rained down, and for some of the good things that you managed to receive. But, damn, they could sure use a break, he didn't mind thinking.

Okay, just a few seconds of self-pity. Something his mother said when he had screwed up or hadn't gotten what he believed he deserved. 'You can have a few seconds of self-pity', she would say. 'A mini pity party if you feel you must. But then get busy.'

As if in answer to some karmic plea of maybe both of theirs, the moon emerged from behind a cloud and lit up the hallway in front of him.

"Okay. Let's go."

As they started forward, he remembered the orange glow he saw from the car and he knew they were headed in the right direction. The sooner they could find Detective Wyld, the sooner they'd be on their way. He'd about had it. No more screwing around. He'd demand they be put on a bus to Arizona first thing in the morning.

He found himself starting to run.

Up a few steps into a living room, he figured. A fireplace, a mile-long couch, and lamps that looked like saucers and sat on thin tables.

"Keep up."

"I am. Is he behind us? After us?"

"No. He can't get out."

"M, how did he find us?"

Michael didn't answer but turned right and headed down the hallway. That was when he knew they were close. He could smell it too. Plants. Humidity. Frosted double glass doors. Beyond them, the same warm glow he'd seen from the car. And voices.

And a gunshot.

CHAPTER 55

No one was eager to see it again Jake knew, but he also knew that all they saw on the first time was the shock of a man's death. No one recorded any details about what they'd seen. As if they'd seen aliens land and pick fruit from the garden. They didn't really accept what they'd seen.

He knew they would watch it over and over. He knew IT would analyze it frame by frame. He knew the FBI or somebody with better technicians than Jeffrey would tell them about everything they could find about this video. Just not yet.

"Wait," Jake said. "Don't restart it yet.

He made sure the video was feeding to the laptop.

"Okay. Go."

Jeffrey remained motionless, staring at the laptop screen.

"Jeffrey," urged Ollestad. "Restart it."

She pushed him in the back and he answered with an indignant, "All right!"

The video started. Once again, the flashes of light and dark, three figures with a white light behind them, then the view centered on what they now knew to be the theater screen in Marston's screening room.

Within seconds the picture went from blurry to focused. Once again, the beekeeper in Blood and Honey scampered away from the slow-moving sloths that were the student zombies, infused with deadly honey.

But nobody was really watching the movie. They were waiting for the view to tilt down and reveal the man sitting in the front row.

They were waiting to watch the last few moments of James Marston's life.

The sick anticipation was like one of Jake's nightmares.

A shiny ball bearing is rolling across a linen tablecloth. He sees it from every angle, mostly from tabletop level, watching the ball bearing rolling with a snakelike hiss toward...something. Somewhere, though he couldn't see it was a wrinkle in the tablecloth and he was terrified what would happen when the ball bearing would hit the wrinkle.

The ball bearing got closer and closer. He could see the wrinkle, hear the growing hiss as it got closer. Something bad was about to happen.

Then it went over the wrinkle and as a kid, he would wake up with the bed heaving from his trembling. He'd lie back down and steadied his breathing as his heart rate returned to normal.

Now, he watched as the video once again tilted downward to reveal the man.

It all played out again. No one wanted to stop it. Watching death is like that. You know what's coming and you can't stop it and you don't want to stop it. Because it's already happened. And then. Here it is again.

The light flickered. The beekeeper fled. The metal noose came up from behind. The legs flailed out in hopeless agony.

Once again, Ilsa Pokovich stood triumphant at last, letting her twenty years of hate cascade in wicked laughter.

"Jesus," whispered Mallory when it was over. She could not lose the image of Ruby Everheart squirming in the back row of the screening room, holding up the bear so it recorded everything. It was surreal.

Sharon tapped Jeffrey on his shoulder. He jumped at her touch. "What?"

"Secure it. Do whatever you need to do to make sure what is on there doesn't go away. Hear me?"

Jeffrey nodded and looked down at his black box and the small memory card that protruded slightly from its side. Probably for the first time in his life he experienced the fear that was shared by those older than himself, those old enough to have lived through the vagaries of DOS and blue screens of death and crashed hard drives and the finality of CTRL-ALT-DELETE.

"Does anyone have a plain paper bag?" asked Jeffrey.

He saw Jake's questioning expression.

"Paper bag. No static," he explained.

Jeffrey disconnected the attachment to the laptop with the gentlest of tugs at the connectors.

"Here you go." Mallory handed Jeffrey a brown paper lunch bag.

He opened the top of the bag, stood it up and lifted his black box with the memory card still in place, and lowered it on the bottom of the bag. He slowly folded over the top four or five times. Only then did he sit back. And looked up at Sharon. "We're good."

Sharon took the bag and addressed Jake. "You guys can work with your copy. We'll send this out. I want to squeeze every damn scrap of pixel it's possible to get from this baby. Helluva thing."

"You're able to use your copy?" Sharon asked.

Jake checked the laptop and nodded. "Got it."

Jeffrey, his youthful and fearless bravado no longer present, touched the laptop's screen with a trembling finger and shut off the playback.

He had to clear his throat before he could ask with any clarity. "Again?"

"No," Jake and Sharon said in unison.

"Yes," said Mallory.

They all stared at her. She had lost all color in her face.

"I... saw something."

CHAPTER 56

"Go back."

"Mallory, why?" asked Jake. "We've seen it three times."

Jeffrey looked back to Ollestad, who nodded.

"Okay, back we go."

Mallory turned to Sharon. "What kind of facial recognition software do you have? I never had a chance to work with it."

"Just the standard stuff. All California IT departments have the same. The super stuff is in Virginia. But we do pretty well."

Jeffrey was watching Sharon like an adoring spaniel.

"And Jeffrey here made a few tweaks that allow us to remote access the mainframe for recognition software, as well as several other databases."

Jeffrey beamed as if he had just been fed.

"Remote access? We can connect from here?" asked Jake.

"Sure," said Jeffrey taking over. "Standard protocol, if you know the link point and have the password. Both of which I do." More beaming.

Jake turned to Mallory. "What's the point? We already know who was there. Ilsa, this Nikolai character and sadly, Peter Berlin and Marston, and Ruby was there recording it. That sick freak. We just saw it three times."

"There were figures or something at the beginning," answered Mallory.

Jake shook his head.

"Humor me." Mallory smiled at Jake.

She tapped Jeffrey on the shoulder. "Let's check."

"Then you mean that very beginning, the blurry part, where you can't really identify anybody because the camera is swishing around before the festivities start. That beginning?"

"That part, yes."

"Come on, Jeffrey," said Sharon. "Justify why I'm paying you so much."

"You've mistaken me for someone who is well-paid, but I'll do what I can."

Jeffrey cranked it back to the beginning and ran it in real time. The scene went by incredibly fast then settled on the movie screen.

He took it back again and then forward at half speed.

Then quarter speed.

He stopped it back at the beginning, turned and looked at Mallory. "What do you expect me to do with this? It lasts all of 1.72 seconds."

"Okay, how many frames in 1.72 seconds?"

Jeffrey did a quick calculation in this head. "Just about 50," he said. "About 50 frames of blurred pieces of shit."

"Then we'll go frame by frame. We'll look at each one."

"You say so," sniffed Jeffrey.

"Stan should see this," said Jake. "I'll try him." He slipped out of the office and took Jake dog with him. "Maybe I'll walk him, too."

Mallory gave Jake a half wave, glued as she was to the screen.

"Okay what are we looking for?" asked Sharon, as she slipped behind Mallory and Jeffrey.

Mallory didn't answer. She didn't want to answer. Growing like an ache, like a floor drop, like a feeling unbalanced.

"Just a hunch Sharon. No not even that. I just need to make sure."

"Let me understand," said Sharon, trying to be nonjudgmental. "You want to make sure that inside this blur are the people we see later right?"

Jeffrey smirked.

Mallory nodded then shook her head. "Yes, but no. There's something else, and I don't believe what I just saw."

CHAPTER 57

"How do you do this?" asked Mallory.

"It's very simple," replied Jeffrey. "You want to see what's totally obscured in what the filmmakers call a 'swish-pan', currently defined in this case as a blur of millions of digital pixels over the course of fewer than two seconds."

"Yes, and?"

"Jeffrey don't be an asshole. Tell her," sighed Sharon.

"Okay. Look, you ever heard of the ancient philosopher guy, Zeno?"

"Can we get on with this, please," said Mallory.

Jeffrey ignored her. "Zeno said that… well, there was this arrow see."

"Jeffrey!"

"You wanted me to explain. I'm explaining." Jeffrey turned back to the screen and found the very first frame of the recording. "This arrow. Zeno said that if you look, if you were to look at the arrow in a fraction of time, if you took a picture of the flying arrow, a still picture, in a very, very small slice of time, it would not appear to be moving. It would be like frozen, in time like they say. Basically, at rest."

He expanded the screen until all anyone saw was a group of dots, colored, some sharp, some smeared. He scanned until he found a distinctive cluster of pixels. It had a distinctive shape, like a horseshoe. He circled it and zoomed back out. The circle was now itself a tiny dot. He froze the screen on a second screen.

"What is that?" questioned Mallory.

"So, Zeno's point was, if, at every instant of time, the arrow is at rest, when does it really move. If you break down time into instants and look at the individual instants, the arrow is always at rest."

Jeffrey pointed to the small dot he drew. "That, my friend, is my anchor. I hope."

"Jeffrey!" said a frustrated Mallory. She'd had enough of a flying, not-flying arrow. "What does that have to do with anything?"

"We are," announced Jeffrey, not disguising the pride in his voice. "We are reversing Zeno's process. We are taking motion and we are creating an instant."

Jeffrey moved on to the next digital frame. Once again, he found the little horseshoe shape, captured it and once again froze the screen.

Jake and the dog rejoined Mallory.

"That was quick," said Mallory. She noticed Jake dog was still pacing.

"He wanted to get back here."

"Right."

Jake moved past her. "How much longer?" he asked, prodding Jeffrey on the shoulder.

Jeffrey moved to the next screen. "One point seven two seconds is approximately 50 frames. Should render each frame in a half a minute. We'll see if that's true in this case."

The room was silent because it was obvious now, that hidden in the blur was a person. Anchoring the same spot in each frame, and overlapping the frames, resizing and sharpening as he went, Jeffrey had built an image.

"Run the program," whispered Mallory.

"I'm only on the 28th frame," said Jeffrey.

"Just run it," said Sharon.

"Won't be accurate."

"Run it," said Mallory. She looked at Jake. He raised his eyebrows, not understanding what she was sure was the case. What she was sure would change everything. There had been someone else there when Marston and Peter Berlin were slaughtered. Someone that was never supposed to be there. She did and didn't want to find out. The sinking feeling had settled and suffused her entirely. She felt as if the world was now moving in slow motion. That her every movement, her every thought was smeared over time. Like Zeno. Time was stopping. And her clock would stop forever the moment she knew.

Jeffrey split the screen. On the right side was the image on which he had been working. On the left, he started the recognition program. It scanned through face after face, its own digital blur. Not stopping on any one image, it sped through the search comparing similar points.

It stopped unexpectedly.

The smiling face it froze on blinked. First bright, then dim, then bright. Ten straight lines connected the face to points on the image.

This was the one.

And it was a face familiar to all of them.

"Oh God," exclaimed Sharon. "Carruthers! Carruthers was there."

Mallory and Jake exchanged looks. The full impact just began to dawn.

"Stan!"

CHAPTER 58

It was Carruthers that at once appeared to be asleep. Stan would know him anywhere by his slicked back hair and sloped shoulders.

"Carruthers?" Stan laughed. "What's all this drama?" Stan tried to sound jovial as he parodied Carruthers' conversation. "Whoa. Come to the Marston mansion, you said. Bring the kids. I have something you must see."

Carruthers stood and turned to Stan. Even in the gentle half-light of the Conservatory, Stan could see the man had lost all color. And his hands shook as he tried to grasp the back of the bench.

"Hey. Carruthers? What's wrong?"

And that's when a man stepped from the shadows.

It took a moment for Stan to realize who he was seeing.

"You?" whispered Stan.

"Yeah," sneered the man "Me and him."

"What is… this?' Stan asked. His words echoed and instantly solidified the strange dynamic between the three of them.

Stan needed just a second to catch up and to remember where he had encountered the man. At first, he thought it might be one of the crew that took care of the grounds, the landscapers. Then it came it to him. The first day he and Rodriguez's crew had searched the place. They'd been interrupted by the owner of the company that cleaned the place for Marston. Blue Bird Cleaning or something like that. The guy was a cleaner. A janitor. But he wasn't dressed in his fancy white suit like before. He looked vaguely out of place in a leather jacket and black turtleneck. And the gun. When it had appeared, Stan didn't know, but it was casually leveled at Stan's center mass.

"So, what is it then?" asked Stan of Carruthers, trying to sound as if he didn't understand and they all might walk out of here, victims of a tense misunderstanding, and be on their carefree way.

When Carruthers didn't answer, Stan continued with the pretense. "So, the janitor here found something?"

"Oh God," mumbled Carruthers. "Don't…"

The Cleaner shoved Carruthers aside and watched, amused, as Carruthers slumped to the bench.

That slow-motion moment of clarity made it obvious to Stan. It wasn't Carruthers who was in charge, it was the Cleaner. And they wouldn't all be walking out. They wouldn't all be just going on their way.

The Cleaner smiled. He turned to Carruthers, who seemed to be staring at his trembling hands.

"Good job getting him here," said the Cleaner. Carruthers had no time to respond because, in one motion, the Cleaner raised the gun and held it to Carruthers' head. Carruthers flinched and tried to back away, but the Cleaner kept the gun pressed to Carruthers' temple.

Carruthers' eyes went scared wide and he tried to form words, but nothing came.

"Now," said the Cleaner to Stan. "Your gun. On the ground. Two fingers."

"Why?"

"Because we'll all be more comfortable that way."

"I think not."

The Cleaner's smile vanished. "I said, two fingers only. Gun on the ground."

Mechanically, Stan unholstered his gun and slid it between them. The clatter of metal sliding, bouncing on the concrete floor was sharp and final.

The Cleaner picked it up, hefted it, then shoved his own gun into a back pocket.

"Now, we wait until my screwup of an assistant drags those two kids and my prize in here and we'll be done."

Stan couldn't take his eyes off the Cleaner and Carruthers, whose shaky pallor contrasted with the red roses and green ferns surrounding him.

"Then we'll be done," repeated the Cleaner with quiet certainty.

And then he put a bullet through Ash Carruthers' head.

CHAPTER 59

Michael dropped the backpack and put his ear to the frosted glass doors.

"M, what is it?

Michael didn't answer but pushed through the glass doors with both hands and froze when he saw the two men. Jessie was right behind. She bumped into him and when she too saw the men, she grabbed Michael's arm.

"We tried to stay in the car like you asked" Michael started but he was out of breath. "But there was that little prick and he..."

That's when he saw the gun. And it wasn't in Detective Wyld's hand.

It was held by a heavily built, bristle-haired foreign-looking guy. It was funny because to Michael he looked like he'd been a wrestler on Saturday morning TV. Some guy named the 'Russian Strangler' or the 'Hungarian Torturer' and now he was too fat and ugly to get in the ring. And he had a gun. And it was pointed at him and Detective Wyld. And they were in a huge greenhouse. And the aroma of growing things surrounded them. And it was warm and pleasant. And there was this hulk with a gun. And they were supposed to be going to Arizona.

It was all too much for Michael.

Fuck this shit.

"What's going on?" he demanded, turning to Stan. "Who is this asshole, and what's his problem?"

"He wants your backpack," Stan replied slowly. "He wants what's inside."

"Screw it! He can't have it. It's mine," answered Michael, spewing words, still trying to figure out what the hell was happening or what movie he was starring in because the unreality of it all was overwhelming.

"I mean, really, who is this dickwad then? Some dumb muscle? And what's with the gun?" Michael raised his chin. "You planning to pistol whip me if I don't give it to you?"

The Cleaner sneered, revealing two broken front teeth. He stood aside, revealing Carruthers' body, collapsed and twisted on the bench, his blood draining out and staining the flagstone floor.

Michael moved Jessie behind him. She buried her face in Michael's back. He could feel her shaking.

The man came to within inches of Michael.

"No, you smart-ass shit," the Cleaner said quietly. "I will break your sister's fingers one by one until you beg to tell me. Then I will shoot your tiny little balls off. One at a time."

Michael's gaze went from the carnage that was Carruthers to the gun in the Cleaner's hand, and up to Stan.

Stan exchanged glances with Michael. It was a look that sunk deep into Michael's gut.

The air had changed, the silence only broken by Stan's voice, delivered in as smooth a tone as Michael had ever heard.

"You can see the kid doesn't have it. If anyone has it, it would be the Davis police department. They confiscated the kids' stuff when they arrested them. I can help arrange to get whatever it is you think is yours, if you can show proof of ownership."

Michael stared at Stan, marveling at the performance, realizing he was buying time.

In one motion, the Cleaner backhanded Stan with the gun barrel. It struck Stan along his cheek. He flinched but recovered, bristling.

"No matter," murmured the Cleaner. "Police don't have it. It is in the vehicle you came in, I'm sure. You were seen carrying it out of the hospital and placing it in the vehicle with these two. It will be brought to me shortly."

"And who do you expect to do that?" sneered Michael, summoning as much bravado as he could. He figured he could stall as easily as their detective.

"You don't mean the little greasy insect of a runt who I've locked into dead Ruby's trailer. That turd? You're expecting him to do anything? Last I heard was him bawling his head off as he banged on the door. Guess he didn't want his fortunes told that much."

The Cleaner's expression never changed but Michael's head was banging in warning as he felt the dead ball of inevitability begin to roll down the hill. Stan, too, knew they had passed that point, probably sealed all their fates when he had pushed through the Conservatory doors.

The Cleaner once again approached Michael. Stan held out his arm across Michael, as much to tell him to shut up as to protect him.

"It will happen this way," began the Cleaner. "There will be a fire. It will be an extremely hot and uncomfortable fire. You will suffer greatly and die."

"Sure, asshole," answered Michael. "You'll burn this place down? I don't think so."

The Cleaner looked conciliatory. "I won't burn this down. This is my home."

"Your home?" asked Stan. "Your home?"

The Cleaner looked straight at Stan. "Those who come after will believe you committed suicide and started the fire."

"Why would I do that?" asked Stan.

The Cleaner smiled and shrugged. He moved toward Carruthers' body, scraped his boot through the pooling blood, then used a palm leaf to wipe it off.

The Cleaner raised Stan's gun, examining it. "Looks like you shot him. Your gun. Your bullet. Your dead Captain."

Stan tried to speak without saliva. His words came out dry and wooden. "Not believable."

The Cleaner continued, "You shot him, then committed suicide. Who knows why? Who knows why anything happens. But they will believe. And I will tell you something else they will come to believe. They will know your great Carruthers was, as you say, a slimy lizard. They will discover how many investigations he steered into nothingness. How much evidence he found that just... vanished. How many people died when he just didn't have the brains to manufacture the evidence. He was a tool, a stupid one."

Stan stood silently as connections formed. Carruthers. He held his breath because he remembered. He remembered what he had been searching for on his computer the night Ilsa Pokovich had appeared.

He'd come from meeting Phil Ginger. He'd wanted to check something out.

He'd pulled right up to where the Marston car had been found. Abandoned car on Jones road.

He'd trudged through the bushes into a nearby neighborhood. One that looked damn familiar. He'd been here before. He recognized the distinctive streetlights. He'd been to a party here. A company party. This was when he first became a detective. And the host lived in this neighborhood.

And the host had been Captain Ash Carruthers.

He remembered he'd been searching for Carruthers' address in the company roster when Ilsa Pokovich had materialized.

"You would start the fire and commit suicide because, with your own weapon, you killed your superior." The Cleaner nodded toward Michael and Jessie. "And these two."

Stan knew now who had killed Phil Ginger. Who had orchestrated the beheading of James Marston. Who had slaughtered Peter Berlin. Who had made his own sister, Ilsa Pokovich, walk into the OID office alone.

This wasn't the Cleaner, the man who cleaned the Marston property. It was what Jake had warned him about. The Bearded Lady.

Stan was staring at the last Pokovich, Nikolai Pokovich.

And this will end very badly.

CHAPTER 60

With his steel-toed boot, Nikolai Pokovich gave a solid kick to the back of Ash Carruthers' head. He put his boot on Carruthers' face, distorting the features.

"As I said, he was a tool. A money-taking, money-making tool." Nikolai held up his hands, weighing the good and bad. "He took my money to start a ridiculous investigation against someone he knew to be not guilty of anything and he took my money to stop investigations. Sound like something you may know?"

It was hard to not watch Pokovich's boot grind into Carruthers' nose, surely splitting the cartilage inside.

"What do you mean?" Stan managed.

"You think I was going to let my brother be arrested?"

"Your brother?"

Pokovich continued as if he had all the time in the world.

"Yes, sure, my brother was a crazy kid hunter. He loved 'em. Loved the little ones. You saw his collection in the woods. Pretending to be this Ruby whatever fortune teller. A silly disguise I told him. Yet, he pulled it off. Everyone believed he was some gypsy. Just some old woman. You probably thought he was a suspect."

Stan nodded. "Yes. He was."

"Except for my bitch, your Captain of Sacramento Police, my Carruthers, who shut down the investigation, deflected suspicion. Of course, you believe my brother was guilty. Naturally you do, because I'm sure for certain he did do all those things you thought he did. He loved them. Kids. Did what he wanted and just kept hiding them."

Pokovich shrugged and pushed down harder with his boot.

"But this guy finally saw our family's side of the story. Of course, it wasn't until after I paid him, he realized my brother couldn't have done it." Pokovich leaned down and regarded Carruthers' smeared features. "Didn't you?"

When the dead head of Carruthers didn't respond, Pokovich shrugged. "This guy put a down payment on some summer cabin, I believe, with what I paid him to clear my brother."

Stan found he couldn't breathe. He remembered Carruthers questioning Ruby Everheart back in the original investigation. Carruthers shaking his head after the interview. 'Not our guy' he'd said. 'Not our guy'. The Olive Park murder investigation went nowhere, died from lack of suspects. Driven to a dead end by Carruthers.

"I see you do believe it." Pokovich removed his boot and nudged Carruthers' cheek. "He wanted to retire. In the end, I thought that he would be more valuable to me as upper management. Funny, huh, some coincidence. Those above him died and my guy here rose in your ranks."

Stan stood stock still as a new solution roiled in his head.

"Marston? What about James Marston?" asked Stan.

"Forget him. Nothing. He needed to go. What he did to my sister. He's nothing now."

"And this guy." Pokovich casually lifted his boot then pressed down, grinding his heel into the side of Carruthers' face.

"This man was stupid, like a stupid pet. Easily broken. Easily led. He took the bit into his mouth like an obedient jackass."

"Peter Berlin and Phil Ginger."

Pokovich shrugged. "Trash. They were meddling trash. But the fire, yes you will start it, and I assure you, you will die. By your own hand they will believe," continued Pokovich. "You would do this because you would not be shamed. You will panic. You will need to cover your heinous crime by taking very special care of the two children who would implicate you because they saw what you did."

"You're mistaken if you believe anyone will buy this," Stan stated.

"Now, move. The bag please," said Pokovich, addressing Michael. "You get it from the vehicle. Your sister and Mr. Detective will stay safe with me."

Michael looked at Stan who nodded.

Michael moved to the double doors, pushed open one of the doors and retrieved the backpack from where he'd dropped it. He moved back to Stan.

Pokovich's eyes widened. "Clever. Now give it to me."

Michael regripped the only strap that was left on the ragged backpack.

"Why?"

"In it is what I need. You know this."

"It has nothing you need," said Stan.

"Yet, he guards it."

"Of course. It's his." Stan calculated the time it would take to get Michael and Jessie back through the double doors. It was their only way out. However, if they tried, not all would make it.

The gun was raised. "The bag. Now."

Stan turned to Michael. "Give me the backpack Michael." At the same time, he mouthed 'Ready to run.'

Stan faced Pokovich and hefted the bag, jerking it up and down. Something inside the backpack rose and fell with weight.

Pokovich's eyes shone. "Hand it here. No, no, slide it over." He pulled a shiny serrated knife out of a scabbard attached to the side of his belt, ready to cut open the backpack.

Stan ignored the instruction. "I'll show you there's nothing you need in here." In one motion Stan uncovered the back flap and turned the backpack upside down.

"No! Do not drop it!"

While all eyes were on the sweaters and jackets and socks and underwear and apples and yogurt containers as they fell one by one into the Carruthers' pooling blood, Stan threw himself at Pokovich.

"Run!" he yelled to Michael.

The knife, when it slashed, ripped into Stan's leg, but his shoulder block sent Pokovich stumbling back, headfirst over the unmoving body of Carruthers. He careened backward and slid, flailing, down into the lily pond.

Stan pushed himself up and limped toward the double doors and hit the light switch that threw the whole conservatory into moonlit dimness.

He turned to grab Michael and Jessie to push them through the doors only to find Michael had run the opposite way and had pulled Jessie behind one of the oversize concrete planters.

"Shit."

He only had seconds to join them behind the planter before Pokovich recovered.

CHAPTER 61

"You were supposed to run," hissed Stan.

"We did."

"You were supposed to run out the door."

"This was closer."

"Now we're trapped."

"Here," said Michael, handing Stan's Glock back.

Stan looked at it as if he'd never seen something so beautiful, then back to Michael.

"I thought we might need it. Asshole dropped it when you hit him." Michael moved back from Stan when he saw the blood.

"You're bleeding! He got you?'

Stan waved the question away. "Nothing."

Michal watched the stain and like a leak that couldn't be plugged, it grew bigger. Drop after insistent drop hit the concrete floor.

"It's not nothing-"

"Shh," Stan cut him off.

The sound of a new magazine being loaded and the slide racked was unmistakable.

A pissed-off Nicholai Pokovich roared out. "I guess I'll have to kill you with my own gun, starting with your dick so you will have nothing to live for and will welcome my final shot. Yes?"

There was no response from Stan.

Pokovich's voice echoed off the glass. "Cop! Send out the kids. I won't hurt them. Right away, anyway. Bastards."

He took a few steps forward.

"Nothing? Okay. I can wait five minutes."

Even though no one was watching he made a show of checking an imaginary watch.

"The answer to your question is five minutes. The question is how long to bleed out when someone severs your femoral artery with this" Pokovich held up the blade, flicked off the blood that clung to it, then held it up so he could admire his distorted reflection.

"It was the serrations that did it. Sure, the blade is so razor sharp that if someone were to, I don't know, nail your hand to the floor and run the edge across your thumb it would slice off the ridges of your fingerprints."

Pokovich seemed to remember where he was. He raised his voice. "If I'm not mistaken the ends of your good old femoral artery are now inches apart and as ragged as a dog's chew rag. Can't put Humpty back together I'm afraid. So yeah, five minutes. Though by now we're down to four. Maybe less if you feel that panic coming on."

He took another step forward in the growing darkness. The moonlight had become muted with the growing cloud cover.

Behind the planter, Stan tried to arrange himself in a better position, one that would allow him to keep a tight hand on his leg.

"Are we going to die?" asked Jessie.

Stan, leaning in with all the pressure he could put on his thigh, could feel the rapid pulse, his heart having found an open and easy path to freedom. The blood streamed from under his leg.

He shook his head. "No, hon. We're going to get out of this."

Michael looked from Stan's leg to Jessie.

A disbelieving tear rolled down her cheek.

Michael scrambled to the side of the planter, cupped his hands to throw his voice.

"You call an ambulance shithead and we'll come out."

"Ah. If it isn't Mr. If-I-had-a-shovel-Cooper. Trying to negotiate, are we? Nice try. Though we are in the Conservatory and I'm sure there is a shovel around here, as that seems to be your weapon of choice."

"Yeah. Well, your brother wasn't too happy to die like a blubbering dog with a shovel stuck up his ass."

The shot ricocheted off the concrete planter and shards stung Michael's face, cutting his chin and cheek. He fell back against Stan.

"You will pay for what you did to my brother," the voice from the darkness shrieked. "You will pay with pain, you little pissant. You will die in screaming agony. I'll cut a hole in your head, hang you upside down you little shit. You hear me? Where is the fucking bear!"

"Eat shit and die," muttered Michael.

Stan put a hand on Michael's arm and shook his head.

"Shh."

Michael wiped the blood off his chin. "What?" he whispered.

Stan sighed and tried to hand Michael his gun, but he couldn't lift his arm.

"I'm coming for you, you little shit," boomed Pokovich. "And when I kill you, I'll watch the cop die in a puddle of blood and piss and then I'll do to your sister what I'm sure my brother had intended."

Michael started to rise, to take the bait, but Stan tightened his grip on Michael's arm to hold him down.

"Take it," Stan whispered as he pushed his useless arm out of the way and pulled the gun from his holster. He forced it into Michael's hands.

Michael's eyes widened. "I can't shoot. I've never shot anything." He dropped the gun.

"You will," whispered Stan. His eyes closed as he paused to breathe.

Michael stared at the gun.

"You will because you have to," repeated Stan.

Stan fished around, then pulled out two rounds. Like a priest at a communion, with a cupped hand, he gave it to Michael.

The copper jacket and dull lead sat lonely in the faint moonlight. The wet blood on them shone black.

Pokovich's voice echoed. "I would give you a count to ten like in the movies, but you have little time. Your life is draining out and running into the sewer. I can wait. It will not be long."

"You can load it?" breathed Stan.

Michael nodded. "I watched you, but…"

"You can do it," sighed Stan. "You can. You have to."

Michael, before he could do anything with them, dropped both onto the concrete floor. Before they disappeared under the planter's edge, he retrieved them. With Stan's nodded encouragement and using all the strength he could, he forced the two rounds into the magazine. When he was finally able to pull the slide back and forth, the sound of it resounded against the glass walls.

"Yes, yes, reload," shouted Pokovich. "Reload and try to shoot me. You are a wounded animal. You will fade and die. I am patient."

"Two shots now," breathed Stan.

"But…"

"Two shots. Remember."

"What do I do? How…"

Stan looked into the boy's eyes. "You kill him. Because if you don't…" The rest withered, unsaid.

"I'm waiting," said Pokovich, nearer now. "Or give up the bear and I'll give you a count of three. Run anywhere you like. Anywhere. I dare you. Hey! I know all about you Cooper boy. Wet your pants because you couldn't save your Mummy. I know you. I own you. I own your life. You're nothing!"

"Stay low," murmured Stan. "Aim up. Center mass." He had lost all color Michael noted.

Michael tried to stop his hand from shaking. He was cold all over.

"What are you going to do?" he hissed.

Stan looked up from his blood-soaked pants and tried a valiant smile.

"Jessie and I are going to give you two extra seconds. We're going to distract him from over here." He raised his chin and indicated toward the door.

"You can't leave cover," hissed Michael. "Not with Jess. Please. Stay here. When he comes around the corner, I can...shoot."

"If he comes around the corner, you won't have time. We have to distract him, so you can fire."

Michael shook his head. "Leave Jess here, then. You go that way, then I'll go this way. She'll be safe."

"Michael, we can't leave her." He gave Michael the look that communicated exactly what would happen if she was found alone. If they both failed.

"We have to try. You know that."

Michael tried swallowing but there was nothing there.

"Listen," panted Stan. "This will not be how you imagine it. It will be different. Expect him not to be right where you think or where you want. Focus. Embrace the difference and expect it. Keep your finger alongside the guard, not on the trigger 'til you're ready to fire. You can do this. I know."

Michael picked up the gun.

"Finger on side of the guard 'til you're gonna fire."

Michael nodded. It was all a dream. Stan floated before him. His head swam. This was not happening. From somewhere he heard himself agree. "Okay. But you can't move."

Stan pushed himself up on with his elbows.

"Can't run the 440... but I'll give you two, maybe four seconds."

Michael looked skeptical.

"I'm good. Michael. I'm good. You do what you must do. And whatever happens, run. Don't stop. If you get him or not. You run."

"But…" And then Michael realized. Then he saw it. Then he saw what he never saw with his father. What he never saw before his father killed his mother. What he finally saw in his mother's dying eyes. How things were going to end. How they had to end. It was as inevitable as breathing, and as dying. It was not only the way it would be, it was the way it had to be.

This time Michael put his hand on Stan's arm. "I'm sorry."

CHAPTER 62

"I'm counting!" came the shrillness from the dark. "And guess what I found. A shovel!" The grating of a metal shovel head scraping on the concrete floor.

"What are we going to do?" whispered Jessie.

Stan winced as Michael pulled him up further against the planter.

"You go," breathed Stan. "Get ready. In position."

Jessie was crying softly. "What is it M? What are we going to do?"

Stan answered before Michael could.

"That door over there?"

Jessie turned. "Way over there?"

"That's it. You and I are going out through that door."

The voice was closer now. "What do you say, big Sacramento detective?"

Jessie looked back at Michael.

"M?"

Michael wiped his mouth with the back of his hand. He nodded at Jessie. Tried to give a reassuring smile. Couldn't.

"We can't stay here because as soon as he thinks we don't have any strength left, he'll come around the corner. You go with him, okay. Do what he says."

The shovel scraped closer. "Oh, come out come out wherever you are."

Michael steadied Stan so he was leaning forward, then helped him so Stan was on his hands and knees. His head hung down and he stared at the blood pumping in an inevitable stream, pooling next to his knee. It was slick black, fringed with swirling stars that clouded his vision.

"Gotta go," Stan managed. "You ready?" His head still hung down.

Michael moved to the other side of the planter. He nodded.

Jessie held onto Stan's arm and whispered in his ear. "He says yes, he's ready."

Stan managed a nod. "Stay low," he whispered to Jessie. "No matter what, get to that door, keep going."

"Without you?"

Stan raised his head. "We'll meet up later."

Before Jessie understood, Stan put a gentle hand on her arm and lurched forward keeping her to his right, toward the wall.

The first bullet caught Stan in his back, spinning him. He dropped to the floor after only two steps.

"No!" yelled Jessie as she tried to pull Stan to his feet.

Pokovich advanced with a gun in one hand, shovel in the other.

"No!" screamed Jessie.

"Shithead!" yelled Michael raising up from the other side of the planter.

Pokovich turned in time as the bullet glanced off the shovel blade, jerking it back, out of his hand.

"You missed you pathetic shit," recovered Pokovich. He swung the gun back to Stan.

Stan raised his arm toward the door. "Go. Now" he panted to Jessie. "Go." The second bullet hit his shoulder forcing him face down.

Jessie stood unmoving, frozen behind Stan, as Pokovich approached.

"Out of blood. Out of bullets, you're out of time you piece of shit," he fumed. "Now the pain."

Stan tried to rise but collapsed onto his back, arms useless at his sides. He didn't hear Jessie. He didn't hear Michael. Sound had left him.

A shovel, point down, high above his head, blocked the reappearance of moonlight.

"No!!" yelled Michael.

Pokovich paused, shovel at full height.

"No!"

Pokovich turned. "What? What you gonna do Cooper boy?"

"I'm going to shoot you."

Nikko smiled. "Your life is a meaningless turd now. You're nothing. You're pain waiting to happen."

"Go Jessie," yelled Michael. "Go now!"

"Yeah, go little Jessie. Run to that door," growled Nikko. "Run to that door if you want. It's locked. Like all the rest. Soon as I smash your brother's face in, soon as I run this shovel into the cop's neck, I'll join you and probably slit your throat. Or, stay and watch. Watch what real life is. Watch and see what agony looks like. Watch as…"

Michael's shot, when it came, ripped through Pokovich's side, propelling him back into the nearest clump of beach grass. He stumbled, finally collapsing into a sitting position against Stan. The shovel beside him.

Disbelieving, Pokovich stared first at his side, then at Michael. "You were out," he managed. "You had… nothing."

Michael lowered the gun.

"You… little… fuck," panted Pokovich. He pushed himself up but instead of turning to Michael, he swiveled and grabbed Jessie's arm, pulling her to him. He stood, swaying, with Jessie before him, seemingly stronger than before, as if the shot had only energized him.

Hoping Stan was wrong and that there was salvation in the gun. Michael raised it and tried to pull pulled the trigger. twice, three times. Nothing.

Pokovich remained standing. "Yeah, yeah, little Cooper boy. Now what? I'm gonna mess her up 'for I kill her. I really don't think she's gonna like what I do."

Michael started for Pokovich. He glanced down at the shovel.

"Yeah?" mocked a wounded Pokovich. "Try it. I will fucking eat you alive."

It happened fast. With all the strength left in him, Stan swung his good leg and connected with the Pokovich's knees.

He went down, flailing. Jessie went tumbling away.

Michael grabbed the shovel and advanced.

Pokovich crabbed backward with one hand gripping his bloody side.

Jessie's fists tightened as she watched Michael raise the shovel.

Pokovich looked up at Michael.

"I know you Cooper boy. I know-"

Jessie's eyes widened as the shovel came screaming in. Pokovich raised his arm in defense. The shovel broke it in two with a wet crack.

Michael raised the shovel head up as high as he could. It happened like a nightmare. Like a release. It was all so right. It was all to be finished. In slow motion. The blue moonlight on Pokovich's face. The smell of the roses. The feel of the shovel. His mother's dying smile. His father's mocking face.

He brought it screaming down. He felt the handle break as the shovel head cut down into Pokovich's neck.

He stared, surprised, at the handle in his hands. But he knew. With the broken handle he knew. He knew to be finished, where it had to go.

With all his might, he brought the broken handle down into the chest of Nikolai Pokovich. He felt it break through ribs. Like a lurid dream, he saw the blood erupt. A crimson fountain of desperation.

He staggered back only then hearing Jessie's screams for him to get somebody. To get somebody. To get help.

He made it through the conservatory's glass doors when he remembered the cell phone in the lining of his jacket. Fumbling with the phone, he found the number and hit Send.

Stan saw her face. The face of a little girl. She was speaking, though he couldn't hear. She was stroking his face though he couldn't feel.

'*Michael, help him…*'

His vision narrowed tenderly, a soft dark mist advanced.

The clerestory, the moon, the stars, all the things he wanted to do, all he should've done. A soft hiss of gentle drops washed his face.

He had saved her.

'*Please…*'

With all his strength, he tells her. She nods.

Her tears. The rain.

And then, his want was gone, his needs fulfilled, his job done.

'*I'm sorry*'.

He was ready. Ready for the place where Bea's soup was never too hot, where single malt was always like the first taste, where cancer was just a word, and the rain, like thankful tears, was always warm and refreshing.

It took as long as the crash of a wave, the flit of a hummingbird, the nod of a friend, for him to surrender. When he did, a soft and knowing hand wiped away his worries, cleansed him of all regret, and soothed and soothed and soothed him until it was over.

CHAPTER 63

Jake couldn't push the pedal any further.

The Corvette raced down the narrow road that led to the Marston mansion, the same place only weeks ago that he and Mallory had come to investigate.

They were almost to the entrance.

"Hold on."

"Jake!" yelled Mallory. "Stop! I'll get the gate. I'll get it."

"Jake!"

Mallory only had time to brace against the crash. The low-slung car met the gate halfway up, sheared it off at its lower hinges. The gate's determined metal pickets ripped up the Corvette's hood, gouging along with iron insistence. Red paint and scored fiberglass peeled off as iron fingers raked the windshield, then slit through the soft top.

Mallory grabbed the dog and pulled him down just in time as they made it through.

As they accelerated up the drive, she looked back between the seats. The gate hung lifelessly askew with the red scrapings as the only evidence it had fought it all.

She wasn't prepared when they crashed over the new the low rock wall. She hit the dashboard with her shoulder and felt something rip inside.

Jake braked to a hard stop, just missing Carruthers' car.

"You stay," Jake said to the dog, as both he and Mallory rolled out of the vehicle.

Jake, with his gun drawn, pulled open the heavy front door. Mallory cradled her right arm as they both rushed in and quickly panic-stopped. They couldn't see anything. The whole house was dead dark. When he hesitated, Mallory blew past him.

"This way."

"Sure?"

"I have a feeling."

Up steps, through rooms, down a hallway, they both pushed through the double conservatory doors at the same time.

Jake started to call out to Stan, but Mallory stopped him.

"Listen," she said.

Jake held his breath so long his laboring lungs and thumping heart would let them hear what he dreaded to hear.

In the distance somewhere among the innocent hibiscus and ferns and cymbidium orchids came the sound of a child plaintively sobbing.

CHAPTER 64

Sharon Ollestad stood behind Jeffrey. They'd been in the same position for three hours, both mesmerized and disgusted by what they were seeing.

There were over 300 separate files, each holding one or two videos. The resolution was on the low end, the lighting haphazard, the locations... almost always the same. A couch. In what appeared to be a house trailer.

The background audio was always a cooing, cajoling grooming drool.

The subject on the screen was always a child.

Each series of videos showed the progression of a relationship between whoever was off camera and the child.

When the video became too specific, they stopped, logged it and moved on.

Plagued by the gross perversity of what was on the bear's recorder, they continued. At about the time they should've been hungry for dinner, they found the faces that matched the pictures Mallory had given them of Michael and Jessie Cooper.

"It's them," murmured Sharon. She held up first Jessie's picture, then after a few minutes, Michael came on the screen. Jeffrey stopped the playback, so she could match the still frame with Michael's picture.

"Jeffrey, you okay?" asked Sharon.

Jeffrey stayed seated, though he wanted to get up and flee.

"There are so many. I guess I don't know. I never thought. I mean I didn't realize people could be so... bad. Not just bad but... sick. I'm just an IT guy. Most think I'm a nerd. That I don't know what's up. Don't know what people do to each other. I've seen a lot. So, yeah, I know people do things to each other. I know that. But this." He pushed back from the table. "This. This is just... shit."

"Just shit," said Sharon. "At least, these two made it. They were meant to disappear."

Jeffrey nodded the same time Sharon's cell went off.

"Mallory?" She listened.

When she didn't say anything for half a minute, Jeffrey swiveled in his seat to see she had turned off the phone and was wiping tears from her face.

Danni Harness liked working at night. There was only one assistant on the night shift and as a bonus, on night duty there weren't as many bureaucratic assholes calling, interrupting and skewing her evening, usually while she had some poor unfortunate cut open and was involved in inventorying what was there, what wasn't, what was damaged and what was still intact.

She finished with the homeless guy who had everything intact except his right leg. At least it shortened the exam.

She straightened up and lit a homemade cheroot while her assistant brought in the next client, a woman who had decided she'd enough of the shit she was going through.

While she was leaning back against the wall watching her assistant open the body bag, the night receptionist came down, lightly knocked on the door frame.

Danni motioned her in, but the receptionist hung around the door. In her hand, she had a note.

Danni's eyes went from the note to the woman's face.

The woman shook her head.

Danni pushed off and met the woman at the doorway. She took the note. The woman immediately turned and headed back down the hall. The assistant, done removing the body bag and setting out the instruments his boss would need, left as well.

Danni unfolded the note. She reread it twice, crumpled it into a ball and dropped it. She moved to the doorway, turned off the light, shut the exam door and, crossed the hall into her office. She collapsed into her seat behind her desk and sat in the dark, feeling more tired than she'd ever felt before.

Susan got Mallory's call at midnight.

She didn't remember dressing. Didn't remember driving but made it to the Marston mansion in twenty minutes. She'd forgotten her SacPD I.D. and the two guys working on prying the busted main gate loose didn't know her. But, after spending two minutes helping them, she pretended her phone vibrated.

"Sorry, they need me up there," she told them. "You're on your own."

She sprinted up the dark drive arriving amidst a mad sea of flashing lights. It seemed as if all of SacPD had turned up.

After asking someone she knew about Mallory's whereabouts, she was informed that Mallory had left.

She plopped down on a low rock wall and watched in awe at the unbelievable scene before her. It was dawn before she left.

In the morning, Rodriguez, after reading Jake's summary of what had happened at the Marston mansion, as well as what they'd found on the recorder hidden in the bear, notified the Mayor of Sacramento.

Within an hour, he had Samuels, Carruthers' right-hand man, standing before him.

It took five minutes for the Mayor to put Samuels on suspension, pending an investigation. He informed the stricken Samuels that he was barred from his own office and that his work and personal computers, as well as both his cell phones, were being confiscated and would be swept.

Pleading innocent of knowing anything about Carruthers' activities and frankly disbelieving of what he was being told, he left the Mayor's office, feeling that special form of nakedness that comes from becoming suddenly and inexplicably powerless.

Days later, in a locked day room in the Sunnyvale nursing facility, one of the young aides sauntered up to the near withdrawn figure of Jane Cooper. The aide slid a newspaper onto the table and pointed to the headline.

"Didn't you tell me you was takin' care of them two kids? Didn't you tell us all that you was their aunty or something?"

When Jane didn't respond, the nurse tapped her finger on the faces of Michael and Jessie staring out from the front page. They were old school pictures and not representative of what they looked like.

"Right here. Thems two." She tapped again.

Aunt Jane looked up finally, drew the paper closer to her. She stared at Michael and Jessie for a long time.

"Well," demanded the aide. "Ain't that them?"

Aunt Jane settled back and returned to watching Oprah on the silent TV monitor.

"Don't know 'em."

Squinty Saunders read the headline before he even got to the elevator. In fact, he stopped in the middle of the building's lobby. He searched out the nearest chair to finish the article. The nearest chair was at the shoeshine stand.

He had received a shine on both shoes before he finished.

Had he had anything resembling a conscience, as an attorney, he might've felt bad for not disclosing everything he knew about the Marston property and ownership thereof when he'd been asked.

He pulled the paper close and examined his shoes. Satisfied, he handed the paper and ten bucks to the shiner and caught the next elevator, all the while wondering if someone in the Marston debacle needed a good lawyer.

Across town, Dr. Avery closed his office door and caught the elevator. He exited the building in the same direction he and Michael had taken the first day Michael had come to see him. He went to the same coffee shop, bought a latte.

He crossed the street to the park and settled on to the same bench he and Michael Copper had sat on watching the inline skaters, mostly girls, whiz around the pond.

He wondered if he had helped Michael at all.

In Arizona, Shippen Travers got off the phone with a nice lady from the Sacramento Police Human Resource department.

The arrangements were made. There would be a car and an officer to meet him when he arrived.

CHAPTER 65

Jake stepped forward. He replaced and smoothed his tie that was teased by the spring breeze. He scanned those surrounding the casket.

Representatives from North, South and Central commands along with Citrus Heights, Rocklin, Elk Grove and, Roseville flanked them. County Sheriff, Highway Patrol, even the District Attorney showed.

Every member of Robbery-Homicide stood stoically

The group from IT hovered off to the side. Danni from Forensics stood alone, her countenance set. She raised her chin so no one saw the quiver.

Jake dared to glance at Mallory. She had her sprained arm through Beatrice's for support. Her other hand held Jake's leash. He saw Mallory had tied a black kerchief around Jake's collar.

There was no way for her to wipe away the gentle tears that graced her cheeks.

Finally, in front was Michael Cooper and his sister, Jessie. Michael's arm surrounded his sister. The two white roses they held swayed in the spring breeze.

Jake removed the frayed paper from his jacket and turned to the crowd, and that's when he saw the glints of the cap bills of six hundred of Sacramento's finest, standing at attention.

Jake lowered his eyes. He found it hard to swallow as he stepped closer to the casket. The edges of the draped American flag rippled gently.

There was no cross. That was the way Stan wanted it.

No pastor. No reverend. No one to represent the great unknowable, to repeat platitudes that held little sway with the life that Stan lived.

His belief was in himself, his family, his partners, his duty, his service, his integrity, his sacrifice.

Instead, resting atop the flag was Stan's shield and three shot glasses. Two brimmed with Stan's favorite Speyburn.

The third was unfilled.

Jake opened the folded paper. The words blurred before him. He closed the paper and replaced it into his jacket pocket.

When he spoke, it was clear and proud.

"And so it is on a day just like today that we gather at the water's edge for, today, our sailor makes his final trip. In the gloaming, he pushes off from the shore and because he has not yet felt the wind and cannot yet raise his sails, he rows with strong determination.

"Every now and then he stops and yells to us who remain on the shore.

"'Remember the time we all...' and, 'Didn't we have fun with...'

"And we do remember.

"And we realize how blessed we were to have had him with us.

"As he gets further away, his voice grows fainter with distance and we strain to hear, and to remember, for we understand at once we shall not hear his voice again. We see him stand and wave. It is for us he is waving, to let us know the wind has filled his sails now, and he has his course.

"We are reminded of what a big man he is... in stature and in heart. Unseen and unknown, except to themselves, are the many lives he made better because he cared. In his wake, our sailor leaves a generous legacy, a deep and respectful compassion for others. A legacy that will endure, for a true inspiration never, ever, dies and remains in that quiet place of the heart.

"Our sailor gives us a final salute and slowly turns away just before the horizon claims him and we see him wave to those on a distant, unseen shore. Those who have gone before will now welcome him home with enthusiasm and gratitude for they know the treasure he brings and the bounty he carries. A bounty of love and quiet determination.

"And so it is on a day just like today that doubt in ourselves and in our own lives, and our continuity can be set aside."

"Because now, as we turn away from the water's edge we see at our feet, a bottle. Inside a piece of sail has been torn. On it, a note, written to us."

Jake paused. He felt the breeze and the wetness on his cheeks. He cleared his throat.

"For you see, thinking only of the anguish of those he left behind, on a piece of sail our sailor has written three words.

"All is well."

Jake stepped to the casket. He placed his hand on the side of the casket. Mallory released Beatrice's arm and joined him on the opposite side. They smiled at each other, knowing that this was the final time the three of them would meet and as usual, Stan was already ahead of them.

They raised their glasses. Together they clinked the side of Stan's empty one. Locking eyes, they downed the drink in one swallow.

Jake quietly arranged the three empty glasses in a row. Mallory stepped back and brought Michael and Jessie forward. Both placed their roses next to the glasses.

As Michael and Mallory stepped back. Jessie leaned close to the casket, whispered a few words, then leaned in and kissed the flag. She resumed her place by Michael. Shippen Travers rested his hands on their shoulders.

Beatrice approached with two red roses tied together with a red ribbon.

She held the roses before her for a minute before undoing the ribbon and placing one of the roses next to his shield. The other she kept and held close to her heart.

Michael started as the casket began lowering. He remembered a bitter grey day how long ago? A year ago? A memory ago? Well, damn. He didn't know why, but there was so much that hurt. So much had gone wrong. So much he couldn't fix. So much he was responsible for and could do nothing about. He had tried so hard to make right. He had done his best.

He kept remembering what Dr. Avery said one time. About how he saved his sister. He hadn't thought that it made a difference. What did it really matter when he couldn't save his mother?

But now, as he looked at the others around him who lost what was precious to them, who lost what they had treasured, he understood. It wasn't what was gone, it was what was here. It was what was meant by a legacy. It's not that nothing lasts. It's that everything changes. It's not what we lose. It's what we keep, what we take with us.

He remembered the man who shook his hand that night so long ago in the woods of Olive Park. The kind detective who when he told him everything would be all right, Michael believed it. Who, when he looked into Stan Wyld's face, Michael had understood someone cared. Detective Stan Wyld made him believe from then on things would be better.

Michael nudged his sister.

She looked quizzically at him, shrugged, smiled.

"What did you say to him?" he asked her.

She looked back at the casket as it disappeared.

"I told him what he told me when he shielded me. Before he died."

"What?"

"I told him he was safe now."

We leave a trail in everyone's heart we touch.

Mallory stood silently next to Jake for a few moments then took his hand.

While the rest of the mourners headed to the main gate, Mallory started in the opposite direction.

"Come with me."

They wended their way past the headstones until they came to a fenced off area. The fence was knee high and made of spindly black iron, not completely straight and with some rust showing its maturity. The opening in the fence was framed with two iron pillars, at the top of which was an arch. In iron was the name of the area.

ANGEL PARK.

Below it in cursive,

Angels At Rest In Loving Arms

Jake knelt and whispered to Jake. "We'll stay here, boy."

Mallory looked back at them and smiled. She raised a finger. I'll be a minute.

The headstone was the newest in Angel Park. She had chosen an open spot near the middle of the cemetery, so her brother wouldn't be lonely. Mallory looked around. There were plenty of kids here. It felt right and just. She knelt to the side and placed her hand on the top of the stone. With her other hand, she started to brush away a few leaves that had gathered at the base, then stopped.

She traced the name chiseled into the stone.

Samuel Anthony Dimante

"I don't know if you can hear me. I don't know if you're there. I don't know if anybody is ever there. But…I hope so. See, there's something I need to tell you."

Mallory looked up and tried to not let her eyes fill. When she looked down tears ran down her cheeks.

"I need you to be brave. And don't wait for me. I'll be a while. I have a few things I need to do. But you probably already know that. You probably already know what I'm going to say, right?"

"You know me, I don't really believe in…the bigger things, God and heaven and all. But, I've always dreamed that you're in a place, a special place. Where there's no hurt. Where there are only good things, where what you've always wanted is there. But, today, I realized you're not up there. Your special place is in my heart. You'll always be with me. I love you my Sam."

She wiped her eyes.

"Now, I need a favor, okay? When you get a chance, I'm asking you to make some room in there for someone else. You've been in my heart for so long you should know how to make him welcome."

She stuck her hands in her jacket pockets and wiped her face.

"Thanks, kiddo."

When she rejoined them, Mallory knelt and hugged the dog for a long time. Then she adjusted his collar, took off the black kerchief and replaced it with a bright crimson one.

"He doesn't need that does he?" asked Jake. He noticed her red-rimmed eyes and said nothing more.

After Mallory finished adjusting the kerchief, she admired her work. "He looks proud. He looks handsome."

"He looks embarrassed."

Mallory stood and moved in front of Jake.

"Some males know how to dress. Others I know from firsthand experience just pull on whatever is on top of the pile in the dirty laundry." She turned to the dog.

"Our dog looks smart!"

Jake moved past Mallory and clicked for Jake, who fell in next to him. Mallory rushed to catch up.

"Where you going so fast? What'd I say?"

Jake ignored her.

"Jake! What is it?"

Jake stopped and looked down at her. His face was set and had that shielded look she hated.

"Jake?" ventured Mallory, softer.

"You said, 'our dog'. Our dog."

Mallory lowered her eyes. "Jake, I know he's yours, I just…"

His hand raised her chin. He was smiling.

"Yeah. Okay," he said lightly. "Our dog."

Mallory's eyes widened, her face exploding into a smile. She reached out and pinched his hand with all her strength.

"Ow! Stop it! I'll sic our dog on you."

"You said 'our' dog."

"Under torture."

Mallory picked up the dog's leash, grabbed Jake's arm and hooked hers into it. She urged him on and the three of them started toward the center of the park. When they reached the big eucalyptus, they stopped. Mallory started to rise up on her toes, but Jake leaned down and met her halfway. He could still taste her tears when he kissed her.

Next to them, Jake dog sat. He scanned the park while he waited for his humans to finish. He checked out the curve in the pathway, 'cause you never knew what was going to come 'round the corner.

And in his crimson kerchief, he knew he looked pretty damn hot.

ABOUT THE AUTHOR

Following his careers in radio and TV broadcasting, motion picture and video production, C. J. brought detectives Stan Wyld, Jake Steiner and Mallory Dimante to life in the PARK trilogy - OLIVE PARK, CRIMSON PARK and ANGEL PARK, the series involving Sacramento Police Department's fictional On-going Investigation Division, the cold case division. Winner of the Bronze medal in Popular Fiction at the 2012 E-Lit awards, named one of the Top 5 Mysteries for 2012 by the Reader's Favorite Awards, OLIVE PARK went on to be awarded the Best Mystery of 2012 at the Global E-Book awards

CRIMSON PARK and ANGEL PARK continue and complete the story of Michael and Jessie Cooper and the detectives of the On-Going Investigation Division of the Sacramento Police Department.

C. J. has studied fiction and creative writing with Judith Guest (ORDINARY PEOPLE), Rebecca Hill (A KILLING TIME IN ST. CLOUD), Christopher Short (THE BLACK CAT), Gary Braver (TUNNEL VISION, SKIN DEEP), Elizabeth Engstrom (LIZZIE BORDEN) and screenwriting with David S. Freeman ("Beyond Structure").

An author of numerous short stories, including Pushcart-nominated "Relentless", he is currently working on a young adult series as well as another mystery-thriller.

C.J. lives with his wife on an island near Seattle, Washington.

Facebook and Twitter @cjboothbooks
Email cjboothbooks@hotmail.com

ACKNOWLEDGMENTS

Those who contributed to the collection are hereby acknowledged.

First, thank you to all the readers who stuck with me and the characters of OLIVE PARK and CRIMSON PARK to make it to the final leg. I hope ANGEL was all you hoped it would be.

Second were the individuals who assisted in ways they could not imagine and to this day probably have no knowledge of their total contributions. I include those who have made an impact on one, or all, of the books of the trilogy: Author and journalist Dawn Ius, Literary agent and author Michael Neff, Literary agent Katherine Sands, Indie publishing expert and author Debbie Young, Attorney Mike Larson, Consultant Derek Pacifico, and Author James Patterson. Special note of merit to Sgt. Robert McCloskey, part of the Cold Case Unit of the Sacramento Police Department, for his insights into the workings of that unit.

Thirdly, Beta readers, whose varying points of view, strict adherence to a rational story timeline and insistence on the correct use of the English language, are essential to any writer. Mine were invaluable. I bow down to their patience and feedback and their time. Elizabeth Booth, Sarah Adams, Michael Brown, David Booth, Trace Adams, Jo Booth, Kayleen Nichols, and Tom Boster.

A book's cover must convey part of the story. For that, I thank Jessica Bell who not only re-designed the cover of OLIVE PARK but with the assistance of Sarah Adams, captured the curiously sinister feeling of CRIMSON PARK and the finality of ANGEL PARK.

Finally, a writer tends to collect an assortment of friends who usually have something to say and add to the development of the story, or if not that, just general cheerleading. They are always appreciated – Julie and George Gorveatt and Teras Karlinsey and Pete Cummings.

As before, and always, at the literal heart of this writer's support is my wife, Elizabeth.

Thanks, my love.

AUTHOR'S NOTES

A trilogy, as many police investigations do, consist of a beginning, middle and end. Angel Park ends the Park trilogy. It only ends the story. The characters, here, once given life though, may at some time find their way into other adventures, in other venues, at other times. I suspect, this might be the case, though they have only hinted to me what their plans are.

Personally, I would like to know what Michael and Jessie do and become. Even though they seem to be headed to a quieter and more sedate existence with Shippen Travers, it seems to me that Michael has a backbone and a strength and energy that will probably complicate and enliven his life going forward. We shall see.

The Sacramento Police Department will soldier on, of course. Danni Harness will still occupy the basement solving the mysteries of the recently deceased. As cyber and IT grow in importance, Sharon Ollestad's status will also rise, as will Jeffrey's and Susan's. It is a fast-moving field and anyone with experience will be valuable and critical in crises to come.

Truth be known, I am a closet romantic. In writing the Park trilogy, I always knew that Jake and Mallory would get together, if not end up together. Throughout all three books, I was only looking for the right way for it to happen. And when it did, it was slightly awkward and unusual, the way romances really happen. It isn't always flowers and music. It is often someone reaching out, hoping the other one takes their hand. And even when they do, the following moments, days, years can be uncertain and probably, sometimes awkward. If I had to place a bet, my money would be on these two, not only making it but having an adventuresome life together. Oh, it might involve solving a crime or two. Again, we'll see.

Finally, I didn't want to leave without a note regarding Stan's eulogy

The idea and image of a boat carrying the dead to another land is ancient, beginning with earliest Greeks and Charon the Ferryman who transported the dead across the River Styx, which was thought to be the boundary between the earth and underworld. Today's eulogies have used many modern interpretations of that myth with the eulogist typically adding personal details from the deceased's life.

In composing Stan's eulogy, I used, as many funeral speeches do, the general image of a sailboat, inspired by Henry Van Dyke's *Gone from My Sight* and *I Am Standing Upon the Seashore* poems. Additionally, the last line of Jake's speech, 'All Is Well' is the last line in the popular funeral eulogy poem, *Death Is Nothing at All* by Henry Scott Holland.

I find the thoughts in the eulogy both moving and comforting. As I hope you do.

C.J. Booth
December 2018